ONE
TRUE
MATE · 3
Shifter's Echo

LISA LADEW

Book cover by The Final Wrap *smooches* Hi, Rebecca!!

Cover model: Jonny Kane

Photographer: Eric Battershell

Special editorial assistance by The Blurb Diva and Savan Robbins. <3 Here's your ode: Monterey Jackass. I laughed for a month.

Thank you, Marci and Chris Passaglia for the dart smacktalk and info!

Mucho thanks to *Kristine Piiparinen* for your above and beyond help and hot—guy scouting skills.

Thank you, beta readers, arc readers, babes, and all my readers. You put the fun in fun.

Thanks, as always, to Amanda Quiles, you are a genius!

And lastly, but firstly in my life, thank you to my husband for your constant support in all things book related, oh, and for raising our boys to be good men.

GLOSSARY

Bearen – bear shifters. Almost always work as firefighters.

Citlali – Spiritual leaders of all *Shiften*. They are able to communicate with the deities telepathically, and sometimes bring back prophecies from these communications.

Deae – goddess.

Dragen – dragon shifter. Rare.

Echo – an animal with the same markings of a *shiften*. Usually seen as a harbinger of bad things, but could also be a messenger from the Light.

Felen – big cat shifters. Almost always work as mercenaries. They are also the protectors of Rhen's physical body and a specially-trained group of them can track Khain when he comes into the *Ula*.

Foxen – the *Foxen* were created when Khain forcibly mated with female *wolfen*.

Haven, The – final resting place of all *shiften*. Where The Light resides.

Impot – a *shiften* that cannot shift because of a genetic defect caused by mating too close to their own bloodline. Trent and Troy are not thought to be *impots* because they were born during a *klukwana*.

Khain – also known as the Divided Demon, the Great Destroyer, and the Matchitehew. The hunter of humans and the main nemesis of all *shiften*.

Klukwana – a ceremony where a full–blooded *shiften* who mates another *shiften* does so with both in animal form, then the mother stays in animal form during the entire pregnancy. The young in the litter are always born as their animal. *Wolven* from a *klukwana* always come in at least 4 to 7 young. *Bearen* are always two cubs, and *felen* are unpredictable, sometimes only one. *Shiften* born from a *klukwana* are almost always more powerful, bigger, and stronger than regular *shiften*, but many parents don't try it because of the inherent risks to the mother during the (shorter) pregnancy and the risk that the *shiften* young may choose not to shift into human form. A lesser known possibility is that the *shiften* young will have a harder time learning to shift into human form, especially if no one shifts near them in the first few days after birth.

KSRT – Kilo Special Response Team, or Khain Special Response team. A group of *wolven* police whose primary goal is to hunt down and kill Khain, if that can be done.

Light, The – The creator of the *Ula*, humans, Rhen, Khain, and the angels.

Moonstruck – Insane. *Shiften* who spend too long indoors or too long in human form can become *moonstruck* slowly and not even realize it.

Pravus – Khain's home. A fiery, desolate dimension that sits alongside ours.

Pumaii – a small group of specialized *felen* tasked with tracking Khain when he crosses over into our dimension.

Renqua – a discoloration in a *shiften's* fur which is also seen as a birthmark in human form. Every *renqua* is different. The original *renquas* were pieces of Rhen she put inside the wolves, bears, and big cats to create the *shiften*. Every pure-blooded shifter born since has also had a *renqua*. Half-breeds may or may not have one. Some *foxen* acquired weak *renquas* when they mated with *shiften*. Also called the mark of life.

Rhen – the creator of all *shiften*. A female deity.

Ruhi – the art of speaking telepathically. No humans are known to possess the power to do this. Not all *shiften* are able to do it. It is the preferred form of speaking for the *dragen*.

Shiften – Shifter-kind.

Ula – earth, in the current dimension and time. The home of the *shiften*.

Vahiy – end of the world.

Wolfen – a wolf shifter. Almost always works as a police officer.

Wolven – wolf shifters, plural.

Zyanya – When a *wolfen* dies, the funeral is for the benefit of humans, but the important ceremony is the *zyanya*. The pack mates of the fallen *wolfen* run in wolf form through the forest, heading north to show the spirit the way to the *Haven*. When they reach a body of water, they all jump in and swim to the other side, then emerge in human form.

Prologue

Serenity Police Department, in Wade Lombard's, Deputy Chief of the Serenity PD and Head of the KSRT, office

Crew Arcoal leaned against the doorway to Wade's office, watching the craziness inside with a heavy heart. Wade and every member of the KSRT, the police special response team made entirely of wolf-shifters, whose only purpose was to fight the demon Khain, were inside. Also present was Graeme, the dragon shifter from Scotland with special abilities none of the wolves had, and the two brothers of the team's lieutenant, Troy and Trent, both of whom could not shift into human form and were wolves bigger than Great Danes. The police department passed them off as dogs, but barely. The nine males, all as big as football players, were yelling over the top of each other while Troy howled and Trent stared on in steely disapproval, making the room seem smaller still.

Crew watched Trevor's face. He was the lieutenant of the team, and the reason they were all gathered there. The worst had happened. His female, the only one true mate found, had been taken by Khain into the *Pravus*, the dimension where Khain lived, that existed alongside the real world. Trevor had no options, no way to get to the *Pravus*, no way to save his female. So he was going to offer himself as a trade.

Crew shuddered, a black darkness consuming his insides, because he knew that would be him soon. Except his female would probably already be dead. He gritted his teeth. Would he survive it? There was nothing in this world he wanted more than a mate. *His* mate. His promised mate who the angel had designated for him alone, but Khain had promised long ago that when Crew had well and truly fallen for her, Khain would end her life. Crew had sensed nothing but truth in the statement, and he knew Khain had the ability to make it happen. *Tricky, merciless, murdering demon.*

Crew felt Wade's energy shoot through the room and all the male voices cut off. Crew flicked the energy away from him with a finger, wondering if Wade had really wanted to bind him, too. Or really thought he still could. Wade was the *citlali* of the Serenity Police Department, the spiritual leader who had the special ability to immobilize *shiften*, their term for shifter-kind, when they got out of hand, and who also could talk to Rhen, the goddess who had created them all, although her communication came in the form of prophecy, which was often not easily interpreted.

Wade lifted his chin and spoke loudly. "Everyone, listen

to me. Graeme says he can't get us over there for twenty-four hours. I say we use that time to plan our offensive. Nothing like this has ever been done before, and we need to have a strategy."

"She'll be dead in twenty-four hours," Trevor said from the couch, his voice shaking in a way Crew had never heard before. He imagined his own voice shaking that way as his female died in front of him.

"She won't," Wade said. "He…" He didn't finish that sentence.

Trevor stood up. "Crew, can you get a message to Khain for me?"

Crew stared at Trevor for a long time. Re-forge the connection between himself and Khain that Crew had foolishly initiated when he was thirteen years old? The connection it had taken ten *citlali* to break? The connection that had sealed his and his one true mate's fates forever? The connection that had split his world into two lives? His two lives were this life, that he thought of as his real life in the real world, and the one he lived when he fell asleep, and thought of as his dream life. Except the dream life had teeth.

Crew hadn't known that Trevor was aware of his ability to converse with Khain. Wade must have told him. When Crew's mother, and almost every other female *shiften* on the planet, had been murdered by Khain, Crew's father had been unable to care for him, and Wade had taken him in. Wade had been against Crew digging around in Khain's mind, but Crew had done it anyway, and had been paying for it every day since then.

Trevor's eyes tried to stay strong as he waited for an answer, but Crew could hear the breath he held captive in his chest, and the way his heart sped up. Crew's answer could determine whether Trevor's mate lived or died... or lived as the concubine of a demon.

Of course, Crew couldn't, *wouldn't*, say no. He nodded.

A sickly, strained hope flooded Trevor's visage. Crew heard his message in *ruhi*, telepathic communication that only certain *shiften* were able to use, loud and clear. *Thank you. Anything I have is yours. Anything I can do for you, ever, it's done. I owe you a pack-debt.*

Crew pressed his lips together, hoping he would never ask Trevor for anything, especially not something as bloody as a pack-debt. If he could find his way out of this world for good, he wouldn't need to ask Trevor for so much as a ride to work.

Trevor spoke. "Tell him he can have me. Tell him if he lets her go, I'll give myself to him. I'll hold my head up so he can cut my throat. Be sure to tell him of the two prophecies that involve me."

The males in the room exploded in opposition to that plan. Crew waited until they quieted and Trevor explained himself, then looked at him one more time, his expression resolute.

Crew nodded stiffly and left.

The trek to his office in the tunnels was quick, but turbulent, his mind whirling. Was he really going to do this? Yes, he'd keep his word. What other choice did he have? He would not let that female die over there if anything could be done. No one deserved that, to be alone in the monster's den, with no help coming.

Once in his office, he tossed piles of books from the floor into the corners. He would need room to pace, to not feel trapped by his own powers.

A path cleared, he bowed his head and began to walk a

circle through the room. He took a deep breath and imagined part of his consciousness as a living thing. An ethereal, amorphous entity the color of smoke that pulled away from his soul with a thick sucking sound, then escaped out of his body through his *renqua*, the markings on his back that connected him to Rhen, their *deae*, or goddess. Contacting Khain in this manner was something he only had an ability to do in this, his real world, not in the world he visited when he slept.

The part of himself floated fluidly to the door, then passed through it like a ghost. Once outside, the smoke entity formed itself upright, in the shape of a male. Crew could imagine all of this, seeing both the image of his consciousness walking away, and what it saw through its eyes. It moved its legs when it walked, but its feet did not touch the ground and the speed of its legs had no bearing on the speed of itself.

Crew felt it throw a wistful glance down a tunnel it passed. That tunnel, if followed far enough, would lead to Rhen's body. As a child, his consciousness had visited Rhen's consciousness many times, in a place he'd never thought to ask the name of. A green meadow with cavorting butterflies and small prey animals that never quite seemed to trust him, although they loved Rhen like a mother. How he and Rhen had laughed and giggled and she'd called him a handsome child and tickled his sides and told him life could be so very good, if he'd let it.

After he'd first visited Khain at the age of thirteen, he'd been forever barred from that meadow, but he did not know why. The Rhen he knew did not get angry, did not punish. So there had to be some other reason…

Once past the area of Rhen's body, his consciousness sped up, gliding down the darker tunnel faster and faster, until it was just a blur. Crew knew the end of the tunnel would come soon and he closed his eyes against the impact that would not happen.

It didn't. His consciousness passed through solid rock the same way it had through open air. Its speed increased even more, until it was fast enough, then

sidestep

The acrid tang of fire filled his nostrils. His consciousness had made it into the *Pravus*, Khain's home in a dimension that stood next to his own. It looked around, taking bearings, feeling for Khain.

But it needn't have. Khain came to it, his massive, skeletal body rushing across the barren landscape like a freight train, plowing through the middle of his consciousness with enough force to batter it to the dirt ceiling.

Crew gathered his consciousness together, his body pacing faster and harder in his office while beads of sweat began to form on his head.

Khain laughed and the sound made Crew think of blood and snakes and murder.

WELCOME, PUP. I'VE MISSED YOU. THOUGHT YOU WERE DEAD. WE STILL HAVE BUSINESS, DO WE NOT?

Crew winced as Khain's voice scattered his consciousness once more. He knew what business Khain spoke of.

That laugh came again. World's biggest fingers on an earth-sized chalkboard.

I can dial it down, for you. I wouldn't want to break your little puppy eardrums.

Crew jutted his chin forward and his consciousness did the same. *I have a message for you, then I'll be gone.*

Of course. You want the female.

Trevor Burbank, the head of the KSRT, and mentioned in

both the Savior Prophesy and the Demon Death Prophecy, also called Khain's downfall, will offer himself as trade for her. But she must be unscathed, untouched, still alive and whole. He says he will give his life for hers.

Khain tsked, his ghastly face twisting. Crew could smell his rotting breath. *What if she's already been… scathed. Should I keep her?*

Crew pulled his shoulders back in his office and his consciousness stood up straighter. *Give her to us now. In whatever condition she is in, and you shall get Burbank.*

Khain tapped a jagged claw against an overgrown fang. *I'll consider Burbank's offering, but whatever shall you give me, son of Amos and Deborah? You already owe me the life of your mate. You haven't forgotten, have you? Do you need a reminder of what I have taken from you so far?*

Crew shuddered at his parent's names in the demon's mouth, then winced but held his ground as the image of his mother in a coma, bleeding internally from Khain's poisoning filled his mind. Then, another death he hadn't seen personally, but had imagined many times, played out in front of his eyes. His dad, drunk, despondent, limping home from the local dive bar after last call. Crew knew his dad had died from falling into a ravine while drunk, pressure from a closed head injury finally choking out his ability to breathe. They'd found him the very next day because Crew had known exactly where to look when his dad hadn't made it into work. Khain had shown him that death when he was thirteen and worked his way into Khain's mind for the first time.

He'd made his father promise, swear on his dead wife's grave, that he would never drink alone, would never walk that particular stretch of road by himself, especially if drunk. Crew remembered standing at the top of the ravine, staring at his father's stiff body as rescue pulled him out, and thinking his Dad might not have forgotten that promise. He might have finally decided he was ready to meet his Deborah again.

Crew's eyes narrowed as the incident played out in front of him. His father, a large male with intense eyes, had stumbled down the street, throwing longing glances at the ravine that tumbled down into darkness. He took a few steps that way, then returned to the street. Crew gritted his teeth and clenched his fists but knew he was unable to stop anything. *This had already happened!*

In Crew's mind, Amos took a long, shuddering breath, pulled his gaze away from the ravine, then headed across the street, toward home. A figure materialized in front of him. Amos dropped into a fighting stance and his look of drunkenness fell away. "You," he snarled. The figure didn't speak. Before Crew could blink, the figure grew to three times Amos' size and hoisted Amos over his shoulder as easily as Crew would a small animal. In two monstrous steps, the giant was at the ravine, throwing Amos to the bottom with no more effort than if he were throwing a baseball. Crew winced at the crunching sound that signified the beginning of his father's end.

In his office, Crew slammed himself into the wall. "Sonofabitch!" he screamed, losing himself for just a moment. His dartboard fell off the wall, clattering to the ground, the darts snapping out. Even before the furious word fully escaped his mouth, he worked on getting himself back under control. His consciousness in the *Pravus* had scattered, and it took several moments for him to pull it together enough to speak to Khain.

When Crew was mostly together again, he faced Khain, whose hulking, skeletal frame shook as if he were laughing.

You can't mark shiften, demon, so how did you know my father was there? And why was there no report of you crossing into the Ula? Tell me, or I will pluck these answers from your mind, and we both know how much you hate that.

Khain tapped a claw against a fang again, causing Crew to shake in *impot*ent rage. He didn't know if he could carry out his threats or not. It had been so long since he'd done anything that required that much power, and he was no longer that foolhardy boy who believed in his own invincibility. Having Khain threaten the life of his father, carry that death out, and threaten the life of his mate, had stripped any sense of power he'd once had.

Khain dropped his arm and stared at him. *You're right. You should know how I did that. In fact, I had always intended to show you… if ever our paths crossed again.*

Khain crouched suddenly, and an energy shot out of him, punching through Crew's consciousness, then following its back trail in a quarter of the time it had taken Crew to get there. Crew sagged against the wall of his office, calling his consciousness back, putting up every defense he had, but it was too late.

Khain's energy punched through his emotional shield like it didn't exist and careened at Crew's face. Crew squeezed his eyes shut tight and struggled mentally. If his consciousness could just make it back in time…

Khain heaved one last time and a tiny bit of him made it into Crew's brain through his eye, even as Crew's consciousness returned, slamming into him, returning the power it had taken. Crew clawed at his own face and dug about in his own mind wildly with his mental talons, trying to find Khain and cast him out.

Khain's abrading mental voice came to him, as if from

far off. "Tell Burbank to be at the red wolf statue, alone, in an hour. He can have his mate, and her sister, too." The words stopped. Crew's awareness of the demon faded.

Crew stood tall in his office, alone, more terrified than he'd ever been in his life. He couldn't feel Khain inside him, but he knew some tiny part of him was there.

Had he just traded the life of his mate for the life of Trevor's mate?

CHAPTER 1

Present Day

*C*rew woke on the couch in his office in the real world all at once, instantly aware that someone else was there. He couldn't contain his violent, defensive shift, even though he knew the male was friend, not foe. The transition between worlds always put him on edge, especially since his body never seemed to actually rest. Go to sleep in one world, wake up in another. Years of the world's most realistic dream was wearing on him.

He twisted off the couch onto all fours, snarling as his mouth elongated and his fangs grew, his hips popping and angling downward, his clothes ripping and falling off of him. He faced the intruder as a wolf, lips pulled back in a snarl.

The other male was shifting also, but Crew didn't have to witness all of it to know who it was. The white wolf with black fur on each foot that looked like boots, or socks, told him right away, even though he'd never seen Beckett shift, but he'd heard other *wolven*, wolf shifters, talk about Beckett's strange markings and Mac had taken to calling him Boots since he'd been shot and had to shift in front of everyone to heal himself.

Crew got himself under control and promised his animal a run as soon as possible, then shifted back into human form. He let himself fall backwards, naked ass hitting the floor, and stared at Beckett, who had done the same.

"Dude," Crew said, rubbing his face with a shaky hand.

"Dude," Beckett agreed, snatching up his camo cap and putting it on his head with a practiced flick. "Who the fuck did you think I was, the ever-loving boogeyman?"

Crew grunted. "I've told you before, the transition puts me on edge."

Beckett's eyes widened. "I saw it! You weren't there, and then you were! You just… appeared."

Crew scowled. "I fucking told you. What, you didn't believe me?"

Beckett picked up his dark pullover and eyed it for rips, not meeting Crew's eyes. "I did. Mostly."

Crew launched himself to his feet and grabbed up his own clothes. His shirt was ruined, but his pants were good, saved by the special velcro pull-aways all their uniforms had in choice locations. He pulled them on.

Beckett made a face. "Dude, change your clothes."

Crew looked him over. "This is the same uniform you were wearing."

"Mine's clean. Don't you ever do laundry?"

Crew unbuttoned the pants and yanked them off, balling them up and throwing them into his overflowing garbage. He crossed the room to a pile of crisp, new pants and shirts, all exactly like what he'd been wearing, taking two off the top, then offering one set to Beckett. "Santa hasn't brought me a washer and dryer yet."

Beckett stared at him for a long moment, before accepting the clothes. "You aren't living here in your office, are you?"

Crew scrubbed his hand over his face again and looked down. What the hell, he could trust Beckett. "Don't tell Wade."

Beckett's eyes narrowed but he gave a tight nod, then blew out a breath. "Why do you have two *renquas*?"

Crew turned away and dressed quickly, then returned to the couch for his boots. "I was born that way." All proper *shiften*, had one *renqua* on the back of their left shoulder, a sign of their creation by the goddess Rhen, and a reminder of their sworn duty to protect humans. He was the only one he knew of who had the same *renqua*, a burst pattern that almost looked like a star, on his right shoulder also. In his human form, he paired them with twisting, inexplicable tattoos over his shoulders and chest, but he had never bothered to try to hide them in his wolf form. Like Beckett, he took great pains not to shift in front of others if possible.

Beckett nodded. "That means something, right? Like it reflects your powers, or maybe it's because you have two lives."

Except one of them only started when he'd first crossed Khain's path. Crew kicked a book out of his way and crossed the messy room to his desk. His pill bottles sitting there looked different than they'd been before he went to sleep. Had Beckett been reading the labels?

He turned quickly. "Why are you here, anyway?"

"Wade sent me. He's worried about you."

Crew snorted. Of course Wade felt it too, knew that

Crew would be next to meet his one true mate. Then, when he was in love with her, Khain would kill her in front of him. Game. Set. Match. No fucking do-overs. Crew shuddered. He wanted out. He would do anything not to have to face that fate. He knew what it felt like to lose those closest to him, and the look on Trevor and Graeme's faces said no one had ever been closer than their new mates, or ever could be.

Crew knocked all of his pill bottles into a drawer and turned to face Beckett, who had hauled himself into the one chair in the room that wasn't covered with books and papers. "Doesn't he have better things to do? I'm not the only one with issues. Is he worried about *you*?"

Beckett dropped his eyes satisfyingly, but Crew felt bad just the same. He and Wade were the only ones who knew about Beckett's loaded-gun of a past, but rubbing it in his friend's face to take the attention off himself felt crappy. "Sorry, Beck, that was messed up."

Beckett flashed him a too-quick smile. "Fucker. You always fall for that."

Crew felt his lips twitch into a sour grin, even though Beckett was a full-on dicksmack sometimes. He dropped back onto the couch and waited for whatever Beckett had been sent in here to say.

Beckett savored his win for a few moments before he took a deep breath and stared at Crew with an intensity that made Crew want to squirm.

"It's about your one true mate."

Crew quirked his head. "Yeah, I gathered that," he said, his voice laced with sarcasm. "I didn't think Wade sent you down here to find out if I'm a Mac or a PC."

Beckett screwed up his face. "A what or a what?"

Crew waved a hand at him. "Nothing. Computer talk. Never mind."

Beckett snorted and flashed him that smile again, the one that showed every one of his teeth. "You think you're fast, but I get you every time. Hi, I'm a Mac, you're a PC. I'm awesome and you suck Bill Gates' crusty right nut."

Crew shook his head but some of the edginess leaked out of him. Beckett was a pain in the ass, but a *fun* pain in the ass. For Crew, fun was rare in this world.

Beckett looked around the room. "Where'd your dartboard go?"

Crew stood, eyeing the spot on the wall where it had been. Oh, right. He pointed it out and Beckett went to it, picking it up and messing with it, obviously hoping a game would make whatever he had to say easier to get out. He muttered something, but the only word Crew could pick out was, "*housekeeper.*" Crew took the interlude to probe around in his mind for Khain's hook, like he always did when he returned to his real world. It was there. He pried at it mentally, circling it, looking for weaknesses or changes. Every time he got too close, the mental pain was unbearable. But he would find a way to get it out or die trying. Maybe the dragon would know. But could the dragon be trusted not to tell anyone?

Beckett found the nail and pushed it back into the wall, then replaced the dartboard and spoke without turning around. "So, Wade wants me to feel you out. He thinks you're planning something. I reckon he's worried you're gonna off yourself, but I tried to tell him you would never do that."

Beckett stopped talking, but Crew didn't respond. He'd been wondering how to bring this exact thing up to Beckett, and here it was. A sign that it was the right course of action?

The dartboard back on the wall, Beckett picked through

the darts, but all of them were busted. He threw them in the trash, then rooted through Crew's desk drawers for more. Crew could hear the sleeping pills rattle in their bottles as the drawer opened and closed, but Beckett didn't look at them or ask about them, telling Crew he already knew what they were.

Beckett pulled out a wrapped gift box and held it up. "Dude, you never even opened it?" His voice was tight, and Crew knew the hurt there probably was real.

"Sorry, I, ah, I knew what they were. Didn't have anyone to play with. Thanks, though."

Beckett shook his head and tore the birthday wrapping paper off the box and pulled out the tungsten darts. "Top of the line darts, and he just throws them in his desk," he said, holding one on his palm, then rolling it to his fingers in a practiced move.

"Who you talking to?"

"Not you," Beckett snapped, standing behind the line on the floor and letting one fly. "501. Beauty before age."

Crew snorted and pushed himself to his feet. "Any day, Socks, I'm gonna beat you like you stole my car."

Beckett shot him a look that said, 'Don't call me Socks again,' but Crew ignored it. He felt almost not awful for the first time in months. He didn't know it was still possible.

Beckett scowled. "No funny business, either."

Crew feigned innocence, then relented, "No Jedi mind tricks, I swear it." He frowned. Sometimes his power got away from him, but if he concentrated he should be OK. The game went quickly, both of them neck and neck, until Beckett finally got out what he'd been chewing on since he'd arrived, causing Crew to falter.

"Wade thinks you need a guard."

Crew kept his composure, but barely, throwing viciously. The dart bounced off a wire and stuck in the floor.

"Hear me out," Beckett said, taking his turn like nothing had happened. "Since Khain can't mark *shiften*, and he doesn't seem to be able to mark the one true mates either, there's some other way he's going to find her, right?"

Crew took some deep breaths and tried to keep himself from snapping.

"Wade and I have been going over and over the incident you were shown, trying to tease clues out of it." Beckett held up a hand, the thumb popped out. "It's dark. There's snow on the ground. You don't know where you are, somewhere in town. He's got her by the throat. You can't see her face because her hair is covering it, so we still don't know what she looks like." He popped out his index finger. "You know she's your one true mate and it's really something that's going to happen and not just some bullshit he's trying to scare you with because, in this vision of her death, you can feel your love for her and your dread of what he's about to do, but you also can feel that you haven't claimed her yet, so your relationship is still very new." He popped out a third finger. "You shift and run for him, but before you can get there, she drops to the ground and he disappears. You reach her and she calls you by name, knowing you in your wolf form, and then she dies. Is that right?"

Crew swallowed hard and nodded, not trusting himself to speak, grinding the dart in his hand.

"Shoot, and then I'll go on."

Crew took a few deep breaths, then lobbed a pathetic attempt at the board. It barely stuck. 2 points. Genius.

Beckett took his place, speaking in a stilted rush, so different from his normal, amused drawl. "If Khain can't mark her, and you haven't known her long, he's got to find her because of your relationship somehow. Something about you is going to lead him to her. Wade's afraid Khain has an emotional connection with you because of the time you spent inside his head when you were thirteen. He thinks that when y'all first touch, and you feel whatever it is the one true mates make the *shiften* feel at that touch, Khain's going to catch it from the *Pravus* and be able to find you." He turned hard eyes to Crew. "Wade also knows you're thinking the same thing but aren't asking any of us for help, even me, and that's why he's worried you're going to go over the waterfall without a bucket."

Crew scowled and turned away, his not-quite-good feelings evaporating, bitterness taking their place. He should have known his questions to Trevor and Graeme wouldn't go unnoticed. *Did you love her right away? How long did it take for the love to develop?* Their answers, that they'd both felt the calling to claim and protect their one true mates immediately, but the love had taken several days to start developing, had calmed him immensely. To him, it meant he still had time. If he didn't love her the moment he saw her, that meant the events in the vision couldn't happen until he'd spent some time with her, something he never intended to let happen.

He glanced at the scoreboard. Fifty even to win and be done with this conversation. He aimed for the outer bull's-eye, resisting the urge to help the dart find its mark with the power of his mind.

Miss. *Damn it.*

Beckett laughed. "I reckon it'd help if I put some hair around it for you."

Crew moved out of the way and indicated Beckett should

take his spot at the line. "How about you? You miss that fucking thing so often, I'm gonna rename it the G-spot."

Beckett chuckled then quirked an eyebrow at him. "You really gonna go there?"

Crew fell back and waited for Beckett's shot. No, he wasn't. Beckett had him beat in the female department, for sure. Or he had, until now. Crew's one true mate was next to be found. He felt it deep in his being, and in the increasingly irritating tug of the tiny scrap of Khain's essence in his brain. Watching. Waiting.

Beckett let a dart fly, then two more. "So, Wade thinks if you always have three or four *wolven* with you, when Khain shows up, he won't be able to get at her, and once that first touch happens, you'll be free and clear."

Crew didn't look at Beckett, trying his turn and failing again to double out. "Won't work," he mumbled, too quickly, thinking of the demon hook in his brain. "If he misses his first try, he'll get another shot. When I claim her or something. Nobody's gonna be in the room then. Or he'll lure me away from the guard or the other way around."

Beckett stared at him, expression hard. "I'm sure you've considered all of this, Crew, but fucking work with us. We're gonna help you, even if that means putting a guard on you whether you like it or not."

"Go," Crew told him, returning the hard expression. Beckett pressed his lips together, but turned to the board and did so. Crew spoke deliberately between Beckett's throws. "There's one place you can't follow me."

Beckett turned his head to toss him a vicious look, then turned back to the board, throwing his arm in a hard, angry arc, a shot that should have struck an inch left of the board. But somehow, he hit double twenty, winning the game.

Beckett stared disbelievingly at the dart, then at Crew, then crossed the room to rip the dart out of the board and snap it in half. "Fuck that with a bull's dick. And fuck you, too, Crew. I knew that was your plan. Is that what the sleeping pills are for? You trying to make your way out of this world permanently?"

Crew stared back, wondering how much he should admit.

CHAPTER 2

*D*ahlia Woodridge squinted out the windshield of her car, cranking her wipers up as fast as they would go. The deluge of fat snowflakes hitting her windshield as she cruised at 47 mph, even though the speed limit was 70, blocked her vision slightly, so she slowed more, then reached down to fiddle with her heater, her eyes still on the road. Great, it was up as high as it would go and she was still freezing. Her piece-of-crap car might not make it through the winter, which was supposed to be a bad one.

Ahead of her, a semi-truck slid to the left, then righted itself. Dahlia stepped on the brakes again, watching it, her heart pounding in her chest for just a moment. When the rig continued on just fine, she took a deep breath and debated trying to pass it. No, she decided. The road was too slick. She would just stay back here like a good girl and make it home al—

The rig swerved wildly, its front end swinging back and its rear crossing both lanes of traffic. The tiny blue sedan to Dahlia's left had no chance, crumpling like a soda can when it impacted the forty tons of steel that hadn't been there a moment before. Dahlia slammed on her brakes and spun her wheel, knowing in her heart she didn't have a chance either, but unable to give in, give up, not at least try to live...

***

Dahlia blinked rapidly, opening her eyes to darkness at her front and cold at her back. The scream that had escaped her lungs as only a hiss when her car had impacted the semi-truck echoed in her ears, but no other body traumas had come with it. Her muscles felt soft, not tense. Her mind wasn't reeling with frantic, adrenaline-laden instinct. She felt normal. Maybe her throat was a little dry?

She twirled her hands and realized she still had them. Feet? Yep, those too. Her vision came into focus and she moved her head on her neck. She was lying down in what felt like snow, staring at a dark, night sky.

Dahlia gaped at the stars, unable to grasp what had happened. Why wasn't she dead? Or even hurt? She hadn't dreamed the car accident. Well, she *had*, but it had still *happened*. She turned over in the snow and pushed up onto her hands and knees, gagging, then retching violently onto the frozen white ground. The memory of the wreck came back to her, stronger, and she replayed every detail. The too-fast-to-comprehend screeching impact of metal against metal, then flesh. The numbing, searing pressure in her throat that she somehow knew was the destroyed steering column invading her.

She sat back on her knees and cradled her head in her hands. She had died. She knew she had. Any attempt to replay the sensations and instinct that told her she had died pushed her onto her knees to retch again, so she stayed away from them. But the fact was burned into her soul. She should be dead.

A familiar noise built up behind her and she whipped her head around, then scrambled backwards in the snow away from it. It was a car, its headlights cutting through the crisp air, cresting a hill on a road that she was sitting approximately twenty feet away from. The car rushed by her as if she wasn't even there. Dahlia watched it go. Would she ever get in one of those again?

She got to her feet slowly, urging her legs to work. Nausea coiled in her stomach, waiting for her to make one wrong move or think one wrong thought. She looked to the sky, turning to her left to catch a slight breeze on her face, trying to cool her burning cheeks and soothe her stomach.

She stared at the sky for several long minutes. Blinking. Turning. Deciding. No. She wasn't in her real world. Nor was she in her dream world anymore, the world she went to almost every night when she slept. Her dream world had been the one she'd just died in.

Died! Dahlia turned in a circle and put her arms out, a new, peculiar emotion flooding her. Was this some sort of a message to her? If she could survive her death in her dream world, did that mean she could survive it in her real world also? She hadn't seen this dream death coming, but she spent most of her moments in the real world looking over her shoulder for signs of the imminent death that was coming to her there. She'd known it for years. Felt it for months. This winter would be her last.

Dahlia shook her head, her hair rustling around her face. A giggle built in her throat and a sudden euphoria made her face break into a wide, uncontrollable smile.

Knowledge of her impending death in her real world had been crushing her, even in the world she visited every night while she slept, but now that weight was lifted somehow. Freed. She felt light, happy, joyful. Maybe she still owed a death to that world, but here and now, in this world, she was alive! Still here on earth. She looked around. Maybe on earth. It looked like earth. Same trees, same sky, same roads and cars. She lifted her head and smelled the air. It smelled like winter in Illinois; cold and clear with a hint of wood smoke. Another car sped by her, heading in the same direction as the last one, and the scent of exhaust reached her. Earth. Definitely.

Her body shook with laughter, and a supreme joy filled her. Leftover chemicals in her blood stream from when she'd died? Who knew. "I don't know what happened, Dahl, but it was good," she said, the sound of her voice cutting through the quiet field surprising her. She sounded like her mother. That thought twinged her heart, but the feeling couldn't withstand the onslaught of joy that kept coming to her in waves.

Smiling, she stood, feeling her fingers, wiggling her toes, stuffing her hands in her pockets but not minding the cold one bit. Proof that she was alive and unhurt and still could feel. She put one foot in front of the other and began to walk just because she could. She pursed her lips and whistled as she walked, realizing after a few moments the tune was Centerfold by the J. Geils band, her mom's favorite song when she'd been little. That thought made her laugh, then almost cry, and she had to stop whistling.

She looked up again at the sky as her boots crunched

through a thin layer of snow over the open field she was walking in. Overhead, what she supposed were constellations twinkled, but none that she recognized. Far ahead of her, she thought she saw the northern lights for a few minutes and she stopped and stared until they faded.

She turned so she was walking backwards and eyed the groupings of stars that way. Nope. No dippers. No Orion or Gemini. A trio of lights so bright they must be planets sat next to a heavy moon. She eyed it, trying to decide if it was full or not, but couldn't tell. It looked lumpy, maybe even lopsided, nothing like her moon did at home.

Dahlia turned around again, her good mood not broken at all. Her dream world had different constellations than her real world too, and people there had still called the planet Earth, the country America, and the state Illinois. Sometimes there were differences, like the fact that there were forty-nine states there, and what she knew as Nevada was called Deseret. Once she got used to them, the differences had never bothered her at all, and she'd learned the names of the constellations in the dream world without a second thought, only occasionally forgetting what was true in which world.

Dahlia's steps faltered as the night's stillness was broken by the sound of two more cars coming over the ridge behind her. She stopped walking and stared at their taillights after they passed her on the long road. Since she had died in her dream world, did that mean she would never return there? Her houseplants, who would water them? And the stray cat that had been meowing on her porch the last two weeks, almost letting her touch it that very morning before she went to work, who would feed it now? What about Fern? Would she never see her best friend again?

Dahlia moved the thoughts around in her mind, trying

to wring some emotional reaction out of them, but all she could feel was joy, no matter what she thought of. She thrust her musings back to the moment of her death. Oof. Instant roiling in her gut and saliva flooding her mouth. *Don't go there. Got it.*

She started walking again, tentatively at first, realizing that although she didn't have a destination in mind, she was heading in the same direction as the cars she had seen. One foot in front of the other. Eventually she would get somewhere.

In front of her, she saw a statue of some sort. She stared at it for a long time in the dim light, having to get within twenty feet of it before she could tell everything she was looking at. A green and white sign that said simply, *Tranquility*. Behind it, a statue of a bear stood, on its hind legs, snarling into the sky. She shivered, wanting to make a note...

Her notebook! She grabbed at her pockets, knowing she didn't have it. For the first time, fear spiked inside her. Of course she didn't have her purse—it had been on the seat beside her in the car—which meant she didn't have her money, i.d., or phone, either. Which would present problems soon, she knew that, but couldn't quite care about that yet, because under the new fear, that triumphant joy was still filling her. If she could cheat death, surely she could bluff her way into a hotel for a night. Somewhere to sleep safely. She might never return to this world again, or maybe she already had a life here, like she had in her other dream world. She just needed to find it. No, that was unlikely. She'd been going to her dream world for as long as she could remember. As a child, probably even as a baby. Her family had existed in both worlds, and she'd never woken up flat on her back in the snow.

So she didn't have a life here, and without her notebook… she felt her palms begin to sweat just thinking about it.

It wasn't in any of her jean pockets. Think…when had she last written in it? After lunch, but before she left work at the ASPCA for the day. That elderly man had surrendered his ex-wife's terrier, saying she had died and he couldn't have dogs, so could they find the little dog a home? Dahlia had promised they would try, then watched as the man had left without a word or a smile. She had taken out her notebook to capture in words the way his left eye had twitched when he said he didn't like the dog anyway. Had her coat been on? She ripped open her jacket zipper and reached in the left inner pocket with her right hand. Yes! She drew the small notebook out and cracked it open, unable to help herself from counting how many blank pages were at the end, even though her fingers were finally starting to feel the chill. Fourteen pages. That was pretty good. She should be able to make it through the night with fourteen pages left, as long as this world wasn't too different. She flipped through the pages aimlessly, wanting to pluck a random captured thought from its paper home, the way she always did when she needed a touchstone.

A doodle caught her eye. A wolf's silhouette in stark relief against an ink moon. She ran her thumb over it and tried to remember when she'd drawn it. Looking at the pages before and after, maybe a week and a half ago. Why couldn't she remember doing it? The wolf commanded her attention, as did the moon. The single ear jutting into the round sphere attracted her eye. She wanted to touch the fur, maybe see the fangs up close. A shiver ran up her spine and she let it, contemplating what it would be like to see a wolf in the flesh. A true wild wolf, or even a werewolf, like they'd discovered actually existed in her dream world.

Dahlia put the thought away and flipped to the first fresh page of her notebook, pulled the tiny pen Fern had given her for her last birthday out of the spiral at the top of the notebook, and began to write. As always, the words poured through her, not out of her, so she discovered them only as they formed on the page.

If I can survive one death, I can survive another. He said I could choose. I choose life, and that means being brave and wild, like I promised myself. Starting now.

Dahlia stared at the words, her brows drawing together. Who was *he*? Everything else made sense to her, but not that part. An image flashed in her mind of Angel, back in her real world, and she smiled. She couldn't wait to see the little bobcat kitten again.

Brave and wild, huh? Starting now, huh? OK then. She shoved the notebook back into her pocket and put one foot in front of the other again, eager to see where the road would take her.

CHAPTER 3

*C*rew's fangs elongated in his mouth as his animal fought for control. He tensed as he sensed Beckett's animal doing the same. And then what? Would they fight? Rip and slash at each other to settle nothing?

Beckett was Crew's best friend in this world, but he didn't understand what it felt like to *know* you were going to lose the only thing that mattered. Crew's mom was gone. His dad was gone. His brothers were scattered around the country working their own jobs, virtual strangers to him. Crew wanted a mate as badly as the rest of them did, and although all the females were constantly in danger, no one else would have to face what Crew was facing... the knowledge that he had doomed his female to death before he'd ever met her. He'd been the one who'd sought out Khain on a mental plane, certain he was a match for the demon in a battle of wits. But he'd been so very wrong.

Crew snarled, gripping the darts still in his hand, waiting for Beckett to make a move. Beckett's eyes flashed, but instead of shifting, he sagged back against the wall, putting his hands up in a gesture of supplication.

Crew's anger seeped out of him. He dropped his darts on the floor and staggered to his couch, weariness flooding him, even though he'd just woken up. "Fuck," he said as his ass hit the cushions. He scrubbed his face with both hands while Beckett made his way to the leather chair opposite him.

"Dude," Beckett said.

"Dude," Crew agreed. Right back to where they'd started.

"So tell me about it."

Crew lifted his head and looked at Beckett questioningly.

Beckett nodded. "Your dream world. Is it a good place? Better than here?"

Crew barked out a disdainful laugh. "I wouldn't say better. It's... different."

"Where is it?"

Crew shook his head. "I don't know."

"But it's real, right? Like I could go there?"

Crew leaned against the back of the couch, fighting the anger that flared inside him at the question, trying to put himself in Beckett's shoes. It was hard to believe in something you'd never seen, felt, or experienced. "Yeah, it's real. Ask the dragon. He travels to different worlds all the time. I don't know if it's on another plane of existence or what. There are so many theories, and most of them are put forward by humans who haven't ever been to another world. Sometimes I read novels that make me believe the author might have found their way to another world, even if only in their dreams, but I've never found one who would admit it."

"Could I go there?"

Crew stared at the wall over Beckett's head, not sure how much he should say. *It's time to quit lying or hiding. Just spill the truth.* "You're already there."

"What?"

"Yeah, you, Mac, a few of the patrol officers. I don't know if everyone from here is there and I just haven't met them, or if only a few people are in both worlds."

Beckett whistled. "Spook."

Crew shot straight up, leaning forward, his gaze locking onto Beckett. "What?"

Beckett held up his hands. "I said spooky. It's creepy to think we are all living lives in another world."

Crew leaned back again and blew out a breath. "Sorry. I just..." He shook his head. "Mac calls me Spook over there and I always get freaked out when there are correlations between the worlds. It's like déjà vu, but it makes me sick to my stomach."

Beckett cursed. "That's Mac, an asshole in every world."

"Actually, he's not. You are, though."

Beckett gave him a look that said he didn't believe it.

Crew nodded hesitantly. "Mac calls you Becky."

Beckett snarled. "You aren't convincing me he's not a dick there."

"Seriously, he's not. You are." Crew looked toward the closed door that led into the hallway, uncomfortable at sharing so much, but excited that someone was finally taking his other life seriously. Finally *believing* it. "Some other people call you Becky, too, but Mac's the only one who has the guts to do it to your face. You and your mom run the Human Eradication League and you aren't exactly forgiving when someone gets in your way. Me and Mac are part of the Human Rights League and you hate us for it."

Crew waited for Beckett's outrage at his other self, nodding when Beckett's mouth dropped open, but not sure what to think when Beckett finally spoke.

"My mother's alive?"

Ah fuck. "Yeah, sorry. All the females are alive over there."

"Khain didn't…"

Crew shook his head. "Khain doesn't exist in that world. And there's no police. Wolf shifters fight against each other, more often than not."

Beckett was still stuck on his family. "My dad? Is he alive?"

Crew winced. "Sorry, I don't know. We aren't friends."

Beckett deflated a bit, seeming to ponder the information, then he looked up again. "You sure it's actually me? Or like my double?"

"Your name is Beckett Oswego. You look just like you. Your mom's name is Moegan. You two are incredibly close."

Beckett shook his head and looked away. Crew looked the opposite way, not wanting to impose on his friend's grief.

Beckett stood and paced the room, stepping over and around books and files. "I'm a dick and Mac's not? I'm eradicating *humans*? What would make our personalities so different from world to world?"

Crew wondered about the implications of telling Beckett these things, like he always second-guessed himself these days, but it was too late to pull back now. "I don't know. Maybe it has something to do with the females living. And it's different over there. Savage. A totally different way of life. I saw a mating dispute end once with the female grabbing the back of her male's head and ripping his trachea open with her fangs, then screaming at him while he shifted to try to heal himself."

Beckett stopped pacing and looked back to Crew, eyes wide.

"Seriously, dude, her fangs were so long I thought she was a vampire at first, but then I learned that females can half shift over there more easily than males can, and some of them have even perfected manipulating the shift so they can go farther in one body part than they normally would. Think saber-toothed tiger."

"Vampires? Why would Rhen make vampires?"

Crew snapped his fingers at Beckett. "You're not getting it, wolf. There's no Rhen over there. She doesn't exist."

"So where did the *shiften* come from?"

Crew rolled his eyes. "There's dozens of creation stories, but I have no idea which to believe. Each faction has a different one."

"What is the *shiften's* creation story?"

"Each type has their own. Some of them are ridiculous, like the rabbits think that The Great Hare created them to take over the land by sheer numbers. They are everywhere in the country, but not too many come into Tranquility because there are so many *wolven* there who love a good chase."

Beckett shook his head, dazed, then sank back into his chair. "Rabbit shifters?" He chuckled under his breath, but his eyes were still far away. He faced Crew again. "Tranquility?"

"That's Serenity's name over there. Lots of little stuff is different while the essence remains the same. It gives me a headache trying to keep it all straight."

Beckett sat back in his chair, throwing a leg over the side, his hand to his forehead, his eyes far away again. "Tell me everything. I want to know it all."

A tiny pang tugged at Crew's midsection. He looked at the clock. He'd only been awake for a bit over an hour, but he wanted to go back. He didn't love that strange, savage world he woke up in when he slept in this world, but something told him he needed to be there early today.

"Dude, I've got work to do. I'm behind on—"

Beckett made a face. "Right. Like you've done any work in months." He faltered for a second and Crew thought he was remembering four weeks ago, when Crew had orchestrated the trade of Trevor for Ella and her sister. Khain hadn't kept his end of the bargain of course, but they had still managed to get the females and Trevor out of the *Pravus* in one piece. Crew knew he might not do a lot of busy work, but he came through when it mattered.

Beckett lifted his chin. "Tell me about the humans and then I'll leave you alone... but I've got to go back to Wade with something. He's worried about you."

Crew sighed. "So you've said." He frowned, but knew he wasn't going to get out of it. "Over there, it's survival of the fittest. The entire world is modern when it comes to cars and computers, but medieval in attitude. The country is still called America, but the government is mainly there to wage war and defend the borders, not for anything like infrastructure or schools. That's where the humans come in. They are weaker than *shiften* without weapons, but they've proved their usefulness because they are willing to work hard labor, which most *shiften* aren't. Plus, they are geniuses with computers. The problem is they are banding together and demanding rights they don't currently have, like the right to vote and the right to drive and the right to travel outside of their city of birth whenever they want. They also want laws put in place that would treat the murder of a human the same as the murder of a *shiften*."

Beckett gaped. "It's not like that now?"

Crew shook his head. "The place is mostly lawless, honestly, but no, there's no punishment imposed on any being who murders a human, even if they do it for no reason at all."

"And you want to live there permanently? How can the worlds be so different?"

Crew dropped his eyes, then looked back, meeting Beckett's gaze with difficulty. "The world may be savage, but over there my fate is not decided. I still could find a mate."

Beckett leaned forward intently. "Crew, I swear, we aren't going to let Khain get your female. We'll do anything we can to stop it. Wade's sitting in repose once a day, asking Rhen for help. He hasn't gotten any answers but—" He stopped talking suddenly and leaned forward in his chair to snatch something out of the pocket of his old pants. "Damn, I forgot I was supposed to give you this. You can watch the video if you want, but this is what Wade said. He went to Rhen specifically with the question, 'Is there any way to save Crew's one true mate?'"

Beckett handed over the scrap of paper and Crew unfolded it, then read it, his mind closed against hope.

The seed of her safety was given to you by he who will kill her.

He held it up and scowled at Beckett. "What does it mean?"

"Wade thinks it's aimed at you. That you have a way to save her. Something that Khain is responsible for, something he did to you."

Crew balled up the piece of paper viciously and threw it in the garbage. "By he who will kill her? It fucking says she's as good as dead." He stood and walked to the door, opening it. "I got shit to do, Beck, so if you don't mind…"

Beckett stood and the pity on his face did not go unnoticed by Crew. Crew growled viciously. He hated pity.

Beckett looked away. "Can I tell Wade you'll accept a guard?"

"Yeah, whatever," Crew said, but in his mind, he was already back in his dream world. The feeling that he needed to get there earlier than usual grew stronger inside him.

Beckett nodded. "Nice. You going to the rut?"

Crew's brows drew together. He didn't even know when the moon would be full in this world, but he wasn't going to tell Beckett there was no way he was going anywhere that there would be females. "When?"

"Tomorrow. Mac's found a bunch of new females."

"You going?"

Beckett stared out into the hallway. "I don't know. It seemed like a good idea a month ago, but now that two one true mates have actually been found, I feel like I want to give mine a chance to show up. I'd rather have her than one night of rut sex, if you want to know the truth. I could run instead. Work off the energy some other way."

Crew nodded. He knew exactly what Beckett meant. He'd keep the fact that he planned on going to a rut in the dream world that very night to himself. There were no one true mates in the dream world, and a rut was the best place to meet a *shiften* mate. Females got just as wild, unpredictable, and aggressive as males did around the time of the full moon. In the dream world, the full moon lasted for three full nights, making all those states three times worse.

***

An hour later, Crew sat on the couch, a bottle of sleeping

pills in one hand, the crumpled piece of paper in the other, gritting his teeth against the hope that was trying to bloom in his rigid countenance. *He who will kill her.* How could she come back from being killed? She couldn't, and he was a fool to even consider there was a way. But that word taunted him.

Safety.

Her safety.

Crew scrunched the paper again and threw it on the floor, then popped the top off the sleeping pill bottle. He eyed how many were left, dreading how they would make him feel once he'd gotten over there, how they would blunt his already dull senses. But there was no way he was falling asleep without them. He'd only been awake for two hours.

He needed to be there. Now.

He put his head back and emptied half the bottle into his mouth, grimacing as he dry swallowed them, then screwed the cap on, dropped the bottle to the floor, flopped onto his side on the couch, and waited for the pills to take effect.

Someday, he'd have the courage to take two or three bottles at once and see what happened.

He didn't want to die. Far from it. But instinct told him a death in this world might mean a permanent stay in the other world.

Savage or not, he would choose a world where his one true mate didn't exist over one in which she was murdered in front of him because of something foolish he'd done when he was young.

If he never met her, she wouldn't have to die.

CHAPTER 4

*D*ahlia stopped and leaned against a tree, circling her ankles and stretching her calves. She wanted to sit down to rest, but the night was getting colder and if she didn't find somewhere to sleep, she'd have to stay awake all night just to keep from freezing to death. She had passed a few houses, but the KEEP OUT signs, closed gates, and high fences hadn't inspired confidence that the occupants would welcome a guest, especially one who had no proof of who she was and no money to pay for anything.

In the distance, on the other side of the trees in front of her, she heard a woman's shrill laughter and a man's jovial yell. She must be close to somewhere! She'd probably walked seven or eight miles and her feet were starting to ache and rub in several spots, but the sounds of civilization gave her new energy. She began to walk again, following the road, thinking about the first time she'd realized not everyone traveled to another world in their sleep.

She'd been young, maybe eight or nine, in Miss Haskell's third grade class and had tried to explain to her best friend Lucinda the experiments she'd been doing every night to see what transferred from one world to the other.

"The beads I hold in my hands when I go to sleep never go with me," she said breathlessly, holding up her hands, gripped tightly like she had something small tucked into the palms. "And my clothes don't either. But look." She pulled up her right sleeve so Lucinda could see the scar on her forearm in the shape of a short, squiggly line. "I did that in my dream world with my uncle's knife, and it shows up over here, but it looks really old over here, like I did it a long time ago. I bet when I go back tonight it will look like a fresh scab."

Lucinda had looked at her like she was crazy. "You cut yourself?"

"Just for an experiment. Haven't you ever done anything like that? Don't you experiment in your dream world?"

"Dreams aren't real, Dahlia."

Dahlia had stopped to think about that. "Of course they are."

But Lucinda had backed away from her and told Miss Haskell, and then Dahlia had been taken to the school psychiatrist.

Dahlia frowned as the snow crunched under her feet, shoving her hands farther into her pockets. Her aunt and uncle hadn't known what to do with her, but the psychiatrist had a few ideas. He'd recommended they pump her full of drugs. The medications did seem to stop her dreams for a long time. But they'd also made her cut herself for real and pull out her own hair in long, lonely strands.

As a pre-teen, she'd stopped taking them, flushing them down the toilet every morning and night. The dreams had started again, shocking her at how much had changed in her second world without her knowledge, like the version of her in her second world didn't need her at all.

Dahlia saw lights ahead of her and she almost cried with relief. She walked faster, trying to push thoughts of her second world out of her mind. She frowned. She couldn't very well call this world the *new* dream world. It would get confusing. Even if this was the only night she ever spent in it, it deserved a name. She refused to think any farther than tonight. It was too scary to do otherwise.

She glanced around, looking for something good to name the world after. Words had power. Names had even more power. She turned and began to walk backwards, noting and discarding the lumpy moon, not letting herself think about how it could possibly be lumpy unless it was created in a vastly different way than her own moon had been. She wasn't going to call the world Lumpy Moon, so no use worrying about it right now. A name, she needed a name.

The three lights next to it caught her eye, the ones she'd decided must be planets. They sat in a canted line, reminding her of Orion's belt back home.

Orion's Belt. That was it! She smiled in satisfaction because her new dream world had a name, and it was everything she thought a name should be. Strong. Mysterious. Resonating. Even if she never came back, she would always remember this world as Orion's Belt.

Maybe she would write a story about Orion's Belt someday, if anything interesting happened here.

Anything more interesting than dying in one world and waking up in another. No one would believe that one.

***

Crew opened his heavy eyes in his dream world and looked around his small room, his gaze settling on the clock. 5:02 in the evening. He was only two hours early. He pushed to his feet and hoped two hours was early enough for... whatever he had sensed he needed to be here for. He hated that he couldn't control exactly when he entered this world by when he went to sleep in the other.

He swayed slightly and held a hand to his head. His senses were always dulled in this world like he really didn't belong in it, but taking the sleeping pills made it so much worse. He felt like his brain was full of sand. He probed for Khain's hook inside him. Gone. Like it always was over here. Relief at that, at least.

He lurched to his dresser and pawed through it for clothes, then headed for the bathroom, wanting a shower badly. He didn't notice a book on the floor and stepped right on it, his foot slipping across the carpet with it, his big body crashing down to his knees.

Outside his room he heard Mac swear, then his door was ripped open and Mac glowered down at him, his face breaking into a welcoming smile Crew never saw in the real world.

"Spook, you're early!" His voice was lowered like he didn't want someone else to hear him. "You're excited about the rut, aren't you?"

"Yeah," Crew managed as he pushed to his feet. "Sure."

A female voice sounded behind Mac. "Is he OK?"

Crew groaned internally. Mac's younger sister was over.

Mackenzie peeked around Mac, her blonde curls bouncing. She looked gorgeous, as always. She pushed past Mac and touched Crew on his sides, just above his hip bones, gazing into his eyes with concern. "Crew, are you hurt? You look awful."

Crew stepped back from her, out of touching range. "I just need a shower." He made his way around Mackenzie and lifted his chin at Mac. "I'm heading out early. You can meet me there if you want. Gonna patrol a bit, just to see what's doing." Normally they patrolled all night, trying to keep human assaults to a minimum, but they had the night off for the rut, trusting the patrolling to one of their trainee groups. Crew wanted out of the house though. Mackenzie was a wild card, always touching him and trying to get close to him. He was glad she wouldn't be allowed at the rut.

"I'm ready whenever you are," Mac said. "Mackenzie's headed out to Loganville for their rut with some of her friends."

"I'll clean up Crew's room first," Mackenzie said, a note of something in her voice Crew couldn't identify.

Crew shook his head. "I wish you wouldn't," he called, then threw his clothes in the bathroom and headed back to the kitchen. Eating something would help him feel more like himself. As much like himself as was possible in this world. At the table, two bowls of half-eaten cereal swimming in milk sat on the table. Crew made a face at Mac, who had followed him into the room. Crew picked up the box of Frosting Flakes. "I don't know how you can eat this shit. Doesn't it give you indigestion?"

"Nah. We don't eat it for the nutrition. We eat it for the prize. Look."

Crew looked. In big letters the box stated *1 of 3 Terrariums Inside.* He grunted. "I almost forgot you two were into that."

Mac picked up the box and shook it, making little bits of

flaked sugar fly out the top. "Since she could first eat cereal, Spook! So that's, what, twenty-eight years now?"

"Dig it out of there. Let's see how awesome this thing is."

"No can do. We have to eat our way to it. No digging. So unless you want a bowl, we won't be seeing that terrarium until tomorrow or the next day. And how could you forget? *Haven't* you seen Mackenzie's cereal prize shrine at her house, and the one in her old room at Mom's house?"

Crew looked away. "I stayed out of her room. And I've never been to her house."

"Yeah, fucker, cuz you never accept any invites to go anywhere." He looked towards Crew's room to make sure Mackenzie couldn't hear them, then lowered his voice. "That's why I broke out this box. Mackenzie was asking questions about you. I had to distract her."

Crew snuck a look that way, too. "What kind of questions?"

"Did you still have your amnesia? Had we ever figured out who you really were?" He dropped his voice farther still. "She wanted to go into your room and see if you were there. She heard a rumor you disappear when you sleep. You're gonna have to put a lock on the door."

Crew looked for something to snatch and work with his restless hands. "Who'd she hear the rumor from?"

"She wouldn't say. But it's an old rumor, from back when you first showed up here. Don't worry. She probably heard it a long time ago and just now got up the courage to ask. I've noticed her looking your way lately."

Crew took a step backwards, eyeing Mac in nervous confusion. "She's not."

Mac nodded. "She is. Don't act surprised. She's always been into you, even you know that. But now that she's not

dating that *bear* any more, she's thinking about you again."
Mac said 'bear' like the word tasted like dirt in his mouth.

Crew snatched up the cereal box and bent it in his hands.
"Don't worry. I'll never go there."

Mac sat down and lifted a spoonful of cereal to his mouth,
speaking while chewing and avoiding Crew's eye. "It wouldn't
be a bad thing if you did. She's a good girl. And there's no one
I trust more than you. In fact, she asked me if I would sign
the waiver to let her into tonight's rut."

Panic seized Crew, and he knew it was bad, because
normally he could feel very little emotion in this world.
But he felt the closing of his throat and the spurt of adren-
aline in his bloodstream. He fell into Mackenzie's chair,
still mangling the cereal box. "I can't. You know I can't.
My secret…"

"She would keep it. You know she would."

"But, but I'm a freak of nature she could never have a
normal life with because I disappear every night. I don't want
her to know that. And she's your little *sister*."

Mac's face grew hard and he lifted his spoon at Crew.
"She's also thirty years old. She wants a mate. If that mate is
you, I'm not going to stand in her way. You just can't fuck
her over."

Crew groaned and put the cereal box on the table, then
stood. His appetite was gone, but the panic was working him
over anyway, making him feel more than he wanted.

Crew desired a mate, too, but could he really try for one
in this world while he still disappeared out of it every night?
And Mac's sister? That would take some getting used to. What
if he fucked it up? Could he chance alienating the only person
in this world who knew his full secret? Who protected it like
it was his own?

He looked down at Mac and shook his head. "I don't think it's a good idea to even go there."

Mac kept eating. "I knew you'd say that. That's why I told her I wouldn't sign the waiver."

Crew nodded. Good. "I'm gonna take a shower."

Crew only had a moment to wonder if Mac's sudden strange expression indicated sadness before Mac twisted his face into a mask and spoke harshly. "Ten minutes, then we're out. Haul ass."

Crew nodded. He would be ready in five.

CHAPTER 5

*D*ahlia pulled her coat tighter around her and watched the other people on the street from behind her hair, noting each time one of them looked at her with surprise. Everyone who noticed her so far looked at her like she was crazy. Or maybe dangerous. She didn't understand it. Her fake-fur-lined tan suede jacket, jeans, and boots looked similar to what everyone else was wearing. The people looked entirely normal, so she shouldn't stand out. But she was.

The smell of searing meat reached her and she took a deep breath, her mouth watering instantly. She was starved. She hadn't eaten dinner before leaving work and she'd been through a lot since then. The smell was coming from a restaurant to her right, across the road. There were no sidewalks, only muddy, snowy trails in front of the buildings. She gazed inside at the diners she could see through the window, wondering what she was going to do. For the first time, her situation hit her fully, causing her mind to stutter in fear. Strange world. No I.D. No money. She knew no one and was already somehow calling attention to herself for being an outsider. If she ended up in jail, at least she wouldn't freeze to death. Maybe it would have been better if she would have actually died when she was supposed to?

Dahlia shook her head. She wanted to live. But maybe if she would have shown back up in her real world she could have lived happily there without ever visiting another world in her dreams. You know, like a normal person.

A dark image filled her mind. *Nighttime. A man stood behind her, holding her by the throat. He did something violent to her and she felt a cold pressure across her windpipe. The strength flooded out of her body and she sagged against him. He laid her down almost gently and she felt a quiet satisfaction from him. Then he was gone, almost like he had never been there. But her throat felt wet and warm and she could barely move. A dark shape loomed above her. Her eyesight was fading but she could tell it was her wolf. "Crew," she whispered, feeling a smile touch her lips and love fill her heart. Then blackness folded over her like a blanket.*

Her heartbeat thudded inside her, dull, like she was sick of being scared of this vision of her own death in her real world. It was coming closer every day, she could feel it, but at least when she wasn't in that world she didn't have to be afraid of it. She stopped walking and her left hand floated up in front of her, the fingers flexing open and closed. A thought squirmed through her mind and she tried to catch it. She was supposed to be here. Had to be here if she was going to live through that death in the other world.

Dahlia pressed her hands to her temples and her knees

bent, sinking her to a crouching position. She tried to stay off the muddy ground, but she was swaying and it was so hard to care. Her mind felt like it was bending, maybe breaking. She'd died. She lived. She was going to die, but she could still live. It didn't make any sense and it was making her crazy.

The sound of a door to one of the buildings around her opening caught her attention. Noise of laughing and talking and dishes knocking together spilled out into the street. *Get it together, Dahl, you can't have a breakdown. Not here. Not now.* She stood.

The door closed again. Dahlia hoped no one would notice her.

"Oy, chippie, what the hell you doin' over there?" a male voice with a strange accent called. Male laughter sounded.

No such luck. Dahlia began to walk again, quickly, like she had somewhere to be. From the corner of her eye, she could see what looked like a group of four males across the street. They matched her direction and pace. Shit. Maybe she should double back and head into the restaurant they had just left. Or maybe it was a coincidence and they weren't interested in her.

Ahead of her, she could hear a low murmur, like from a crowd. She walked on her tiptoes for a few steps to try to see over the slight hill ahead. A building, like a school gymnasium was there, with hundreds of people in two lines snaking out from it. A rock concert? A Black Friday sale?

She put her head down and kept walking. People meant safety in numbers.

Then the group of men across the street began to cross towards her. Her heart leapt into her throat and she quickened her pace. They broke into an easy run, laughing. She heard something in that laughter that drove icicles of cold fear through her middle.

One of the men caught her elbow in an iron grip and pulled her around to face him. He was tall and strong-looking, with a scar bisecting his right eyebrow, the planes of his face unforgiving. "You don't need to head to the rut, chippie, we'll take care of you right here."

His accent threw her, throaty like German, but the r in rut and right were both trilled. Dahlia's eyes almost rolled back in her head when she realized she was dissecting his accent instead of attempting to run away. She tried to yank her elbow out of his grip but her strength was no match for his. "Let me go," she said, her voice way too quiet.

The man pulled her closer. "First, I want to see what you are. I've never seen a female walk alone in Tranquility before. You must have some big balls."

His friends laughed at that, making him smile. She'd seen smiles like that before in mental institutions. He pulled her closer and smelled her hair, then pushed her away slightly, then shook her. "You smell like nothing." His eyebrows drew down. "What are you?"

Dahlia ignored the question that made no sense and tried to pull away again, then opened her mouth to scream. He slapped his free hand over it and one of his friends moved behind her, taking over the job of covering her mouth.

Dahlia struggled. Was she about to die again?

"What does she smell like to you?" the meathead who was doing most of the talking asked his buddy who had ahold of her from behind.

"Nothing. I get nothing," the second meathead said, his fingers grinding on her mouth.

Dahlia's fright spilled up and over her decorum and she

went wild, twisting her head back and forth. When she got her mouth free, she screamed as loud as she could while lifting her legs to push against the man behind her, catching the first guy right in the gut with her boots. Too high! She tried again, aiming for his crotch this time, but he'd doubled over and her knee hit his face, causing a satisfying crunching sound.

Meathead number one stood, his arm still laced around his gut, his face pained. "You're gonna pay for that, chippie. Pay in flesh," he said, causing Dahlia to lose her nerve for a moment, her eyes going wide. She tried to scream again. Someone had to hear her, there had to be a cop around. Meathead number one grabbed at her hair and pulled her head back to bare her throat. She groaned in pain.

Scuffling sounded next to her and meathead number one looked that way, losing his grip on her hair, his eyes growing shrewd. Dahlia whipped her head towards the noise as meathead number two's grip also slackened a bit. Not enough that she could get away, but enough that she could see help had arrived. *Thank God.*

Her chest heaved as meathead number two let her go completely, pushing her away from him. She almost fell, but scrambled for balance. Two men had put meathead number one and two's friends on the ground with some well-timed punches and now they were advancing on the two who were left, lips curled back, expressions grim. Dahlia backed away, not wanting to be anywhere near the fight she saw coming.

Were they police? They wore no badges or guns. Only dark pants and boots, one in a light jacket and the other in a black pullover with orange trim. Even as Dahlia's blood thundered in her ears and her thoughts zoomed by in overdrive, she couldn't help but notice how handsome they both were, especially the one in the pullover. He looked over six feet tall, with a trim waist and shoulders so broad she knew that sweatshirt hid a body to die for. His hair was dark and cut short enough that it almost looked like a military style. His amber eyes held an intensity she'd never seen before, like he hid secrets upon secrets behind them.

Meathead number one crouched and something like a snarl erupted from his throat. Dahlia gasped as his face changed shape and his teeth seemed to grow longer. He threw a look to his only friend who was still standing that seemed to say *come on, let's do this.* Too bad for him, his friend backed away instead, then turned tail and ran.

Her savior with the intense eyes closed in on meathead number one, his voice coming out in a growl. "Do it asshole, but if I have to shift, I'm going to kill you, instead of just teaching you a lesson about keeping your filthy hands to yourself."

Dahlia swallowed hard, her hands flying to her throat. Shift? Kill?

The other savior zeroed in on her, flanking meathead number one to get to her. "Where are your friends?" he asked in a low voice, looking around.

Dahlia looked around too, as if some might appear for her to claim. "Friends?" Her eyes made their own way back to *his* friend.

"Your pack, your clutch, your clan, whatever. Who are you out with?" he asked in an insistent voice, like it would be suicide for her to be alone. She was learning things about this world the hard way.

Next to them, meathead number one had straightened, his teeth normal size again. He held his hands up and backed away from the man she couldn't take her eyes off of.

"They're up there," she said, pointing to the lines snaking out from the building a football field away.

"Go then. I'll watch you till you're safe. Unless you want to see this guy lose his arms."

Dahlia gulped. She most definitely did *not* want to see that. She turned on her heel and took off, walking at first, then almost-jogging.

When she heard a man's scream behind her, she began to sprint.

CHAPTER 6

*D*ahlia stood in the very back of the line, her head down, trying to look as small and unobtrusive as possible, hoping she seemed like she was with the group in front of her. It consisted of five females, all dressed in tight skirts, knee-high boots or strappy high heels, and low cut tops under dark jackets, all five with hair that looked straight out of a music video from the 80s. Full on hair band groupies. She watched them out of the corner of her eye as a group filed in the line behind her, three males and two females who had an awkward air like they didn't know each other well. She stepped back slightly, hoping now she could look like she belonged to either group.

She lifted her head and took a deep breath, then stared down the hill, but the spot where she'd almost been—what? Groped? Raped? Killed?—stood empty. No meatheads. No good samaritans. *Warriors.*

She clawed for her notebook and began to write in it, thinking she would record the entire experience, but not surprised at the words that ended up on the page.

I would guess him at six foot, two inches, maybe taller. His hands were strong, incredibly masculine, with thick veins wrapping around to his fingers. His mouth was sexy as hell, his bottom lip twice as thick as his top lip, and his face was perfectly symmetrical, his expression intense. The scruff on his chin and cheeks made me want to bite him. Hard maybe. But what did he mean by 'if I have to shift I'm going to kill you'?

Dahlia's pen faltered as she mused and her body lit up from the inside at the memory of his intensity. What would he look like during sex? She bit her lip and tried not to go there. Could he possibly be a werewolf? Did they exist in this world? In her real world, werewolves didn't exist outside of stories, but four years ago, something had happened in her dream world that had changed her idea of reality more than she'd ever imagined possible.

A website called *wikireveal* had insisted that a werewolf had been captured by the government who was holding it in a cell and torturing it to make it shift into its wolf form so they could study it. The story had been accompanied by a research video so compelling, the internet had made it go viral. The news outlets picked up the story, and soon protesters began marching on government institutions, demanding they *show the werewolf.* The government had staunchly insisted they had no such animal and the video was a clever fake.

Until a military convoy, heading into Area 51, a flight testing facility in Nevada run by the Air Force, had found everyone on the base slaughtered. Rumors had flown fast and furious for weeks, until the president of the United States had called an emergency State of the Union address and admitted everything.

Dahlia would never forget that moment. Everyone in the country, probably the world, watched as the president admitted the government had captured a werewolf and held him in a secret underground facility called Operation Arma. The voice of the quiet, eloquent speaker, who was nearing the end of his last term in office, shook as he relayed the details. He then showed video of the underground base that had sent Dahlia, and probably everyone in the world, into a panic. The place looked like a horror movie. Blood sprayed the walls. The camera panned onto the dozens of bodies clad in military uniforms, but Dahlia had looked away each time it did, not wanting to see the carnage. Bullet casings literally littered the floor, blaring the evidence that the soldiers had sprayed bullets like in a gangster film. And still not one of them had lived. At the cell where the werewolf had been held, the steel bars had been wrenched apart with strength greater than any ten regular men could have displayed.

The camera room had been destroyed, any video of the incident taken. The president had said he had not known about the werewolf until after the slaughter. As soon as he knew, he made the decision to share the news with the American people, not wanting to induce panic, but rather wanting to inform them.

His voice had been grim as he relayed the facts. The team investigating the underground tunnels had determined a rogue group had infiltrated the base with the purpose of rescuing the werewolf. Probably a group of werewolves, and there was a good chance they couldn't be harmed by bullet wounds. Everyone needed to keep a calm head, but understand why martial law was being declared. The president signed a bill into law that day making being a werewolf illegal, and authorizing the use of military force against anyone who 'showed signs of being a werewolf.'

The next day, the stock market had crashed, all planes stopped flying, police and rescue workers had gone insanely understaffed, and the country had bedded down, afraid to go even to the grocery store.

Dahlia could remember those tense months like they were yesterday. She'd just turned twenty and had moved out of her aunt and uncle's house the year before, going to school at night and working at the ASPCA during the day. Fern had moved into her place so neither of them would have to be alone, and they had even slept in the same bed, terrified of werewolves but at the same time strangely fascinated by them.

Nothing more had happened. Over time, the panic faded. A new movement began, saying the government had faked *werewolfgate* in order to put martial law into effect. The then ex-president received more death threats than he ever did when he'd been president. Protestors marched on Washington, and eventually the entire world decided the whole thing had been a hoax. After two years, things had died down. Now, four years later, people barely seemed to remember it.

Not Dahlia, though. She believed it with her whole heart, thinking the werewolves had just been saving one of their own, wanting only to live a quiet life away from the prying of human eyes. Maybe she even knew one. She and Fern often spent hours in coffee shops and bars playing *spot the werewolf.*

In her real world, none of that had happened. Dahlia often found herself frustrated at the disparity between the worlds, having a hard time making the switch from frantic the-sky-is-falling-we're-all-going-to-die life over to business-as-usual, nothing-to-see-here life.

And here she was again. How would she ever go about her regular life in her first world knowing that when she slept, she might slip back into this crazy place?

"Go!" someone behind her grunted and shoved at Dahlia.

She whipped her head up, sick to realize the line had moved several feet and she'd been ruminating. She jogged to catch up with the ones in front of her, then shoved her notebook back in her jacket pocket.

No sense making herself look more out of place than she already did by scribbling in her notebook like a crazy person.

***

"Where'd she go?" Crew asked, wiping his knuckles on his dark jeans and hoping the blood wouldn't show.

Mac looked up the hill. "I saw her get in line."

"For the rut?" A tingling excitement filled Crew. She'd been gorgeous. Foolhardy, but a more gorgeous female than he'd ever seen. He called her image into his mind again, caressing each feature in his memory. Short and petite, with long brown hair that flew every which way when she moved and big, wild eyes. She'd looked almost haunted and for some reason that attracted him in a way he couldn't describe. He wanted badly to see her again.

Mac frowned. "Did you see...?"

"See what?"

"As we were running over, the males in blue uniforms right over there?" He pointed to the street corner a few feet away. "They were shimmery, like I could see the trees through them, but they were running this way—" He got a look at Crew's face and stopped. "Never mind. I must be seeing things." He shook his head and changed the subject. "I couldn't tell what she was."

"What?"

Mac waved a hand in front of him. "Her scent. She didn't have one. She didn't smell like anything to me. What about you?"

Crew grimaced.

Mac shook his head. "I forgot you can barely smell anything, anyway. Take my word for it. She didn't have an identifying scent. She can't be human, though. One would never dare to be out past their curfew, especially not alone."

Crew stared up at the crowd, trying to pick her out. "Maybe she's something you've never smelled before." Witch? Vampire? If he knew she was one of those things, would he still be as attracted to her? *Undeniably.* He turned to Mac, wanting to ask if different species could mate. He knew *shiften* and humans could, and he knew different kinds of *shiften* could, although they almost never did. But he knew very little about any other species mating in this world. Tranquility was almost all *shiften* and humans. Rarely did they run across anything else, and he had never been outside of Tranquility.

Mac was staring at him. "Nah, Spook. It doesn't work that way. Even if you've never smelled it before, instinct still tells you what it is. Besides, there ain't nothing I've never run across. Slept with most of 'em, too."

Crew broke off his searching and stared at Mac, believing him, almost.

Mac laughed. "I never accept a rumor about how a species is in bed. Gotta test it for myself or I won't know what I'm missing. Come on, let's get our asses in line. If we're lucky, we'll get another sniff at her."

CHAPTER 7

*D*ahlia pressed close to the group of women in front of her as the line moved. They were near the front and she needed to see exactly what happened when they got to the burly, no-neck security dude with the clipboard who was letting people in. What was he checking off on his clipboard? Did it cost money to get in? If it did, would she casually slip out of the line, or try to bluff her way in?

The women were talking and the youngest-looking one spoke in a whiny voice that set Dahlia's teeth on edge. "I don't understand why the ruts have such stupid rules. It's a rut. There should be no rules. I want to go to the Loganville rut with Rusty! I know he's there right now." Dahlia thought she heard the woman's teeth grind.

An older woman, not enough resemblance to be her mother, but maybe an aunt or older sibling, answered. "Think about your Uncle Donald. Would you want to see him naked or prowling one of your friends?"

"Ew! No!"

The older woman rolled her eyes. "Yeah, and they don't want to see you, either. That's why females under fifty are never allowed to go to the same rut as their male relatives. It cuts down on fights between potential mates and protective brothers or fathers. Plus it helps you find a mate you've never met before. If you've got someone in mind in your own town, you just meet them on your own. No rut needed."

Rut. Dahlia's fingers itched to get out her notebook. She knew rut meant a groove or a habit, or periodic sexual excitement in animals like deer. But could it possibly mean what it sounded like in this world?

The younger woman pouted and twisted her lips as she raised her hand to gesticulate a biting reply but her friend or relative silenced her with a shove. "Go, it's our turn."

Dahlia stood on tiptoes and craned her neck over their shoulders to see if they produced any money. None that she could see.

"Last names?" security dude asked in a bored voice. The older woman gave two last names, her eyes raking over security dude's biceps and chest. He wore no coat and a short sleeved shirt. Dahlia shivered and pulled her own jacket tighter around her.

From behind, a hand grasped her hip. She whirled around and stepped out of reach. The man who had touched her smiled and leaned forward. Close enough that she could count all of his teeth.

"How come I can't smell you, love? What exactly are you?"

Dahlia stared at him, eyes wide, mind racing. The same

question the meathead had asked her, and apparently not a socially inappropriate one. *A human* jumped to her lips but she bit it back, something inside her telling her it would not be safe to admit that.

He stepped in closer and his hand landed on her hip again. Dahlia bit back a scream, hating this world and how two men had already put their unwelcome hands on her. It made her feel small, weak, and cowardly and called up a memory of a time she'd been cowardly, letting her date force himself on her without fighting him hard enough, staying still to save herself pain in the moment, not realizing what it would cost her emotionally. She gritted her teeth, remembering what she'd promised herself after that incident. *Brave and wild, brave and wild. I will never stay quiet and complacent again.*

The internal chant gave her strength. She peeled meathead number three's fingers off her and shoved his hand back at him. "Keep your hands off me," she said, jaw clenched.

He frowned. "You sure, love? Because we'll be inside in just a minute, and then you'll be begging me."

Dahlia's thoughts stuttered. Begging him for what? What would be so different inside?

"Last names?" security dude boomed, making Dahlia jump. *Her turn!* She whirled around and scooted to the front of the line, trying to keep an eye on meathead number three at the same time.

"Ah, Woodridge."

Security dude looked at his clipboard.

"Town of residence?"

Oh no. "Loganville," her mouth supplied with no help from her brain. She held her breath, her hands clenching and unclenching, wishing for the familiarity of a pen in her hand.

If only she could write something, anything, down. It soothed her like a sensory blanket.

Security dude sniffed, then frowned, lowering his sunglasses to look at her. "Species?"

Ah crud. Now what? She took a deep breath and tried to think of what to say, shoving her hands in her pockets to hide their shaking.

Security dude took his glasses all the way off, his stare intensifying.

Brave and wild. Say something. She gave him a cool smile and twirled so he could see her back, then faced him again. "Can't you tell?"

He frowned. "You're not a *prey* animal, are you?"

Dahlia widened her eyes and pulled her head back like that was crazy talk. *Prey animal, what in the world was she getting herself into?* She looked around. Maybe she should just step out of line and try her luck somewhere else. Anywhere else. But in the line next to her she saw *him*. Hot samaritan warrior guy. The security guard on that side waved him and his friend out of the line and they headed in the door while others looked on like they were celebrities. She faced her security dude with renewed intent. She would get in that building. Somehow.

Brave and wild. "No, not a prey animal." She bared her tiny white teeth.

His lips curled up in a hint of a smile. "So why can't I smell you?"

She waved her hand airily in front of her. "I don't know. Maybe because my nose is stuffed up."

He stared at her and she let him, then he laughed and marked something on his clipboard. "Go right in."

Yes! Dahlia scrambled past the table that divided her from the doors ahead and pushed her way inside.

To a sight she never imagined she would see in her life.

The atmosphere was warm and smelled of food, people, and a sweet smoke. Her mouth watered even as her eyes roamed everywhere, unable to believe anything they were seeing.

The room was as large as a high school gymnasium, the lights darkened, with high disco balls sending colored streams of light everywhere. In the middle of the room stood a dance floor, the biggest she'd ever seen, with hundreds of people on it, gyrating alone or in groups or pairs. As Dahlia's eyes adjusted, she saw more and more people who were actually having *sex* on the dance floor. Naked people. No one paid them any attention, as if they didn't stand out any more than the ones who still had their clothes on.

Dahlia stopped in the middle of the entrance, unable to get her feet to carry her any farther. Her eyes locked on a naked hulking man who had ahold of a woman's long black hair and was guiding her down, down to—

The door opened behind her. "There you are, love."

Dahlia uttered a single startled scream that she cut short, then rushed forward, acting like she had somewhere in mind to go. She skirted the dance floor, winding her way between tables filled with people laughing and drinking and couches that she kept her eyes away from. Along the back wall, she saw counters loaded with plates of food, bowls of punch, and tubs full of ice and drinks. People just grabbed whatever they wanted. No money needed. Pay dirt. She headed that way, eyes on the floor, wanting to get a plate of something, find a corner to hole up in, and figure out just what in the hell was going on here.

Before she got there, she saw something she just couldn't ignore. A man kneeling in front of an oversized couch, his muscled ass bunching as he thrust into a woman reclined in a state of obvious bliss. On either side of them, two other woman lay, and the man was fingering both of them vigorously, as they writhed and moaned.

Dahlia stood stock still, her stomach forgotten, unable to tear herself away. *Three women.* He was pleasing three women at once. Dahlia caught herself wondering what it would be like to be with someone like that. The man felt her stare and looked around, holding her gaze with intention, then he shifted his position, laying back on the couch. The three women all moved quickly to be back within his reach. He lifted his chin at her from his reclined position. "Come on over, then, sweetheart. Thrasher's still got one more seat available." He looked straight up, lifting his chin again and thrusting his tongue between his lips, licking at nothing.

Dahlia's eyes went wide as her unruly imagination saw herself there, sitting on his face. The space between her legs heated, then throbbed, and a blush flew to her cheeks. But in her mind, when she looked down, it was not *Thrasher* who was beneath her, but rather her good samaritan.

Dahlia mentally shook herself and strode quickly away with no destination in mind. Just away. She backed against a wall, unable to believe what she was seeing. What was this world? She'd never dreamed anyone could be so open about sex, and she wasn't sure if she wanted to stay or go. She seemed safer in here than outside, but what if someone approached her?

To her left, a stately brunette with teased, curled hair that stood at least four inches off her head in all directions snapped at a man who had touched her shoulder. "Move that hand or lose that hand," she snarled, her lips curled back from her teeth, showing *fangs.*

"Oh my God," Dahlia breathed, unable to tear her eyes away from those gleaming fangs. She wasn't in Kansas anymore. Unfortunately, she had somehow stumbled into a world so startlingly different from hers that she almost wondered if she'd been saved from the car wreck in order to become somebody's lunch over here.

Someone saved me. Who?

The question roared through her mind and she fumbled for her notebook. She had to write it down. Had to ponder it, even if she was in something akin to a lion's den. She could just find a corner and sink into it. No one would notice her for the (hopefully) few moments it took her to get her squirming thoughts on paper. Could all this have happened for a reason?

Over the music, a devastating growl sounded to her left, near the dance floor. The hand seeking her notebook faltered as she looked that way. Two men circled each other and both were swiftly changing into something that didn't look so much like men anymore. They dropped to all fours, their eyes locked on each other. Their faces changed, elongating into muzzles, their heads flattened until their ears almost reached the tops of their heads, then grew pointed and hairy. As Dahlia watched their faces, she missed most of what was going on with their bodies, but in under twenty seconds they were both wolves, piles of torn clothing lying under and around them. *Big* wolves with murder in their flat gazes and snarling lips.

They sprang at each other and the cracking of their skulls meeting burst through the room. People backed away from them, but few watched, and no one screamed or ran to get away.

Dahlia's empty hand fell back to her side and she stared, open-mouthed. *Werewolves. She was at a werewolf orgy.* She absently rubbed the tattoo behind her ear as she watched, wide-eyed, denying the feelings that rose inside her.

The fight lasted only for a few minutes, until one wolf was able to get under the other one and sink his teeth into its throat. He shook the throat until the other wolf fell to its side, panting, blood spilling onto the floor. The winner let go and turned back into a man, then stood. Dahlia gasped at her full view of his lean, naked body. He didn't seem to care that he was naked. He looked past the wolf on the floor, who was also shifting back into a man, and held his hand out to a woman to his right. Dancing people spilled out onto the carpet, the shifting crowd blocking Dahlia's view.

Her hand fluttered to her throat and she clutched at nothing. *Brave and wild.* Her mind clung to her mantra like a life preserver. But she could never be half as brave and wild as anyone in here. She *was* prey. Her fingers began to shake as her mind lost its moorings.

"You really shouldn't be alone," a deep male voice sounded to her right. "Didn't you come with friends?"

A startled squeak escaped Dahlia's lips before she bit it back and turned that way. The man from earlier, who had saved her from the meatheads. A rush of relief hit her as she saw his handsome face. He wouldn't hurt her. He had helped her, with no reason other than he was a good guy. He looked like a good guy. But she remembered what he had said. *If I have to shift, I'm going to kill you.* He was one of *them.*

Of course he was! Everyone here was. She had stumbled into some strange Planet of the Werewolves reality and if she were determined to look for someone human to help her, she was probably signing her own death warrant.

She tried to answer. Her voice shook as words came out of her mouth. "Are you real?"

His eyes narrowed and she clutched tighter at the hollow at the base of her throat, scratching herself with her own nails.

She'd just given herself away.

CHAPTER 8

*D*ahlia played her inane question over in her mind, trying to think of how to excuse it, as the man stared at her, his expression turbulent.

But then his forehead smoothed out. He stepped closer to her, standing next to her and slipping his arm around her shoulders. "Hey, you're safe here. No one is going to hurt you."

The heat of his hand penetrated all the way through her jacket and she shuddered, then scooted closer to him, trying not to bury her face into his chest. She needed his protection. She *wanted* his comfort and his touch. She couldn't explain it, but the feeling was clear and commanding.

His other hand grazed the bare flesh at her wrist and the touch seared into her, bringing feelings she opened herself to. *Relief. Coming home. Goodness. Protector. Powerful.* Somehow, knowledge of who he was at his very core filled her. She cried out at the onslaught of it, which brought back her joy and contentment from earlier. That rush of chemicals that had overwhelmed her when she'd realized she was still alive.

"Hey, what's going on, doll? Are you ok?"

Dahlia shuddered at the endearment, unable to speak. He didn't even know her name, and yet he had just called her what her mother had called her, and what Fern called her, what she called herself sometimes. She gazed into his eyes, her lips parting as she tried to think of something to say to him to explain what she was feeling inside, but her body wouldn't let her think. It was like she was suddenly a giant tuning fork for all the sexual energy in the room.

His own eyes widened and he raised a hand to his temple. His cheeks flooded with color and his eyes glazed, focusing on the far wall of the massive room. Dahlia's heart thumped in time with the heavy beat of the song that was playing. His hand tightened on her shoulder and she could hear his breath suck into his lungs.

She stared hard at him, somehow knowing he was feeling the same thing she was.

***

Crew swallowed convulsively, trying to get himself under control. He'd been thrilled when he saw her inside, then crushed when Thrasher had noticed her. No female ever turned Thrasher down, and that male frequently went all night, pleasing dozens of females in an hour. They lined up to get a chance with him. He was a legendary fighter, too, and Crew didn't know if he could beat Thrasher in a battle for the petite and gorgeous female he was so taken with. Not in this world, where he was never quite at full strength. He would have tried, though. Tried to the death. She deserved it.

But she'd turned away, running from Thrasher, making Crew light up from the inside.

Then when he'd touched her…

Crew's eyes dropped shut as good feelings slipped through him and blissful sensations wracked him, pleasure curling down his spine to coil at the base. His cock hardened, making him piston his hips forward. The pleasure of it! The desire, the wanting! So different from how he normally felt here. He came to the ruts when he had to, not necessarily looking for a mate, but feeling the pull of the moon, even if it was muted. But now? Blood rushed to his erection, leaving him in no doubt of what he wanted.

He forced his eyes open and looked down at the petite female. The smell of the food hit him and he looked up for just a second, frowning, realizing for some reason he could suddenly smell almost as well as he could in his real world. He leaned in close, trying to catch the scent of the female in his arms, his soul on fire with the desire to learn her. Like Mac had said, she did not have the woodsy, wild smell of a female *wolfen*, nor the airy, light smell of a human, but what he detected set him ablaze on the inside. Was it lavender? Lavender with a sweet tang that bordered on citrusy. He decided she was a *shiften*, had to be a *wolfen*, because how could any other species attract him so strongly? And because he wanted her to be more than he wanted his next breath. When he looked at her the thoughts MATE and MINE emblazoned across his brain, which had never happened to him before in any world.

Their eyes met and her hand reached up to touch him on his chin, softly. Her touch felt sweet but branding, like she was claiming him in some way. He didn't even know her name, but she could brand and claim him any way she wanted. His mind turned over, spilling sexual thoughts like candy out of a broken piñata. He held perfectly still, willing her to do what she would with him, whatever she wanted, as *shiften* moved about them in time with the music, ignoring them completely.

He watched her closely, reading her every move. The pink of her tongue dipped out to wet her lips as her eyes raked over his face, then his chest. Her hand lowered to touch him above his right pectoral and he couldn't help but groan as the sensation shot to his throbbing cock.

When he groaned, she made a tiny noise and her eyelids lowered, then her hands went to her throat. He tracked them as they caressed the hollow between her collarbones, then dropped to her barely visible cleavage behind the open zipper of her jacket and under the sensible neckline of her shirt.

Did she want to aggress? Or be aggressed upon? Once the first move was made, he knew his part and would play it to perfection, but if he screwed up this portion of the dance, she might not give him another chance.

Female *shiften* were strong beings in their own right, loving to test the males of the species. They always had the advantage emotionally and intellectually, so most preferred a male to physically dominate them in shows of sexual aggression in order to prove their worth as a potential mate. But all females differed in how soon they wanted the domination to start and how far out of the bedroom it could be carried. He would learn this female's preferences as if his life depended on it. Her name was less important than what she wanted from him. For now.

She turned her face up to his and her lips parted again, her big eyes eating up her face. The heat in her gaze was all he needed. He threaded his right hand into her hair and his left hand around her waist and moved in slowly. He saw fear and indecision in her expression but only for a moment, then whatever was passing between them took over. He tugged on her jacket, slipping it off her arms and letting it fall to the floor, then sliding his hand around her waist again as her fingers floated up to his shoulders.

As the distance between them closed, he pulled lightly on her hair and whispered, "You are the most beautiful female I've ever seen." Her eyes slipped closed and he felt her return his desire. Their lips met. She opened for him immediately, meeting his kiss hesitantly at first, then stronger, as her hands gripped his shoulders and pulled him closer to her.

She tasted sweet and for just a moment he forgot where he was. Forgot everything. Only she existed. Only that moment. Only their exploration of each other. He pulled every inch of her body to his, pressing his erection against her stomach, but paying it no mind. This moment was about their kiss and the heat building between them. Heat he could scarcely handle. It rocketed up from inside him, creating a frenzied need to touch more of her. He hooked his fingers under her shirt and caressed her back, alternating between light, barely-there butterfly touches and deep presses. She moaned into his mouth and slung her hands around his neck, directing him, urging him on.

Crew broke the kiss. "I have to know your name," he rasped. "Tell me."

"Dahlia Woodridge," she said opening her eyes for just a second, then standing on tiptoe to pull him back down to her.

Dahlia. *Dahlia. Mine.* Mine. Now he just had to show her that she was his and he hers. Something about the name pushed at him but he dismissed it, not wanting to think, only wanting to feel, to take, to command, to give, to provide, and to protect. His body shuddered at the need growing inside him.

A male got too close to them and Crew pulled back from her, eyes narrowing as the male addressed Dahlia and raised his hand to touch her shoulder. "So, love, you found what you were looking for, then? Any chance you'd be interested in doubles?"

Crew lost himself, instinct taking over his body. He began to shift, putting Dahlia behind him, a killing snarl erupting from him. Before he completely lost himself to his animal, he caught the male's hand and squeezed it, hearing the satisfying crunch of bone and tendon. "Touch her and die," he growled, pushing the male backwards, barely holding on to his human form.

CHAPTER 9

*N*o!" Dahlia cried, pulling at the sleeve of the man who had made her lose her mind with his kisses. His eyes turned an angry yellow and his canine teeth grew long in his mouth, making Dahlia back away from him, her hands clutching at her throat.

Werewolf. Not man. Just how dangerous was he? And was he dangerous to her? He seemed to grow in front of her eyes, taller, bigger. Fury and power leaked out of him. She didn't even know his name to call it. Why hadn't she asked?

So scared she was almost shaking, she decided to try one more time, and if he didn't calm, she was going to get the hell away. *And go where?*

She reached out, trying to think of what to say. She touched his hand and, like a bubble popping, he relaxed slightly, then looked at her, his eyes the warm amber she remembered from before. He grabbed her hand, gave her a look of concern, then shot his gaze back to the interloper, who was backing away.

"Let him go," she said, running her fingers up the werewolf's wrist. "He's just stupid, that's all."

"Yes, stupid," her werewolf agreed, watching the other male go with his eyes narrowed. His canines were normal length again.

She looked around. "Is there… somewhere we can go?" She wanted more of him, werewolf or not.

He squeezed her hand and looked down at her. "Go? You want to leave?"

She caught her breath, her body throbbing with want for him. Leave? He had a home somewhere. She couldn't quite handle the thought of being alone with him yet, no matter how much her body said that was just what she needed. She scanned the crowd. Not that there was anyone here to help her if he turned on her. *He wouldn't do that!* She shook her head. What she knew about him wouldn't fill an acorn cap, but on some deep level she did know he wouldn't hurt her. She'd always liked powerful men, but this one was scary powerful.

"No," she breathed. "Not yet," she added quickly as his gaze darkened. "Is there somewhere quieter?"

He held her hand to his lips, his intense gaze boring into her. "Yeah, there is, forgive me for not taking you there already," he murmured and her heart turned over. She was falling for him. And she still didn't know his name.

He picked her coat up from the floor and began walking fast, pulling her to the very back of the room, behind the dance floor, past the tables of food, to the left to check her coat. She stared at the food as they waited for the slip and her stomach gurgled loudly. He noticed her looking. "You're hungry?"

She nodded.

He didn't respond, but went to a table and gathered up a plate, napkin, and silverware. He stopped at each dish and looked at her questioningly. *He was going to serve her.* She nodded at the beef glazed with something that smelled sweet, then at the coleslaw and the fries, but shook her head at everything else. He picked through the drinks, showing them to her: Coca-Cola, Pepsi, Sprite, then something called Dragon's Best Sparkling Tea, in an aluminum can with a swirly label like the sodas. She nodded at the tea and asked for a water, too, just in case she didn't like the tea, wondering if there was anything in this world that could hurt her.

No sense worrying since there wasn't anything she could do about it.

Plate and drinks in his hand, he put out his elbow and waited for her to hook her arm through. She did, almost shyly, embarrassed at what she had to ask him.

She stood on tiptoe to be closer to his ear, not wanting to shout over the music. "Ah, what's your name?" A hot blush stained her cheeks. She'd practically climbed him like a tree just a few moments ago, and now she had to ask him his name. Something about the heat between them made it hard for her to think.

"Crew," he told her, with a smile that made her heart stop. Crew. An unusual name and one that made her frown as he began walking again. Why did it make her heart speed up and the back of her neck feel clammy? He picked his way through the crowd, then entered a doorway she hadn't seen. Inside, the light was low, but there were no flashing disco balls and the music from outside was muted to a comfortable level. Tables and chairs lined the left side of the room and couches lined the right. They had it to themselves, except for one young couple sitting on the first couch, their heads together as they whispered and giggled, not even looking up as Crew and Dahlia entered.

Crew led her to the very back table and put her food down. He pulled out the chair for her and she sat, the entire scenario feeling surreal. But her stomach didn't care. It wanted food.

She waited until he sat across from her to pick up her fork. He watched her intently, making her squirm.

"You aren't, ah, hungry?" she asked.

"Not for food." His voice was low, raspy, sexy as hell.

Oh man, what could she say to that? She fiddled with her fork for a moment, then put it down, popped the top on her tea, and took a small sip. Yum. A mild green tea with a sweetness she hadn't expected and a slight carbonation. She drank it down quickly, forgetting the eyes on her for just a second.

When she finished it, Crew watched her hand drop the empty can to the table. "I want to get you another one, but I don't want to leave you here alone," he said, looking around as if men were waiting in the wings to accost her.

She watched him, wondering that he seemed to care so much about what she liked and wanted. "I can drink the water."

He frowned, as if that wasn't good enough, but nodded slightly. She dug into her food, and it was good enough that she almost didn't start obsessing about what she had just done. How fast she had moved with a man—werewolf!—she had just met. Almost.

She tried to slow her thoughts, knowing if she focused too much on everything that had happened that night she might lose it. Just freak out at how crazy the night had been. How much should not have been possible, but somehow was.

"Where are you from, Dahlia?" he asked, his voice still heavy from their kisses.

She shuddered when he said her name, even as fright crept into her thoughts. *What was she going to tell him?* Instead of telling him anything, she asked her own question. "You called me 'doll' earlier. Why?" *Because you call all women that before you know their name?*

He frowned as if he was thinking about it and a vertical line appeared between his eyebrows. "I'm not sure." He canted his head to the right and gazed at her from his peripheral vision. "Unless... my mom used to collect dolls. Her favorite was a Burgundian Victoria that my dad gave me to remember her by after she died. The doll looks a lot like you. The same lush brown hair and the large, gorgeous eyes. Maybe I was thinking of it. I'll have to show—" He broke off, then looked away.

Dahlia's mouth fell open. Was he for real? *Watch yourself, Dahl, he's too good to be true.* But she didn't believe that. He was good, and he was true. She'd felt it.

His silence felt heavy and weighted. She wanted to break it. "My mom used to call me Dahl, but short for my name." She exaggerated the drawled A sound. "My friend Fern calls me Doll, like the doll your mom had."

He looked back at her and gave her that smile again. The one she felt all the way to her toes. "I like both," he said. "Your name is beautiful."

Dahlia looked down at her food and snatched up a French fry. See? They knew each others' names now, and were sharing pleasantries like normal people. He hadn't completely turned her into some sex-crazed lunatic.

But now that her thirst was slaked and her hunger partially dealt with, why was getting her lips back on his all she could think about?

***

Crew watched Dahlia eat, an unfamiliar smile on his face. The longer he watched her, the calmer he felt, like maybe life would slow down and was going to treat him right for once. Her scent swirled around him, heady and soothing, making him take long breaths through his nose. He wanted her right up next to him, on his lap maybe, but he also wanted her to eat. Somehow, he held himself back until she had finished everything on her plate.

When she was done, he policed her dishes, then held out his hand to her. She took it, her eyes guileless, but scared. He pulled her to her feet and positioned her close to him, whispering in her ear. "Don't be scared of me, doll—Dahlia, I'll never hurt you, I swear it."

Her fingers clutched at his chest and she nodded, her hair bouncing around his face. He took some in his hand and smelled it, his eyes rolling back in his head, his muscles relaxing, his mind unraveling. *Heaven.*

A couple entered the room and he lifted his head to watch them. They took a seat next to the other couple near the doors. Crew turned to the couch farthest away from them, at the very back of the wall. His cock had wilted only slightly, but it jerked as he thought about kissing her again, running his fingers through her hair, caressing her skin. He wouldn't do any more than that, though. Not here. He growled low in his throat at the thought of anyone other than him seeing her bare skin, her breasts, the scoop of her stomach. *No.* He would take her alone or not at all.

She pulled back from him and looked around, then at his face. "Crew?"

"Sorry, doll. It's nothing."

She smiled at the endearment and he drew her to the couch, then sat, pulling her, wanting her on his lap. She sat sideways, leaning her torso against him, waiting for his next move. *Good girl.*

He pinned her arms to her sides with his body and his left hand, then fisted her hair again, slowly pulling her mouth to his, watching her eyes. They widened in surprise, then lowered in compliance. Her scent flared and he smiled again. Surprise. More smiles in one night than in the last ten years, in either world. He could get used to it. He *wanted* to get used to it.

He kissed her then, gently, taking the long way around her lips and her tongue, until they were both breathing heavily and his cock felt barely contained in his pants. He ran his hands over her back, up and over her shoulders, under all that hair. When his hand grazed the skin where her shoulder met her neck, he paid close attention. The skin there was smooth, completely unmarred. She'd never been claimed. The realization almost made him come in his pants.

They explored each other with such intensity he lost track of time. He felt like a teenager again, learning to kiss, not needing anything more than her hot, wet mouth against his. He could kiss her all night. He pulled back and put his forehead against hers. "You're driving me crazy," he rasped.

"I'm not trying to."

Crew laughed, surprised into it, then startled at its heartiness and the way it loosened knots inside him he didn't even know had been there. "You're special," he whispered. "I'm glad we met."

"Me, too," she whispered back, staring into his eyes. "Thank you for saving me from those men."

He frowned and pulled back slightly so he could see her face better. "They weren't men."

Her cheeks colored and she nodded, too quickly. "Right. I know."

Crew stared at her for a long time, knowing she was hiding something from him, but not wanting to push her. She could be his mate, he was certain of it, but *wolven* females could be capricious before they were claimed, and they didn't like to be pushed. *But if she's not wolven?*

The thought took him by surprise, bothering him more than he wanted to admit to himself. He licked his lips, then made himself ask the question. "Excuse me for asking, but I don't scent well. Old injury. You are *wolven*, aren't you?"

Her hand flew to her throat, twisting at nothing and her eyes grew haunted again, more scared than she'd looked even when he'd pulled those males off of her. She hopped off his lap and tried to back away but he caught her hand and pulled her gently back down, brushing her hair away from her face. "Hey," he said gently. "I meant it when I said I wouldn't hurt you. I won't let anyone else hurt you, either. You can tell me."

She couldn't possibly be human?

CHAPTER 10

*D*ahlia's voice shook as she tried to think of what to say. She wanted to admit that she knew nothing about this world and she was not a werewolf, but on some deep level, she knew that would put her in danger. Maybe not with Crew, but certainly with everyone else.

"I-I," she stuttered, twisting her fingers at her throat. Normally she wore a necklace that she rubbed if she were nervous or deep in thought, but it hadn't made the transition between worlds with her. A slip-sliding vision of the pressure at her throat at the moment of impact made her wonder if her necklace was colored with her blood in the other world.

The food she had eaten turned in her stomach and she gagged slightly. What was she doing? She'd died. She'd lived. She was in a world she didn't belong in and she'd been *making out* with a werewolf! Like it was Saturday night and she had no greater care in the world than to find a hook-up. She pulled her hand out of Crew's grasp and put it to her head. "Oh, God," she whispered under her breath, not looking at Crew. She knew he had to be staring at her like she was crazed. She felt crazed.

Think! She needed a place to stay. That was job one. A place to sleep. Maybe when she went to sleep and woke up in her first world (please God, let that be what happens) she would stay there permanently and not travel in her dreams anymore. Maybe she would never come back to this place at all. If she could just get through the night until she slept, maybe she would never have to answer the question Crew had asked her.

She looked at him then, steeling herself for the pity or indecision or maybe irritation she would see on his face, but there was nothing there except concern. Her knees buckled slightly at it. If she never came back to this world, she would never see him again. The thought went through her like a knife. He was special. Strong. Handsome. Sexy. Insanely good kisser. Valiant. *Werewolf.* Sweet. Thoughtful. Why couldn't she meet a man like him in a normal world?

"Dahlia?" he asked, standing, grasping her elbow.

Dahlia swallowed a sob. She didn't want to use him. Didn't want to tell him lies. Didn't want to never see him again. Her hands shook and she pressed them against her temples. She wanted her notebook. Wanted to write in it. Needed the soothing calm it provided as she put her thoughts on paper.

"Crew, I'm sorry," she gasped. "Just, give me a minute. I was in an accident…"

He pressed against her and moved her to the couch. "Sit. Here." He grabbed her water off the table and gave it to her. She took a drink, then capped it.

He took it from her gently and peered into her face. "When was this accident?"

"Earlier tonight."

Dahlia chewed on her lip and tried not to cry, staring hard at the floor. She didn't want him to think she was crazy, or lying, or both.

"A car accident?"

She nodded.

"Where?"

What could she say? Could he find out there had been no accident? Loganville popped into her mind, the town where the whiny female had been from, but she really didn't want to lie to him. "I... I don't remember."

He brushed her hair behind her ear. "Did you hit your head?"

She looked up at him. "I—I might have."

His eyes scanned her hair. She touched a spot just above her left ear, grimacing. "It hurts here. I might have a little bump."

He looked at her sideways. "Did you shift? You can heal that."

Dahlia sucked in a breath and looked down again, her cheeks coloring. *She was an idiot!*

"Are you not able to shift?"

His voice held such concern that Dahlia thought she might die of shame. She had no idea what she could or should say, and agreeing to anything felt like a complete betrayal of him. Anything she said, he would believe, she could tell.

She shook her head, trying to hide behind her hair. "I don't remember."

He touched her under her chin, urging her to look at

him. "Hey, it happens. I've heard of it before. Don't be scared. Did you go to a doctor?"

"Not yet."

He nodded like that was completely normal. He climbed onto the couch next to her and put an arm around her. "You're really here alone, aren't you?" he said softly.

She looked at him, eyes wide. Did he know already that she was lying? "I am."

He chewed on the inside of his lip and stared down at her, something she couldn't read on his face. "How old are you?"

"Twenty-five," she whispered. "How old are you?"

He looked away, for a moment, then back at her. "Thirty-five," he said, almost apologetically. She smiled to let him know a ten-year age gap didn't bother her at all. He was sexy as hell, and *mature*. She loved that about him.

"Have you ever been to a rut before?"

Dahlia looked past him, toward the open door. Outside of it, she could see bodies writhing in open sexual displays. She looked away, cheeks reddening again. "No."

"Have you…? Ah, Dahlia…" His voice trailed off.

"I've had sex, Crew. I know what it's all about. But no, not like this. Not out in the open. And I was kind of forced into it, so—"

She cut off as a low growl came from his throat. She looked up at him, alarmed. His eyes were deadly yellow.

"Who? Tell me his name and where I can find him." His voice was as deadly as his eyes. She felt afraid, but not for herself.

"Crew, he doesn't live near here."

"Tell me, Dahlia. I want his name."

"Donnie Bryan," she said, unable to not tell him. Donnie lived in another world.

She watched as Crew filed the information away in his mind, then visibly calmed himself. His eyes warmed, the gorgeous amber coming back.

She went to touch his chest but he caught her hand and looked at the inside of her wrist, then pushed her sleeve up, his brow furrowing. One of her tattoos.

His eyes found hers. "That's amazing for a white tattoo. So crisp."

She nodded and bit her lip, not trusting herself to say anything, her eyes on the small moon just under her palm. White tattoos were rare because tattoo artists didn't like to do them for so many reasons, but when she'd gotten that tattoo in her real world, it had been black. One of her tests to see what transferred from world to world. All of her tattoos still showed in the world she hadn't gotten them in, but in their inverse colors, like a negative. His eyes on it made her nervous. She pulled her hand gently away.

"Crew," she said. "Can you take me home—to your home? I don't want to be alone tonight."

Brave and wild. If she only had one night with this amazing man, she would make the most of it. She would keep him so busy he wouldn't ask her any more questions.

***

Crew jumped to his feet, knowing a distracting tactic when he saw one, but not caring. She might be hiding something, but he was hardwired to get his mate whatever she wanted. She wasn't his mate yet, but if she wanted to go home with him, maybe she was feeling the same things he was. She'd never been claimed, so what she was hiding wouldn't come between them.

"You don't have to be alone," he told her, his voice lowering, as he slid his fingers down the soft skin of her arm. He cursed lightly as he remembered he and Mac had walked there. They tried to walk everywhere, taking it upon themselves to patrol Tranquility constantly, stopping exactly the kind of crap that had introduced him to Dahlia.

"What?" she asked him, looking haunted.

"We can't drive. I walked here."

"How far is it?"

"Half a mile or so."

She smiled at him, making his fangs grow in his mouth. He itched to claim her even though he'd only just met her and knew nothing about her. That's how it was with your mate, he'd heard, but never experienced. Thoughts of taking her from behind filled his mind. He could see it, her head rising and falling and her hair flying everywhere. When he bent over her to bite that spot where her shoulder met her neck, her hair would be all over him, rubbing against his face, tickling his chest, spilling her scent all over him. His eyes slipped shut for just a moment and his cock jumped behind the zipper of his pants.

"Crew, I can walk a half mile."

What? Oh. "I'm sure you can, but we shouldn't."

She frowned but didn't say anything, only watched him with those big eyes. He shook his head. "I might walk alone if it were just me, but with you, I need at least one other male with me. It's not safe otherwise."

Her frown deepened and he looked at her, really looked at her reaction for the first time. She hadn't known that. She wasn't from around here. But where in this world was it any different? Unless she was from another wo—. No. Impossible. He cut the thought off at its knees then circled back for another slice.

He quickly pulled her toward the door. "My roommate Mac will walk us home."

They entered the open area of music and twined bodies and Crew wanted only to get her out of there as quickly as possible.

She pressed against him, holding onto his arm. "Is that who you were with earlier? When you, ah…"

"Yeah, that's Mac. He's a good male. One of the best. Strong. Loyal. Never runs from a fight."

She didn't answer but her grip on him tightened. Crew looked over the crowd, threading his way between couples pressed so close to each other they might as well be one person.

A male approached him that he recognized, a flamboyant female on his arm. He lifted his chin in greeting, then remembered what Beckett represented in this world and snarled instead. Beckett snarled back and his female eyed Crew, then gave Dahlia a dangerous look. When they passed, Crew pulled Dahlia to the other side of him, just in case Beckett attacked. When he didn't, Crew relaxed slightly.

On the other side of the dance floor, he found Mac on a couch, reclining as two females licked whipped cream off of him. Crew skirted around the back of the couch, holding Dahlia slightly behind him.

"Mac!" he yelled over the music until Mac looked up and back at him. One of the females smiled and nodded invitingly at him, including Dahlia in her stare. He ignored her, leaning close to Mac's ear. "Sorry, dude, but when you get a break can you walk me and Dahlia home?"

Mac twisted to see, but Crew kept Dahlia behind him. Mac grabbed him by the back of his neck and pulled him closer so he could talk directly into Crew's ear. "I know you don't go to a lot of these, Spook, but you don't take females home from the rut. That's what the rut is for."

Crew pulled away and gave Mac a challenging stare. "She's special."

Mac twisted again, trying to see Dahlia. He must have gotten a partial look and realized who she was because his eyes widened. "Her?" Crew nodded tightly. Mac tried to say something to her but Crew lifted his lip so Mac got a good view of his teeth, and gave a warning growl.

Mac's eyebrows lifted and he locked eyes with Crew, a question in his gaze. Crew nodded again. "Shit, Spook, you shoulda said something! Congratufuckinglations."

He turned back to the females, standing up, pulling his body out of their reach and grabbing for his pants. "Sorry, ladies, but I need to help a friend get his female home safely. I'll be back before you can miss me."

But they were already turning away, looking for someone else to hold their attention.

"Sorry," Crew offered.

Mac pulled on the rest of his clothes. "No stress. There's hundreds of females here who would pay to be the bread in a Mac sandwich. My night is young."

He held up his hand and Crew clasped it. Too late, Crew realized he was using the gesture as a way to get another look at Dahlia. Crew pulled her closer and put a possessive arm around her.

Mac smiled at her and Crew felt like killing him.

"You're Dahlia," he said. "Groovy."

Dahlia smiled back but stayed close to Crew and didn't say a word. Good girl. He'd show her how good when they got home. He was going to make her come three times before he took his dick out of his pants.

If she just wanted to cuddle, that would be good, but if she wanted more, she would be in for a ride she'd never forget. A memory that would still get them hot when they were grandparents. He would make sure of it.

CHAPTER 11

*A*s they walked, Mac slightly in front, she and Crew behind, Dahlia held tightly to Crew. He was tense, much more tense than he'd been inside. His eyes moved constantly and when other people passed them, he tensed even more. The street was festive, with several boister-ous groups walking through the area. They passed two males fighting and neither Mac nor Crew even looked their way.

They were in a residential area and Dahlia watched the houses closely, thinking they looked familiar. When they passed a two-story beige house with a wrap-around porch, she frowned as she examined it. She knew that house. She'd babysat there in both her real and her dream world, except in those worlds, the fence had been a small picket one, not the monstrosity topped with barbed wire that this one had. Tranquility had to be this world's version of Serenity, which had been where she'd lived in both worlds she lived in. She shuddered. It was not named well. If she had written a town like this into a story, she would have called it something different, dangerous-sounding. Like Where the Wolves Play or...

Two large animals shot out of the darkness straight towards them, both black with teeth that gleamed in the moonlight, startling a scream from Dahlia. Crew pulled her to the side and behind him, but the wolves—they had to be wolves, they were both as big as Great Danes but looked like dark huskies—ran straight by them.

"What the hell?" Mac grated. "Keep her quiet. We don't need to look like we spook easy."

Crew gave her a questioning look that made her feel like a complete idiot. Females in this world didn't scream when they saw wolves. They *were* wolves.

"Sorry," she whispered to Crew.

"Shh. Don't worry about it. They startled you."

Mac turned left in an alley in front of them and Crew steered her that way, where they followed Mac through a gate that towered over her head. Inside the gate, Mac wrestled with several locks on a steel door. When he got them all unlocked, he held the door for her and Crew, then waved. "See you two later." He turned and disappeared back out the gate.

"Is he going to be ok by himself?" Dahlia whispered.

"Mac's strong and fast. He'll be fine over that short distance. And we have lots of friends patrolling tonight. If he gets in trouble, he'll howl."

Crew led her up the dark stairs, worked several more locks at the top, then clicked on some lights and smiled at her, holding out his hand so she would enter first.

Dahlia looked around curiously. A large, open room greeted her, looking like any other house she'd ever been in, except there were no pictures on the walls, no plants, no decorations of any kind. That didn't surprise her overmuch. "Is it just you and Mac here?"

"Yes." Crew walked past her and turned on lights in rooms off the main room, then headed into the kitchen area. He dug four candles out of a drawer and lit them, then took some drinks out of the refrigerator and placed them on the counter. Dragon's Best Sparkling Tea and two water bottles. He pulled his sweatshirt over his head and tossed it on the back of a chair, then looked at her and picked it back up, taking it to a closet, turning the main lights down low on his way. "Can I take your jacket?"

Dahlia gave it to him, feeling nervous all of a sudden, hoping things weren't about to get awkward between them. From across the room she could see he had a tattoo on his right forearm but she couldn't tell what it was.

He hung her jacket on a hanger, then turned to her and stared at her, his expression smoldering. Dahlia half-smiled, nervous still. He crossed the room to where she stood, holding her in place with his eyes, then dipped a hand around her waist and another into her hair. "I'm so glad you came home with me tonight."

Dahlia's cheeks heated up at his straightforwardness. He wasn't feeling awkward at all. Maybe he did this a lot. His hand in her hair tugged slightly, sending sensation down her spine. She smiled at him again. *Brave and wild.* "Me too." She touched her tongue to her top lip, feeling ridiculous at first but then triumphant when his gaze flew to it and he made a noise deep in his throat, like a growl. His every sound and gesture was incredibly sexy and she wanted more.

He stepped away from her, pulling at her with just two

fingers, heading for the couch. He let go, then sat down and looked at her. "Come here."

The command in his voice was unmistakable and it sent heat straight to her core. She didn't care how often he did it. She wanted to experience it.

She walked to him, almost sat next to him, then changed her mind and straddled him instead, facing forward, locking gazes with him.

The intensity in his eyes as he nodded his approval overwhelmed her. "Good girl," he rasped.

He leaned back and put his hands on the couch, palms up, fingers curled slightly, touching her only with his gaze. "Touch me," he told her. She looked at him questioningly. "Anywhere you want. I like how it feels when you touch me but I don't want you uncomfortable."

Her fingers crept to his belly, flat and muscled under his shirt. She dropped her eyes to it as she lightly caressed it. Power rippled through his muscles as they jumped at her touch. Greedy to know more of him, she ran her hands up to his chest muscles, then down again, lifting his shirt. He sat forward and took it over his head. She gasped at the sheer perfection of his chest, running her hands over the bulging muscles. He was heavenly to look at. His tattoos caught her eye and she traced them with her fingers.

"What does this mean?" she asked, her hand on a large tattoo of wings over feminine eyes on his chest.

His lips quirked slightly and he didn't speak for a long moment. She wondered if he resented her asking.

When he finally spoke, his tone was contemplative. "I did some stupid shit when I was thirteen. It cost me something very dear and this is my reminder."

"You got that at thirteen?" she asked, her fingers

memorizing his pecs and shoulders. He dropped his head to the back of the couch and closed his eyes, as if her touch was bliss.

"Fourteen."

"Your parents let you get a tattoo at fourteen?"

"My mom was dead. My dad… wasn't around."

Dahlia sucked in a breath. "I'm sorry."

He opened his eyes and caught her hand. "Don't be sorry for asking questions. You can ask me anything and I'll never get upset."

She dipped her head. "Why are you being so sweet to me?"

He stared at her so long, with such intensity, that she squirmed in his lap. Finally he spoke. "Because you deserve it. Because I want you to be mine."

She sucked in a breath, her hand flying to her throat to twist nothing. "We just met," she said softly.

"I know. But I can feel we are right for each other. Tell me you feel it, too."

Dahlia looked back down at his muscles. What could she possibly say to that? This intense, sexy, strong man, in another place or circumstance? *Yes.* She would say yes to that in a heartbeat. But here? She hoped she would never see this place again. She'd been through dying, without the heaven or hell, and had no idea what the future held. What would he say if he knew that?

But she did feel it and she had no choice but to admit it. "I do feel it."

Relief spread across his face. "I will always be sweet to you, Dahlia. I don't know any other way to be to my mate."

Dahlia's eyes went wide at that word. Mate. So animalistic yet strangely attractive. Way stronger than girlfriend. *Too bad she didn't know how any of this worked!* Would he give her a ring? Want her to move in? Be destroyed if she somehow disappeared from this world?

The thoughts came quickly, overwhelmingly, and she leaned forward into his chest to hide her face. She'd been hoping that when she went to sleep she would wake up back in her real world and never come to this world again. Something that had happened to her after she died and before she arrived in this world—something she couldn't quite remember—made her think that was what would happen.

Now she wondered if she really wanted to go back to the world where she was only a few weeks from dying... for good.

Dahlia's breaths came too quickly and for the second time that evening she felt close to losing it. To just curling up on the floor and crying or screaming until she passed out. *Crew.* She remembered now what that name was from.

The name she would whisper to the dark wolf who bounded to her side as she lay dying in the snow.

***

Crew put his arms around Dahlia, sensing the change that had come over her. She shivered against his chest and he felt anxiety swirl around her. He couldn't take the words back, and he didn't want to. He spoke his heart, or nothing. She deserved his heart.

But when she didn't calm, he got worried. "Dahlia, hey, talk to me. It's ok. I swear. No matter what's wrong, I'm going to make sure it's ok."

The room shimmered and he tensed, eyes widening, ready to throw Dahlia behind him and fight. But fight what? His eyes narrowed as he realized he was seeing something, but that he could see right through it, almost like a movie projected on a transparent screen. In the scene that was playing out in front of him, his viewpoint was from on the ground. He could see trees and the sky. A wolf bounded into view and Crew swallowed, hard. He was staring at himself.

He felt her eyelashes flutter against his chest and her voice was muffled but understandable. "Do you believe in fate?"

At her question, the scene disappeared and his living room looked normal again, leaving Crew shaken.

Crew considered for a long time, looking around as he hugged Dahlia to him. When he decided the phenomena wasn't going to reappear, he pulled his mind back to Dahlia.

Fate. He knew fate was a real live thing, and it had a strong pull over his real world, but this world? He wasn't so sure. But since this world seemed to be a distorted version of that world, it must. He kneaded Dahlia's shoulders, trying to work out the knots there. "Yes, I do believe in fate."

His answer forced a sob out of her, but only a single one. He felt her getting herself under control by sheer force of will and wondered what secrets she was hiding. He ran his hands lightly down her back. "You can tell me anything."

Her silence seemed to indicate she didn't agree. He swallowed but didn't force her. He had enough secrets of his own to deal with. Maybe he could distract her.

"Tell me what you like to do." he said, kneading the muscles in the small of her back, enjoying the way her ass looked as she bent over him. By Rhen, she was lovely and he was enjoying her closeness more than he should in the wake of her distress.

"Like to do?"

"Hobbies. For fun."

"Oh. Right. I write."

"You write?"

"Stories. I make stuff up and I put it on the Internet for people to read."

He smiled into her hair. She was creative. An artist. He should have known. Her haunted eyes spoke of many worlds inside her head. She stiffened suddenly, as if she'd realized she'd said something she shouldn't have. He worked her back more, then dropped his hands to her hips. "I'd like to read one of your stories." She softened slightly.

"Oh, ah, I don't think you would like them."

"Why?"

"Mostly, ah." He could feel the heat of her cheeks against his chest. Was she embarrassed?

She sat up and looked at him, her lips pressed resolutely together, her cheeks bright. "Romance. I write romance stories."

Crew felt a rush of pride at her will and her passion and the fact that she could put a story together. He respected writers as artists who could do what he did; live in two worlds at the same time. "I definitely want to read them."

Her brow furrowed. "You read romance?"

He dug around in his mind to find a quote in his eidetic memory that she might consider romantic. "Whatever our souls are made of, his and mine are the same."

She frowned and he had a moment of panic during which he tried to remember if Wuthering Heights existed in this world.

But she knew it. Her face turned skeptical. "*Contemporary* romance. With sex."

Blood surged to his groin. She wrote sex. He wanted to peel her clothes off right there and give her something to write about. Instead, he found another quote for her, trying to speak in Graeme's accent. "When the day shall come that we do part, if my last words are not 'I love you'—ye'll ken it was because I didna have time."

Her eyes widened. "Outlander?"

"Aye."

She laughed at that, making him smile. He would give anything to get her to do it again.

CHAPTER 12

*H*e was well-read. The kind of books she liked. She should have known. His eyes said he was intelligent and a deep thinker, and the quotes he pulled off the top of his head? She wouldn't have thought anything could have made him sexier, but they did. And he wanted to read her books. The last time she'd told a man she wrote romance, he had rolled his eyes at her. But not Crew.

Something had brought them together. Maybe fate, maybe something else, but she wasn't going to question it anymore. All she'd wanted for years was to die well, without crying or running from it. She'd known she was going to die when she was twenty-five for years, and now that her 25th birthday was three days in the past, she felt like she was living on borrowed time. Time to be done with all her fears, her doubts, anything that held her back from doing what she wanted. Her time left grew shorter every second. *Brave and wild*. From here on out.

She stared at him, then brought her hands to her shirt slowly, pulling it up over her head and casting it on the floor. His eyes raked her body, the smooth skin of her stomach, her small breasts contained by a pink bra. He didn't smile, didn't encourage or discourage her, just stared as if she were something beautiful and amazing. A sunset on a watery horizon, perhaps.

She hooked her fingers around her back and unclasped her bra, casting it aside also. His fingers convulsed on her hips but he made no move to touch her, still staring intensely. She brought her own fingers up to her nipples, which he couldn't take his eyes off of. She pinched them, watching him. His face hardened and he shifted his body, then brought his hands up to her hair. He pulled it forward so it fell in two sheets down to her breasts.

"You're stunning," he rasped, and his words felt like power to her. She wanted to thank him, to ask him to say it again, to write it down in her notebook. She'd never been called stunning before. She positioned her hair so it hid her nipples in a kind of peekaboo, watching as he licked his lips. His hands slid down her sides and cupped her breasts from below, barely touching the skin there. His thumbs slid across the groove where her breasts met her torso, causing goose bumps to ripple out across her body. His eyes lowered with heat. He liked the anticipation, and discovering that burned her up from the inside. He didn't want the release. He burned for the discovery, for the playing. Oh shit, now he was even sexier. Had she ever met a more interesting man?

"Tell me again," she said, dropping her eyes to his jeans. He was hard, his erection straining against the stiff fabric.

She'd felt it earlier, against her stomach, but it looked bigger than she remembered. Really big. Her turn to lick her lips. The way he made her feel, she didn't care if it hurt when he took her. She wanted it to hurt. He made her feel wicked in the most delicious way and she wanted to see how far he could push her past what she was used to and comfortable with.

She wanted to feel *alive*.

***

"You're stunning. Beguiling. Your breasts make me wish I were a poet," he said, his breath coming faster. She didn't have more than a handful, which was just how Crew liked them. He itched to palm them and tweak the nipples like she was doing, but watching was better, especially when her yards of hair covered the nipples so he could hardly see them. He shifted underneath her, trying to keep from adjusting himself. The only way he was going to get relief was by getting his jeans off, and he did not want to do that yet. He could watch her play with herself all night.

He licked his lips and she took it as an invitation, placing her hands on his shoulders and raising up so her breasts met his mouth, her hair tickling his cheeks. Heaven. He licked one nipple, then the other, watching as she closed her eyes and arched her back. He took her hands and held them behind her back, clasping the wrists with one hand, working his other hand back to her breast. He did palm it then, feeling how perfectly it fit there. He moaned into her skin at how good she felt.

He released her breast and plunged his hand into her hair, pulling until she came down and he could capture her mouth with his. They kissed and all the secrets between them ceased to matter. They knew what they needed to know about the other right then. Crew knew she was stunning, sweet, artistic, and that they fit together. And that she wanted him.

He released her, and pulled back so she could see his eyes. "Stand up," he told her. "I want you naked."

She licked her lips and nodded, then glanced down at his painful erection which was still clothed. He smiled wickedly. "You want me naked, too?"

She nodded, and when a whispered, tortured "Yes," escaped her lips, he groaned.

"You first, doll," he said, grasping her by her hips and placing her on her feet. With her every movement, her hair swayed around her shoulders and breasts, her bare skin making him bite back a moan. He loved a female with a lot of hair. He was already imagining holding onto it, gathering it into a ponytail, and using it to direct her lips down his shaft.

She stepped out of her pants so quickly he never even got to see her panties. Next time, he'd spend more time undressing her. He raked his eyes down her body, starting at all that delicious hair, past her breasts, to the softness of her middle, down to her flaring hips and thighs, her strong calves, delicate ankles, and tiny feet. Her hands dangled loosely by her sides as she let him look his full. "Doll." He was barely able to speak. "Dahlia."

"Tell me I'm pretty, then take your pants off," she said, a sinful smile on her face.

Oh, he had his hands full with this one. Which he loved. He couldn't have ordered a female more perfect than her. "You are pretty. So pretty."

He kicked off his boots, then unzipped his pants and lifted his hips, yanking all his clothes off at once and kicking them away, watching her reaction closely. Her eyes widened and her lips parted as she took him in. Her hands closed reflexively at her sides and he smiled. She wanted to touch him.

She straddled him again, her hands on his thighs, her eyes on his cock. "Crew, it's just so big."

He chuckled, then ran his hand over the head, loving that her hands clutched his legs when he did, her nails scratching at him. He gave his cock a thick stroke, his eyes on her face. "You know how to make a male feel good."

"No, I mean, it's really big. I'm almost afraid."

He stroked it again for her benefit, then pulled her up against him, his hands spanning her hips. "If we do it right, it won't hurt, if that's what you're worried about."

She looked at his eyes for a moment, her expression brimming with trust, and he vowed to himself he would never take that trust for granted. She would know all his secrets. Then she moved so that her wetness rubbed against his hardness. He groaned at the connection and closed his eyes, then opened them again when he felt her hands on him. She wrapped one hand around his shaft exactly like he had, and stroked it.

"Is that how you like it?" she asked, her breath heavy. He could hear his blood pounding in his ears and he wondered why he hadn't turned any music on.

"Just like that, doll. That feels so good."

He pulled her forward to kiss her again, but her hands, wrapped around him, pulling as she shifted her weight, felt so good he worried he was going to come before they ever got a chance to get started. He reached for her sex, dipping his thumb into her wetness, then gliding up to her clit. She cried out, her hands tightening wonderfully on his cock, then bucked her hips forward. She was swollen, deliciously swollen, and he was gratified to find she was as close as he was.

Her hips bucked forward again, and she ground into his available flesh, pulling at his cock in a forceful way he'd never experienced before. He put his head back, holding on for the ride as pleasure built inside him to an unbearable peak.

***

"Oh God," Dahlia cried out, her eyes slitted shut, blocking out the visual world so she could only *feel* as an orgasm pounded through her. Thick waves of pleasure pulsed at her harder and faster than she'd ever experienced. She hadn't realized she'd been on the verge until he'd touched her the first time and she almost went off right then. The spasms intensified, making her cry out again. Dimly, she heard Crew's husky groan as his own orgasm took him, and she felt his seed spill over her hands, hot and thick.

As the all-consuming sensations receded, a sense of goodness, of rightness filled her.

Then a sense of tearing loss that he would be taken from her soon. If not when she next went to sleep, then surely when she died, whenever that would be. Sometime in the next three hundred and sixty two days, she knew, before she turned twenty-six.

CHAPTER 13

*D*ahlia watched as Crew cleaned up, then got her a blanket and some water, his muscles flexing beautifully as he moved about the room, naked. On his back, on each of his shoulders, was a tattoo of a starburst pattern, not quite a five-pointed star, but almost. She touched the tattoo behind her ear, rubbing it, her thoughts racing.

"What time is it?" she asked Crew, exhaustion settling in on her.

He looked at the window on the far side of the room. "Almost daylight. I would guess 6:30."

Dahlia gasped. She'd been up all night? "Won't Mac be coming home soon? I should get dressed."

His eyes raked over her body, mostly covered by the blanket. "Don't put on a stitch. We'll move into my bedroom."

A sound at the door caught her attention and she looked that way. *Too late.*

But when the door opened, it wasn't Mac. It was a beautiful woman with long, blonde hair who entered with a key, saw Crew first and beamed at him.

Oh no. She's in love with him. Is she his girlfriend?

Dahlia's heart split in two pieces. She froze, unable to think of what to say or do, taking in the scene in some sort of awful slow motion that made her want to puke.

Crew looked up, nervousness clear on his face. He glanced at Dahlia, then looked back at the new woman. "Mackenzie," he said tightly. Her brow furrowed and she checked to see what he had looked at. When she saw Dahlia, a furious understanding crossed her features and she stepped all the way inside, bowing her shoulders and clenching her fists.

"Mackenzie, no," Crew warned.

Mackenzie didn't listen. She dropped the purse she was holding and began to crouch. Before Dahlia understood what was going on, Mackenzie had turned, shifting into her werewolf form. Dahlia shook herself, trying to unfreeze, knowing she was about to be torn to pieces and there was nothing she could do about it.

Crew ran for Mackenzie but Mackenzie was closer, jumping for Dahlia even as her body was still twisting, changing, conforming to fit the white and deadly wolf shape it sought. Just before Mackenzie's teeth closed around her throat, Dahlia forced herself to move. She ducked and slid under Mackenzie, rolling onto the floor, getting caught in the blanket. Mackenzie's claws raked painfully across her shoulder and tore the blanket to shreds.

"No!" Crew shouted, running full speed, catching Mackenzie in a flying tackle, his arms around her, pulling her to his chest. She ripped at him with her claws and bit at his head. Blood flew and Dahlia scrambled away, looking around for a weapon. Anything to protect herself with.

The door opened again. "What in the hell?" Mac asked, his voice strangely calm. "Mackenzie, shit, girl, didn't we talk about this already!" He shifted into a white wolf just like Mackenzie's but bigger, his clothes tearing and falling off him. Dahlia gathered her blanket around her and backed into a wall, breathless with shock, her shoulder throbbing. Mac jumped on top of Mackenzie, grabbing her throat in his teeth and shaking until she let go of Crew and turned to fight Mac. As soon as she did, Mac shifted until he lay on the floor as a man, her teeth clamped around his throat.

"You gonna kill me, Mackenzie? Will that make you feel better?" he yelled, and he almost sounded like he was laughing. He was completely naked, but Dahlia couldn't look away.

Crew scrambled to his feet and skirted both of them, picking up his and Dahlia's clothes and pushing her into a bedroom. "What about Mac?" she forced out as he slammed the door, cutting off her view.

"She won't hurt him. They fight like that all the time."

Dahlia eyed him, not sure what to think. Flesh hung from his skull in flaps and blood flowed freely from his shoulders and arms. She backed away from him, running into something. She turned and it was a dresser with a mirror on the top. In the lower right corner was a heart drawn in lipstick. Dahlia stared at it, unable to think.

Facing away from him, she watched Crew in the mirror. He examined the wounds on his arms and shoulders and held a hand to his head. He pressed his lips together and seemed to concentrate, then he crouched like Mackenzie had done. Hair grew where only skin had been, his face changed shape, and his ears grew and moved. She whirled around, wide-eyed.

Unable to run, unable to hide, as he turned into a gorgeous but deadly silvery-white wolf with black-tipped ears and fur, his eyes that flat orange-yellow she'd seen earlier. But he was only a wolf for a second, not long enough for her to get a good look at him. As soon as the transformation was complete, he reversed it, and stood there as a man again, his wounds gone. Her mouth dropped open. He was completely healed, blood on his skin the only reminder left of his injuries.

When he saw her look of astonishment, his eyes narrowed in confusion. "You're hurt," he said, almost gently.

Dahlia swallowed hard.

Was he about to discover she was human? She almost hoped so. She felt like she was lying to him by not admitting it.

She held her breath as he approached her, then brushed her hair away from her shoulder to get a better look at the scratches there. "It's nothing," she murmured, hoping that was true. With their regenerative ability, they probably didn't own even a tube of Bacitracin.

She realized he was standing stock still and she looked up at him. "Crew?"

He stared at her neck, his hand frozen against her hair. She frowned. Was he staring at her tattoo there? He should like that one. Or was there some taboo against a tattoo of a wolf here? Nerves fluttered in her belly. He pulled his eyes away, to her shoulder.

"You should shift."

"I can't," she bit out.

"You can't," he repeated, then his eyes met hers.

"Crew..." she said, but a pained look in his expression stopped her. He didn't want to know the truth. But she did. "The woman, Mackenzie, is she an ex?"

"No," he said absently, like it was no big deal.

Her jaw clenched. "A current?"

That shook him. "No! She's Mac's sister. I've never encouraged her attentions."

Dahlia stepped to the side and indicated the heart drawn in lipstick on the mirror.

"She must have done that earlier this evening, before the rut."

"She was in your room?"

Crew touched her elbow softly, his voice low. "She's nothing to me, never has been. She cleans up here sometimes. But I won't let her in my room again. It's hard to talk her out of things she wants—"

"—and she wants you."

Crew smiled sadly. "Even if I were interested, which I am not, Mac is my best friend in this world. I would not date his sister."

Dahlia stiffened, playing those words back over in her mind. *This world.* Surely, he'd meant, *the world.*

Dahlia pulled her hair forward, covering her shoulder and her tattoo, then gathered her clothes. "Ok," she said simply. She believed him and exhaustion was hitting her hard. Her eyelids drooped, her real world called. "Crew, I—do you mind if I sleep here, with you?"

He nodded vehemently. "I want you to."

Then why did his face look panicked, like she had asked him for something he couldn't possibly provide?

***

Crew hurried into the living room, glad to find Mackenzie gone and Mac eating cereal again. "Was Mackenzie ok?" he asked, his mind still mostly on the black and silver tattoo of the wolf behind Dahlia's ear. A shot from above, showing the wolf's back, and the two white stars on its shoulders, just like his *renqua*. He shuddered, knowing it meant something that he did not want to face. Not now.

Mac waved his spoon at him. "She'll get over it. She was upset when I told her you thought you'd found your mate, but it probably makes her doubly determined to find her own. Congrats again, wolf, how did it go here, with her? I stayed away as long as I could."

Crew grunted and ignored the question, not sure how he could respond. It had gone both wonderfully, and awfully. "You could have come home about three minutes earlier."

Mac laughed at that. "Nah. Then I woulda missed you rolling around on the floor naked with Mackenzie in your arms. I bet she loved that."

"Fuck off," Crew said companionably enough, crossing the room to get Dahlia's notebook out of her jacket that she had asked for. He resisted the urge to look inside it.

On his way back to his room, he stopped at the kitchen table. "She wants to sleep here. I told her she could."

Mac froze, his spoon halfway to his mouth. "She wants you in there with her, right?"

"Yeah. I'm not sure what to do."

Mac waved the spoon at him and milk splattered across the table. "Go, lie down with her. Make sure she falls asleep first. If she wakes up before you get back, I'll tell her you had an emergency at work and you'll be back soon."

Crew resisted the strong urge to shift and fight at the thought of Mac even *talking* to Dahlia. It was the only thing that would work, and he needed Mac. Plus, he trusted him. And he had no other choice. He hated this affliction more than he ever had before. Maybe today would be the day to take enough sleeping pills to make him sleep permanently. *If only he knew what would happen!*

"Mac, there's one more thing." He glanced towards his room where the door was still shut. "She hasn't come out and said it, but she's implied that she got hit on the head and has amnesia." *And she can't shift.*

Mac whistled and shook his head. "Just like you, Spook, when I first discovered you in our barn stealing eggs, twenty-two years ago."

"Yeah." Crew grimaced. Exactly like him.

Mac leaned forward. "Could she be from your world?"

Crew clenched his fists so hard he felt his nails slice his palms.

Rhen help him if she was.

CHAPTER 14

*D*ahlia woke up slowly, confused at first as to where she was. Her head felt dull and thick, her eyes gritty, like she hadn't slept at all. She blinked, saw her own bedroom, groaned and sat up straight, clutching at her shoulder. Blood had seeped through her shirt.

Emotions warred within her as she jumped to her feet and padded into the bathroom for bandages and antiseptic. Relief to be home, in her own bed, in her real world, hit her strongly. But the weight of missing Crew already sat on her chest, making it hard for her to breathe. Back in her own house, with her belief she'd never see him again, she regretted not sleeping with him. What they shared had been amazing, but not everything she wanted from him.

Their last few moments together had been bliss. He'd brought her notebook to her, smiled acceptingly at her while she half-heartedly wrote a few things down, then he'd crawled into bed facing her and stroked her hair until she fell asleep, her notebook clutched to her chest. She hadn't felt so loved and cared for since her mom had been alive.

Dahlia peeled off her shirt and dropped it to the floor so she could clean the deep scratches in her shoulder, wondering about infection. She carefully taped a bandage over the wound, then stared at the shirt on her floor. It was the same shirt she'd been wearing when she went to sleep, which had never happened before. When she went to sleep, normally she entered her dream world sometimes with her life there already in motion, the dream Dahlia going about her business like normal. But whenever she had woken up still in bed in that world, she'd never been wearing what she'd been wearing when she went to sleep in the real world. And vice versa. It didn't appear back on her body until she woke up in her real world.

Her notebook! Dahlia squeezed her hands open and shut then ran back to her bed. Her notebook was there, pushed partially under the pillow. It had made the transition with her. That had never happened before either.

So what? That was different. That wasn't your dream world. You died in your dream world. You'll never go back there, and you'll never go back to Orion's Belt, either.

Panic made her muscles cramp. She still wasn't used to thinking that she'd died. She would miss her second life. A noise sounded somewhere else in her house and she jumped, a small scream erupting from her throat.

She grabbed onto her notebook and squeezed it in her hands. *Oh, goodie.* Back in the real world with its impending death. Fun times to be scared of noises in your own house.

She heard a yowling from the other room. The sound had been the rescued bobkitten coming in his cat door. "Angel!"

she called, rushing out to see him. He bounded up to her immediately, looking like he'd grown overnight. She picked him up, smoothing the black tufts on his ears, nuzzling him into her neck.

She picked a burr off his fur, wondering if he'd ventured into the woods behind her house yet, like she encouraged him to do. So far, he seemed like he would rather stay in the house and yard. She felt guilty keeping him, but his mom hadn't been around when she'd found him and he'd been too young to survive on his own. She should have let the veterinarian at her work—her old work—decide what to do about him but instead, she'd quit that night, taken him home, and never gone back. She winced, knowing it had been shameful and impulsive, but she'd been less and less able to control her impulses lately. Maybe knowing you were going to die did that to a person. She had enough money in savings to pay rent and eat for a year, if her death didn't happen soon.

She inspected the sores on his back. When she'd found him, or rather when her friend, Heather, had found him and several housecats, plus a woodchuck, inexplicably caught in monster spider webs on the other side of the forest she lived near, he'd been missing fur in a patch on each of his shoulders. Now all that hair was grown in nicely, although strangely.

He was an atypical bobkitten, in that he had much more white fur than most. He wasn't albino; he still had the black patterns and spots of a bobcat, but the white coloring was unusual. The bare patches had grown in completely black with no pattern to them. When she petted his hair straight down towards his tail, they looked like short, stubby angel's wings, which was how she had named him.

She squinted at them, then brushed his fur the wrong

way. She frowned and put him down so she could see him from above.

Dahlia gasped. Now the black patches looked like the almost-stars she'd seen tattooed on Crew's back. Her feelings for him came flooding back to her and her knees felt weak. She stared at Angel, then sat straight down on the floor, tears threatening. Angel made a dangerous cat noise, then ran up to her, putting his paws on her chest, pulling at her chin with one velvet paw until she stared into his eyes. He liked to do that for several minutes each day, and she didn't know why. She'd taken care of a lot of cats at her time at the ASPCA, maybe thousands, and she'd never seen a cat or wild animal do it.

She stared into his eyes, not thinking, letting her mind drift, her hands reaching up to her throat. She normally wore a necklace in this world, too, but it was not there. As her fingers brushed her skin, a memory slammed into her, making bile rise in her throat. She retched dryly, broke eye contact with Angel, and fell backwards to the floor, remembering everything that had happened at the moment she died in a rush of images and sounds.

Dahlia slammed on her brakes and spun her wheel, knowing in her heart she didn't have a chance, either, but unable to give in, give up, not at least try to live, but she impacted the truck anyway. She screamed inside her head as her car crumpled, metal and flesh melding.

Silence. Dahlia screamed, throwing her hands in front of her, turning her head to the side, but it was over. Just over. She looked straight up into nothing. Complete darkness. She blinked, feeling her eyelids scrape against her corneas, but open or closed, she saw nothing different. She tried to get her bearings. She was lying on something soft. She felt around with her hands and found only the softest fur she'd ever felt in her life.

Heaven? Hell? Purgatory? She rolled over and gagged, then got herself under control and tried to stand. Her body worked, but felt stiff and rusty. "Hello?" she called. The sound coming back to her told her she was in a vast open space, but she felt no wind on her face, no atmosphere.

Everything shifted in a nanosecond. The fur underneath her became hard ground, a soft light appeared, and four walls rushed at her until they stopped fifty feet away on all sides. Two of the walls had one ordinary-looking door set in them.

"Hello, ayasha," sounded, and she couldn't decide if the booming voice was in her mind or in her ears. She turned frantically.

Behind her, sat Angel, looking up at her with intelligence in his eyes. No one else was in the room.

"Am I dead?" she said, looking up for the source of the voice, turning in another circle.

"You are. In that world."

Was the voice coming from Angel? Her stomach rolled and she moaned at the saliva filling her mouth, as intense nausea hit her. Around her, in the room, a vision like a movie began to play in the very air. If she wanted to, she could walk right through it. It was the semi-truck, swerving the first time on the road, the point of view of the person watching was hers, in her car behind it. She swallowed hard and put her hands in her hair, pulling on it. "No, no, I don't want to see this again. I'm dead, I'm dead, I died."

"Stop it, then."

The semi swerved again, crossing the lanes of traffic and Dahlia couldn't tear her eyes away. The car next to her was *about to impact and she squeezed her eyes shut, but she could still hear it, so faintly.*

"Ayasha, calm yourself. You are creating this vision. You can control it if you try. Take a deep breath. Imagine only blank space, whiteness, goodness."

Her tires squealed and remembered momentum grabbed at her, but she did as the voice told her, seeing the light inside her head.

"Good. Remember that your emotions may spark the chimera, but your intellect controls it. You will need the power in the future."

Dahlia opened her eyes. The room was only a room again. She blinked, then looked at Angel, still sitting and staring at her. She had a thousand questions, but sensed she wasn't going to get to ask them all.

"Ask the most important ones, ayasha, our time here is short."

"What does that mean—ayasha?"

"It means young one, little one, precious one."

Dozens more questions sprang to her mind at that, but he'd said important ones, so she forced her mind to focus.

"Good," the voice boomed. "Focus is everything."

"Why am I here?" she asked, holding a hand to her head. She could feel he wanted her to ask it, so she did. Why the hell not, right? Crazy or not, she wanted to play by the rules. Rules meant safety.

"You must choose to move on."

"Move on to where?"

Angel's eyes shifted to the door behind her and she looked over her shoulder at it. "Where does it lead?"

"To another world. You will only have one night there, and you must find him in that time."

"Who?"

"He who will hold you above all others."

Dahlia looked at the door again. She liked the sound of that, but what did it mean? Even though the situation was crazy, it was also familiar to her, like she'd been waiting for something like this to happen her entire life. Like it was something she glimpsed in the spaces between going to sleep in her real world and waking up in her dream world.

"How will I know him?"

"By how he treats you, and how he makes you feel."

Dahlia stared at the ceiling. She knew what Angel wanted her to ask next, but she wasn't going to. Instead, she would ask her own question. "Did I die in my dream world so this could happen?"

"No, ayasha, your time was up there, as it soon is in the world where we first met."

Dahlia winced at that. She'd known she was going to die, but here was confirmation. She sighed, and went back on course. "Why must I find him?"

"He is the key to your fate, your destiny, your unification with your true family. If he does not meet you in this manner, he will never let himself love you, because he believes if he does not let himself love you, you do not have to die. But he is wrong. If he does not fulfill his destiny in regards to you, you will still die, and he will be lost."

Dahlia clenched her teeth. "Didn't I just freaking die? Are you playing games with me?"

"No, ayasha, no games. Only life. You must die again."

"Is there no way out of it?"

"There is but one way. Another could take the death for you. You can choose that in the moment, if you like."

That didn't sound good either. Why was on her lips, but the voice spoke quickly, as if heading her question off.

"If you choose to go through the door, you will only have until you fall asleep in the world, and there is much to be accomplished, so listen to me now. Walk in to town, go to the event that all are attending. When you are inside, he will find you. He will be helpless not to."

Angel shifted and the room seemed to grow smaller. "We only have a few minutes left here, ayasha, do not be scared. Your father knew the road ahead of you and your sisters and your mates would be long and dangerous, so he gave you tools, both internal and external to help you find your way. Go, find your mate. It is he who will save you and lead you to your true life."

"Save me from? From my death?"

"No. From what happens after." The small bobkitten stood and crossed the room to the door, where he sat again. "Hurry. No door stays open forever. Do you choose to move forward?"

"What if I don't?"

"Your lives in this plane will be over, an innocent one will die instead of you, and your mate will be lost."

That got Dahlia moving to the door. She could feel the urgency now. She grasped the doorknob. Turning it felt like the end of everything she'd ever known. As it opened a crack and cold wind rushed in at her, her mind slip-slid, like on ice, the conversation she'd just had skittering away. "No! Am I forgetting?"

"You must, ayasha. He who will hold you above all others is powerful and willful. He cannot read your mind but he can sense your being and sometimes your intentions. If you enter this world with an aim, he will resist you."

She chose.

CHAPTER 15

Crew woke up all at once, knowing his office was empty. His hands clenched. "No! Goddammit, no!" he shouted, twisting off his couch to his feet, kicking at the books that lay on his floor. Fierce hatred for this world flooded him. He wanted back with Dahlia.

He strode to his desk and yanked open the drawer, pawing at his right temple with his hand. Directly behind there, that was where he felt Khain's hook. With him again. In the drawer, instead of his pills, he found a note.

Shit's going down. Find me. Don't make me find you.

Beckett's handwriting. Fucker had his pills. Crew would get them back. He strode out of the office, plucking at the hook in his mind as he went. He had to get rid of that thing. He would find the dragon soon and see if he had any ideas on how to get rid of it. But he would do it himself and never go to Wade under any circumstance.

He found Beckett upstairs in the strangely empty duty room. Beckett stood near the back door, arguing with a male who was almost as big as Beckett. *Wolfen?* Crew loped over, listening, but realized as he got closer that the male was human.

Beckett's tone was icy. "Look, I know there's nobody available to take your report right now. You're just going to have to wait or come back later. Go through the front door and wait in the lobby like everybody else. Come back here again, it will be in handcuffs."

The man's eyes narrowed and he poked a finger in Beckett's chest. "You're a cop. Do your fucking job. Shay Carmi, she's my girlfriend. She's been missing for two weeks now."

Beckett's eyes went colder than his tone. "Touch me again and I still won't take your report, but you'll be spending a cold night on a cement floor."

Crew hurried over to keep Beckett from popping the guy. He leaned over to whisper to Beckett. "Carmi."

Beckett whipped his way. "There you are." He turned back to the man. "Get the hell out of here before I do something you'll regret."

Crew shook his head and held up a finger to the man. "Just wait a second." He pulled Beckett around the corner and spoke softly to Beckett. "Carmi is Ella's last name. Shay is her sister. The one who Khain took to the *Pravus*. The one in the hospital now."

Anger leaked out of Beckett's countenance. "Ah fuck," he said softly. "Just what we need today. Do that shit you do and tell Wade. He's around somewhere, waiting for you to show up."

Crew quirked an eyebrow but sought out Wade with his

mind. *We need you in the duty room. Someone reporting Ella's sister missing.*

Wade's voice came back at once. *Not what we need today. Put him in a room. I'll call Trevor in.*

After they did as Wade had asked, Beckett shook his head and pulled Crew to his desk. "Good thing you're finally here. We need everyone on this, especially you. Khain's been popping over here all day long. We think he's trying to find one true mates. He only stays for a moment, so by the time we scramble anyone to the area, there's no trace of him. Plus, there's been a kidnapping. Four-year-old girl. We hope it's not related, but in case it is, the KSRT are actively investigating it. We've pulled everyone in from duty out at Trevor's place except the *bearen*, Graeme, and Trevor. We were supposed to have the induction ceremony today but it's been postponed, indefinitely."

"What ceremony?"

"Graeme, Trent, and Troy are all being sworn into the KSRT."

Pills forgotten, Crew nodded. "About time. What am I supposed to be doing?"

Beckett pulled out a stack of papers. "Here's what we've got." The first paper showed a sketch of a pretty young female. "Possible one true mate. Possible name is *Leilani*. Other than that, we know nothing about who she is or where she lives. She might be in the hospital. Mac and Bruin are looking for her."

"Bruin the bear?"

"Yeah, his chief has loaned him to us. Seems happy to be rid of him. He can stand to be around Mac, so Wade paired them up." Beckett turned that paper over. The next was a picture of a compact, mousy looking male with a large question mark over his head. "This is Boe, the escaped *fox-en* from the *Pravus*. Wade thinks there's a one true mate associated with him somehow, but we have no picture, so we're looking for him. Canyon and Timber are running the network for him while Harlan and Jaggar are out looking for him."

Beckett turned over that paper and Crew's heart and breath stopped. Staring at him was an unsmiling picture of Dahlia, apparently blown up from some sort of work badge. Waves of heat covered his body while his stomach cramped and his mind revolted.

"Dahlia Page. Graeme recognized her as a possible one true mate two weeks ago when she recovered the animals from the forest after the spider incident, working as an ASPCA officer..."

Crew felt his blood pressure drop and his brain go fuzzy. He didn't fight it, he encouraged it. His body tipped to his left and he let himself go completely, until everything was dark.

*

Crew opened his eyes in his dream world, knowing exactly what he was going to see. His arms and bed were empty. Dahlia was not there. He jumped to his feet. "Dahlia, Dahlia!" He ripped open the door to the rest of the house as Mac came running. "Dahlia, where is she?"

Mac shook his head, concern lining his face. "That door hasn't opened."

Crew felt his consciousness waver. Mac's brows drew down over his eyes. "Spook, I can see through you."

Crew tried to speak but his vocal cords didn't want to work. He put out a hand for Mac, but could see the floor through it. The very thoughts in his head went hazy and he felt a strange pulling/drawing sensation.

*

"Crew!" Beckett said, shaking him by the shoulders.

Crew shook his head. He was on the floor… and dripping wet, with ice cubes slipping off of him, plunking into puddles on the floor. He pushed at Beckett. "Why am I wet?"

"Oh, shit, sorry, dude. When you fainted, I didn't know what else to do. You hit the floor and then your body faded. I thought you were going to disappear completely so I poured my soda on you."

"I didn't faint," Crew growled, knowing he had.

"Ok…" Beckett drawled, moving back a bit. "Were you testing the floor for hardness with your face?"

Crew rubbed a hand over his mouth and tried to speak coherently. "Dahlia. I met her last night in my dream world." He scrambled up to his knees and grabbed Beckett by the shirt. "Beck, I—she's my one true mate. And I fell for her already. I might love her."

Beckett stared into Crew's eyes, his expression changing first to shock, then to pity. "Dude."

Crew let go of him. "Do you know where to look for her?"

Beckett shook his head slowly, his eyes wide. "Graeme didn't tell anyone about her until a few days later because he was over in Scotland, but when we finally went to the ASPCA, it turns out she had quit that night. Dropped off the animals and left. No one has seen her since. She doesn't answer her phone and the address they had for her is occupied by someone who's never heard of her. No records under that name and all possible relatives in the city say they don't know her, except for one couple who is overseas. We've left several messages for them and their neighbors say they used to have someone who lived with them who matched Dahlia's description, but no one has seen her there in years."

Wade entered the duty room and both *wolven* scrambled to their feet. "What's going on here?"

Crew didn't know what to say or do. He stood quietly, trying to think of his next move, giving his heart time to stitch itself back together so he could function. Beckett stepped in for him, explaining the situation. When Wade's face filled with pity, too, Crew felt like running. He stood his ground.

"We'll find her," Beckett promised.

"We'll pull everyone off of everything else. Dahlia is our priority," Wade said.

"Woodridge," Crew tried to say, but his voice was too soft. "What?"

"Her last name is Woodridge. Maybe she changed it, I don't know, but look for Dahlia Woodridge." Crew wondered if he were helping her or hurting her by telling them that. "I want to help look for her."

Wade stepped forward and touched Crew on the shoulder. "That's not a good idea. You know why."

Crew rubbed the back of his neck. "I can't just stay here."

Wade nodded. "You're right. Here's what you're going to do. A little girl disappeared today. Paisley White. Her mother is under sedation at the hospital and we need someone from the KSRT to go talk to her great-grandmother, Abigail White. Beckett has the address. You take Trent and Troy with you, and call me immediately if there's any sign of your one true mate."

Crew squeezed his eyes shut. "You gotta find her."

"We will, I swear it," both males said at the same time.

But Crew knew they'd already failed. Something he'd done, or said, or didn't do had already sealed Dahlia's fate.

CHAPTER 16

*D*ahlia pushed herself up into a seated position on her floor and grabbed for Angel. "Angel, you're in on it. Oh my God, what are you?"

The bobkitten yowled in her arms and she realized she was squeezing him. She loosened her hold. No booming voice worked through her consciousness. Desperation caught hold of her. "Angel, how will I meet Crew again if I never go back to Orion's Belt?"

Nothing. The kitten did his version of purring and tried to snuggle into Dahlia's arms. She put him down and stared at him as he nudged her with his furry face, her mind racing.

Her phone rang. She got up to grab it, feeling dazed. More messages from work. She hadn't listened to any of them over the last two weeks, not wanting to hear what her old boss had to say. But now she pressed the button, wanting some sort of normalcy, something to bring her back to reality.

The first few messages were normal. *Dahlia, are you ok, Dahlia, what happened, Dahlia are you coming in today, Dahlia this isn't like you.* No mention of Angel though. Hopefully no one at the office even realized she had him. She'd put him in her car before she'd carried the other animals in, so the only record of him even existing would have been from Heather or that guy she had been with. Dahlia didn't know if she could get in trouble for what she had done, but she thought the answer was probably yes.

The tone of the eighth message was different. *Dahlia, the police are looking for you, they say you don't live at the address you gave us.* Dahlia stared at the phone, then pressed delete all. She didn't want to hear one more message.

She paced around her apartment, trying to think of what to do next, although when she finally decided, she realized she had known all along. Nothing for now. Go to sleep and see what happened. Would she go anywhere? Would she somehow see Crew or talk to Angel again?

She took a deep breath. "Ok," she said to no one, not even Angel. She loved the furry little guy but was miffed that he wouldn't talk to her, or couldn't talk to her. Maybe she could direct him in her dreams.

"Oh!" she said to no one. She remembered the scene of the semi-truck playing over, scaring her, and remembered Angel telling her she had caused it. She'd seen things like that before, but never attributed it to herself. Now she *had* to know for sure.

She looked around. Where was a good place to attempt an experiment? Finally she entered her bedroom and sat cross-legged on the middle of the bed, her back against the headboard.

She closed her eyes, feeling silly. What had Angel said?

Your emotions may spark the chimera, but your intellect controls it.

Emotions. Think of an emotion. Happiness. Joy. She opened her eyes. Nothing. She laughed at herself, then closed her eyes again. She probably had to *feel* the emotion, but how? If she wanted to feel happiness, what would cause it? She slouched against the wall and imagined Crew's intense, handsome face in her mind. He smiled at her and her soul lit up. She placed him a few feet away so she could see his body, then made him naked. Whoa. Good thing nobody could see her thoughts. Her body responded immediately, her breasts growing heavy and her spine tingling, a wicked smile fixed on her face.

This isn't joy, it's lust. Clothes back on. Now what? Maybe we do something fun together. Go on vacation? A sandy beach and a moving blue ocean slid around Crew, his work attire replaced by board shorts and bare feet. He beckoned to her. She took his hand and they ran into the waves together, laughing. She put everything she had into it, coloring each aspect of the scene as if it were real life, holding up her hand to shade the glare of the sun from her eyes. She smelled the salt of the ocean and heard the caw of a seagull.

Angel chattered from in the living room and Dahlia opened her eyes as the image in her mind ripped apart. Her mouth dropped open as she saw that her room was drenched in sunshine. As she watched, a white bird flew from nowhere to swoop over Angel's head into the living room. Angel crouched and made a twisting leap for it, but couldn't reach that high.

The sunshine faded.

Dahlia gaped at the light, until it was completely gone,

her room her own once again. She shook her head. Creepy? Or awesome? She couldn't decide.

She slammed her eyes shut, wanting to see exactly how *real* the chimera was. Another scene came to her. Jungle. Plants everywhere. Ferns. Heavy, hot air. Struggle to breathe it in. Mud that never quite dries underfoot. The incessant call of bugs on all sides. Dahlia peeked with one eye. Her room was bare.

She frowned. Oh, yeah, emotion. What exactly would she feel in the jungle scene she had created? She crossed her hands over her chest and tried to imagine how she would end up there. What if she'd been born in the jungle, one of those tribes untouched by Western civilization? She'd be a hunter with a spear, stalking an animal who would kill her if she didn't kill it first. She needed it for food... or for medicine for her younger sister who lay dying of—of something... and the lion's blood, once treated, would provide a cure.

Dahlia ignored the absurdity of her creation. In her imagination, anything could work.

She crouched in the bed, her right hand clenched on air, her left hand moving plants out of the way in front of her. A wary thrill coursed through her, along with her concern for the sister, and measured apprehension at the danger she was undertaking. Her closed eyes looked down at nothing, but saw a lion track. A big one sunk deep into the mud. The thick, heady scent of rotting vegetation forced its way into her nostrils.

She forgot to check the real world until Angel yowled, then she opened her eyes slowly. All around her, jungle leaves, vines, and foliage closed in. She looked up. Instead of her ceiling, treetops soared overhead. Dahlia scrambled to her feet and pushed backwards through the jungle, feeling the leaves scrape at her arms. "Angel?"

A massive roar split the room, making her jump and utter a scream that she quickly cut off. Plants in front of her quaked, the leaves shaking, making her throw her arms up in a defensive gesture, but it was only Angel, streaking into her arms and quaking there in fear.

White light! Nothingness! She took several gulping deep breaths and squeezed her eyes shut to imagine blankness and the absence of fear.

Dahlia opened her eyes and looked around.

Her room was back, the jungle gone, but still the small, white-striped kitty in her arms trembled and hid its face in her chest.

CHAPTER 17

*C*rew downshifted the truck and cruised to a stop at the light, his mind far away. Trent sat next to him and Troy behind. Crew didn't mind working with the two non-shifting wolves, because both of them talked a lot less than anyone else on the KSRT, and when they did talk, they spoke in *ruhi*, which Crew preferred. Plus, they were vicious and strong, always in wolf form, and both had been in the *Pravus* to fight Khain on his home turf, two of only four *wolven* who had ever done so. If Khain showed up, neither would hesitate to attack with intent to kill.

Trent interrupted his thoughts. *Tell me about traveling.*
What?

Troy perked up from the back seat and put his head over the divider, looking at each of them in turn.

Traveling, isn't that what it's called when you live a second life in your dreams?

Crew frowned. No one had asked him about it in twenty years, and now Beckett *and* Trent in two days? *I guess that's what it's called. Mostly nobody calls it anything because no one does it but me, that I know of.*

You talked to the dragon yet? He says eight to ten percent of all humans and shiften are travelers, but half of them don't realize it and the rest don't talk about it.

The light changed and Crew drove on, mystified.

Troy sneezed, his version of a scoff, then faced Trent. *When did you talk to him? And why didn't you tell me?*

I don't tell you everything.

Maybe you should.

Crew held up a hand to interrupt them. *Wait, you said humans are travelers, too? Why? What is the point of it?*

You really have to talk to Graeme. It's something about keeping continuity between worlds and spreading ideas. He says traveling is not his expertise, but I think that male has forgotten more shiften and dragen lore than the rest of us will ever know, and the dragen were great travelers, even the ones who didn't do it in their dreams. It's a dragen skill, being able to force their way between worlds.

Crew fell silent, thinking. He wasn't a natural traveler, he knew that much, he'd only started doing it after his showdown with Khain so many years ago, but what if Dahlia was? Would that explain how he met her in his dream world? But had she disappeared from there while she slept? He'd been brushing her hair back from her face and only would let himself fall asleep after he was certain she already had. Had he been wrong about when she'd fallen asleep? Or did she not disappear?

Trent cleared his throat. *So is it like a realistic dream? Or do you fall asleep and wake up in a completely different kind of existence and you know that you couldn't possibly be dreaming?*

Crew looked at him questioningly. *Anyone who travels the way I do, knows it. Injuries you get in one world transfer to the next if you don't heal them. Tattoos, too. Haircuts, that kind of stuff. They don't always look exactly like they did in the other world, but there's always some sort of transference. At least for me.*

Troy chuffed. *Why are you asking, Trent? Does this have anything to do with the big slice on your foot that you can't explain?*

Trent lifted his foot and looked at it. Crew could see a nasty gouge there that had taken most of the pad of his big toe. Trent set his foot down and faced forward. *Just curious.*

Troy stood up in the back seat and his voice grew soft in both their heads. *And with all those wolf documentaries you watch? You looking for someone or something, Trent? I'm your brother, you can tell me.*

There's nothing to tell, Trent said, his tone contemplative.

Crew wondered. Trent wasn't one to waste words, one reason why Crew liked him. He hooked a left turn and parked in front of their destination, looking out the window at the red and white door and the sign over it reading *You Need It.*

We've been here before, Troy said. *Trevor bought Ella's pendant here.*

Trent sat up straighter. *Right. This is Mrs. White's second store. Ella blew up the first one when Khain tried to snatch her from downtown.*

Crew grabbed his notebook off the dash and flipped through it. *Mrs. White. That's who I'm interviewing. Her great-granddaughter disappeared earlier today.*

The mood in the truck shifted. This was no longer busy

work or just-in-case work. Coincidences always meant Khain or Rhen or maybe both were involved, shaping reality in a way the *citlali*, the spiritual leaders of the *shiften*, tried to interpret.

Crew jumped out quickly, but it was Trent who took command. *Troy, you go inside with Crew, I'll wait at the door so I don't upset her. Both of you pay close attention to her emotional state and whatever you can get from it. I'll have Wade assign someone to start digging into her family and see if she's connected to us at all.*

Crew nodded. He wasn't so good at spotting lying, especially if the subject was a good liar, but he had other mental skills. Between him and Troy, they would know exactly what had happened.

Once inside, he crossed the room quickly, with Troy on his heels, straight to the cabinet of curios with the elderly woman behind it, a look of absolute disgust on her face. She was short with a heavily-lined face, and dressed extravagantly, a stole around her shoulders. Crew sniffed. Mink. Old, but impeccably preserved.

"You the cop, pretty boy?" she asked, contempt on her face. "You found my great-granddaughter yet?"

"No. I needed to ask you some questions."

She waved a hand. "How many cops am I going to have to talk to before one of you remembers what I say?"

"We're trying to be thorough."

She sniffed at that and her eyes landed on Troy, sitting attentively next to Crew, watching her. She curled her lip in distaste.

"I need to know exactly what happened. Tell me everything from when you woke up."

The woman pressed her lips together, but Crew could feel

her dredging the memory up. He joined it, grimacing at the nastiness of her thoughts, but not shying away. He watched the picture in her mind, instead of listening to her words, only asking her questions when she didn't mention something he could see. Troy stayed quiet, meaning she was telling the truth.

When she described the empty yard as she and her grand-daughter ran out to look for Paisley, Crew caught a faint hint of an acrid, fiery smell in her memory. He clenched his fists and tried not to curse. Troy looked at him questioningly.

Crew held it together until the old woman was done talking. He wanted to murder Khain. How dare he? He took a few deep breaths and got himself under control. "Is there anything else you think we should know?"

Mrs. White's demeanor had cracked slightly while recounting her tale, and now her voice was much softer than before. "She's only four, officer. So little and innocent. You have to find her quickly."

Crew had been trained never to promise humans anything—they died so easily—but he couldn't help the pledge that rose to his lips. "We will. I swear it."

Mrs. White's hand trembled as she reached across the counter to grasp Crew's arm in a surprisingly tight grip. "You're the first person who's told me there was a chance. Please, you personally, go out and look for her. I feel like you could succeed where others have failed. There's something about you."

Crew didn't answer. At her touch, another scene thrust into his mind. Not from that day, but from maybe a week before. Paisley's face looked overly beautiful and angelic as she spoke in Mrs. White's memories. "I don't remember, Nana."

Crew looked down in Mrs. White's memory, running a

gnarled thumb over the scar on Paisley's arm. "You scratched yourself in your sleep?"

"No, Nana, I…" Her voice faltered and she looked down. "Maybe I did."

Crew stared through Mrs. White's eyes at the scar on Paisley's arm that looked at least a month old, but hadn't been there the day before.

CHAPTER 18

*D*ahlia wrote furiously, doing the only thing that could disengage her mind from her troubles, so she didn't have to think about other worlds, lost loves, or strange jungles that shouldn't have ever been there.

Her fingers pounded against the keyboard until they hurt, until six hours later, when she finally typed the two words she'd been seeking since she'd started to write her short story about the werewolf who fell in love with a human woman, and how exactly they made their life work.

She read over the last few paragraphs:

Cole held out a hand to her. Danielle took it, trying to keep her fingers from shaking, as he spoke with an amber eye to the horizon. "We'll go, then. If we can't build a life here, we'll go somewhere we can. No matter what our differences, we can make it work. I knew I had to have you the moment I saw you, and that hasn't changed, human or not."

Hope soared inside Danielle. But... "Cole, can we, well, do you want..."

"Babies? Yes. We can have babies, Danielle. They'll be strong warriors like their father, or beautiful, proud vixens like their mother."

He pulled her close and stared down into her eyes, wiping away one errant tear. "Don't worry, baby, I'll take care of you from now on. You'll never have to be afraid of anything again."

They kissed, the sun finally slipping below the horizon as their lips met. Danielle's eyes were slightly open, so she saw the flash of light in the sky as it went down, like the very gods were blessing them.

She grimaced. Cheesy. Awful. But even as she criticized herself, she knew she could fix it up into something her fan base would love. She'd been writing for years without ever trying to get a book published. She did it because she had to, because the stories filled her mind and tore at her brain until she put them out into the world.

Last year, she'd worked sixteen-hour shifts for over a week when a neighboring town flooded and homeowners had to abandon their animals on their land. During that week, with its constant flow of injured and flood-water-poisoned animals, she hadn't had time to write even a word before falling into bed, and the build-up of stories in her imagination had made it hard for her to tell fantasy from reality by the fifth day. Her boss had finally forced her to go home sick because of her *mental state*, and she'd spent that day writing eighteen hours straight, not even stopping to eat. She'd completed a full thirty-two thousand words and put it up on the online storytelling community where she had almost six hundred followers who devoured every word she wrote.

Her avatar there was Accalia, which meant she-wolf. She'd chosen it when Acca Larentia, who had been the adoptive mother of Romulus and Remus from Roman times, had been taken. She'd always loved all things wolf, and after the captured werewolf had been discovered in her dream world was when the urge to write had overtaken her.

She pressed 'publish' on her story, no sense waiting when she didn't know how long she had to live, and wondered why she never wrote in her dream world. She wrote in her notebook there, but had never crafted and recorded a story.

The website wanted a title, which she hadn't thought of yet. She sat in her comfy chair, absently petting Angel, who was in her lap, and let her mind wander, ignoring a howling noise she heard from outside, somewhere far away. Her fingers typed *Second Chances* on their own.

Good enough. She pressed 'publish' again and put Angel on the ground so she could stand and stretch.

Was the noise someone crying? A little girl? Dahlia opened her front door, listening hard, unable to tell if the noise was inside her own mind or coming from outside. It seemed to come from all directions at once.

Troubled, she walked down her front stoop, her body pulling her mind along.

Angel growled from in the house.

Dahlia ignored him, and kept walking, not even stopping to get a coat, lured by the sound of the girl wailing as if her heart were broken.

***

Crew strode inside the duty room, praying they'd found Dahlia while he'd been with Mrs. White. Mac, Bruin, Beckett and Wade were huddled over a computer, making Crew's heart fall. He could read in each of their beings that they had not found her. His hands clenched as he overheard Beckett say, "The restraining order says he assaulted her, then stalked her while he was waiting for his court date. That must be when she changed her name, moved, and didn't tell anyone her new address, not even the post office box where she got her mail. She gave them her aunt and uncle's address."

"Have the cell phone company trace her phone's location," the bear suggested.

"We tried that already, she's got an app on it that makes it untraceable. This guy must have really messed with her."

Crew's teeth squeaked, he was grinding them together so hard. Donnie Bryan was the name she had given him. He didn't care what world Bryan was in, Crew would find him and make sure he was counting worms before the next full moon.

Wade sensed him and turned to him, giving him a questioning look.

He gave his report in *ruhi*, unable to speak out loud. *Khain's got her. The old lady didn't see it, but I could smell him through her memory.*

Wade took it as hard as Crew had known he would. His back stiffened, but his spirit curdled. A missing human on his watch. A little girl. Khain hadn't acted as a real threat to humans in the area for years, but now that had changed.

Jaggar sprinted into the duty room, a piece of paper held aloft. "We found her! Canyon hacked into her credit card records and found a package delivered to 4123 Ashland Court. That's less than a mile away."

Crew's emotions spiked as he turned to run out the door, but Wade caught him as he was hitting the handle with the heel of his hand. "Us first. You give us five minutes to secure her, then follow. Where's Trent and Troy?"

"Outside somewhere," Crew mumbled, motioning for Wade and the others to go, listening for Khain's footprint inside his head.

"Bring them when you come. We're gone."

The duty room emptied and Crew only stared at the wall, knowing it was wrong. Wrong. He'd done it all wrong. Khain was already at her house.

Don't worry, pup, she's not at home, I checked, Khain said inside his head.

Crew shouted in rage, then grabbed his short hair in his hands and tugged, ripping some out by the roots. He dropped to the ground and shifted, knowing his human form did not have the fortitude for what he was about to do.

Standing as a wolf just inside the exit, he imagined his being as an amorphous but powerful knife inside his body and hacked at his own brain, biting back the screams of pain that his wolf vocal cords couldn't even make.

In a moment, it was over. He slumped to the ground, and blood leaked out his ear. Just before he passed out, he pulled himself together enough to shift, not knowing if his brain would heal or not.

***

Crew, wake the fuck up! Troy screamed inside his head as Trent licked his face mercilessly.

"Ugh," Crew muttered, shoving Trent away.

Back at you, Trent muttered.

How long was I out?

Couldn't have been more than a few moments.

Trent cocked his head to the left. *Hear that?*

Crew pushed himself to his feet and hurriedly pulled on his clothes, not bothering to inspect them for rips. *Hear what?*

But he heard it, too. A little girl crying. His heart seized up, and he headed for the door.

Once outside, the one man and two wolves all tried to go in different directions.

It's this way.

No, it's coming from this way.

Crew ignored them and started running. He knew it was coming from straight ahead, across the parking lot, just on the other side of the grassy field.

Wade spoke inside his head. *Crew, she's not here. Don't come out here yet. Her front door is open, so we don't think she's far. We're looking for her now.*

Crew didn't bother to answer. He'd seen this in his mind a thousand times. He knew how it turned out. His heart burned like fire in his chest and still he was unable to not play his part if it meant seeing her one more time.

The snow in the field crunched under his boots and the winter wind whipped around his face. He saw Khain, looking like a normal man near a copse of trees, the snow around him melted. In his arms, he held not Dahlia, but Paisley. She was asleep with color in her cheeks and a sweet smile on her face. The crying came from Khain's body, like a record on repeat.

Crew skidded to a stop, noting the placement of Khain's fingers around Paisley's neck. Only they revealed his true nature. The nails were hooked claws, sharp as daggers, the threat clear.

He felt, rather than saw, Dahlia emerge from behind a tree to his left. He held out a hand to her, his eyes never leaving Khain's fingers. He'd always thought he would fight Khain to the death, but now he knew why he couldn't. Why he would have to hand over his one true mate without so much as a word of protest. He didn't even stop to consider if she would go.

Dahlia's fingers wound around his, but she didn't look at him. "Oh," she said lightly, as her gaze landed upon the little girl in the monster's arms.

"Dahlia," he said, wanting to explain it to her. To apologize. To tell her there was nothing he could do, but he wished there was with every bit of his being. That he would remember her forever, love her for eternity, never dream of taking another, for what he hoped was an extremely short life.

She turned to him for just a moment, her eyes no longer looking haunted. Now she looked only at peace. She smiled at him. "It's ok. I know what happens now. I've seen it in my daydreams many times."

He tried to speak but she held her finger to his lips. "Me too. Forever."

She turned away from him and went to the monster, only letting go of Crew's fingers when her forward motion forced her to. She stopped three feet from Khain. "Give the girl to Crew and I'll come to you," she said, her voice clear and strong.

Khain juggled Paisley into one arm, caught Dahlia in the other, then floated Paisley across the field to Crew. Khain's jagged claws found Dahlia's throat instead.

All around Crew, the yelling and shouts of his pack reached his ears. Too late. The first one to him took Paisley from his arms, and that was all he needed to fulfill his part of the transaction. He shifted and ran for Khain, his thoughts in slow motion, his emotions on hold.

Khain's hand jerked and Dahlia slumped, then fell to the ground as Khain disappeared. Crew's animal howled in despair even as it ran to her.

She lifted a hand to him. "Crew," she said weakly, then her eyes slipped closed and she died.

CHAPTER 19

*D*ahlia stirred, then opened her eyes on the same carpet of fur. She jumped to her feet, her hands flying to her throat. It was intact, the pain of her death already fading.

"Angel!" she shouted, as the room lit with the northern lights, greens and blues and a pink so intense it hurt her eyes.

The walls slid in close and quickly and, this time, there were three doors. Angel sat in the same spot he had the first time.

"Well done, ayasha. You truly did die well."

"So now I'm dead for good?"

"Of course not, no one ever dies for good."

"The little girl?"

"—will be fine."

The lights flared and Dahlia stared at them, encouraging them, until they blinded her, then she imagined them away.

"And Crew?"

"He suffers, but he will not for long. When he realizes you can be recovered, he will set out to find you, and the trek will soothe his despair."

"What about you, Angel? Will you be ok?"

"The wolves will find me soon. The dragon will know what to do with me."

Dahlia blinked and shook her head. Dragon? Instead of wasting time on that, she asked the most important question. "Will Crew recover me?"

"He will have to make a choice, just like you will, and the sum of your choices will determine your fate."

"You didn't answer my question."

"I do not know the answer, ayasha. I believe he will. I hope he will. If he does not, the world will still spin and the fight against the demon will go on, but without the two of you."

Dahlia swallowed hard, then decided she only had one choice, and that was to decide, and know, with all her being, that Crew would find her. "Is the demon the one who killed me?"

"Yes. Khain is the name he uses. He will hunt you and your sisters as long as he draws breath, but you are strong, all of you."

"I don't have any sisters, Angel."

Angel chuckled and the noise in her head made her think of rainbows and babies laughing. "But you do, ayasha. Thousands of sisters."

"What is that, some kind of metaphor?"

Angel laughed again, making her smile. "No. No metaphor. But your sisters are not what we are needing to discuss now."

"Let me ask you an *important* question. Are you God?"

"I am but one aspect of God, as are you."

She frowned at that but felt he would not answer any other questions along that line. That was ok, she had other questions. Many others. "Why are we here? Why do we live?"

"For the fun of it, for the joy of it, for the love that we feel when we come together."

"Hm. It didn't feel very fun while I was dying."

"That is only because you do not understand your true nature and power."

Ok. He could out-answer her like she was a toddler. "Do you mean the things I can create with my mind when I imagine with emotion?"

"No, although I enjoy them immensely. Imagining is not the only time you can do that. You create entire universes when you write stories."

"I—I what?"

"A discussion for another time, ayasha, perhaps in your dreams. Time again grows short, and you have a choice to make."

She stared at the doors. "Does it matter which one I choose?"

"All things rest upon your decision, but you are not the only one making decisions."

"Enough with the puzzles already, Angel, I'm full up," she said, holding her hand, palm-down, at the level of her nose.

Angel laughed again in her mind, although the bobkitten on the floor did not move at all. "I apologize. The answers to your questions are complex. Now, we cannot tarry. You must choose a door and no matter which you choose, your aim is the same. There is a—he made some noise in his throat that she couldn't quite follow—that you must find."

"Wait, a what?"

He made the noise again, like he was spitting the word out, a word full of throaty consonants. Then he changed it. "I apologize. We shall call it a trinket, or a bauble, or perhaps a talisman will do."

A picture rose to her mind of a pendant approximately an inch and a half high. It rotated in her imagination and her mouth dropped open as she saw both sides. On one side was an angel in flowing robes with a bowed head and wings peeking from its back, on the other, a snarling wolf with amber eyes.

"I've seen that. I had that! My mother—" she broke off, remembering the last time she had seen it. She'd been so very young, maybe four years old, and her mother had come to her in her room and sat on the floor next to her. She remembered her mother's flowing hair and kind eyes and the way she spoke, like Dahlia was the most important thing in the world. She'd held up the pendant so that Dahlia could see it and said, "This is yours, Dahl. Your father left it for you. I see him in my dreams sometimes and I think he wants me to show this to you." She'd spoken of Dahlia's father in that way many times, but not giving his name or telling Dahlia any more about him. She'd just said she would tell Dahlia more when she was older.

Dahlia had held up a finger to touch the pendant, not knowing if she wanted to touch the angel or the wolf more, but when her finger grazed it, her mother had disappeared. Dahlia's throat constricted and she couldn't breathe over the lump. That had been the last time she'd seen her mother in that world. Two days later a delivery man had found her home alone, eating spaghetti raw from the pantry, and had called the authorities. Dahlia had gone to live with her mother's sister, who had just gotten married. Neither Aunt Angela or Uncle Dan had seemed to like her much, but they had taken care of her. No one had ever discovered what had happened to her mom, and young Dahlia was unable to tell them what she didn't understand.

In her dream world, her mother had still been there. Dahlia had relished going to sleep every night, knowing she would see her mother. Every time she'd tried to explain to her dream mother that she'd disappeared in the real world her mother had pulled her into a hug and told her she had such a big imagination, and that she would be a writer someday. She hadn't had to go live with her aunt and uncle in her dream world until she had been fourteen years old, and her mother had died of something the doctors never had been able to explain. Dahlia had treasured every year she'd had her there, understanding that most kids who lost their parents did not get to still see them in another world.

"Yes, ayasha." Angel's voice was gentle. "You remember true." He waited for a moment until she calmed herself, then went on. "You must choose a door, then you must find the talisman, no matter which door you go through. There is one in each world. You must procure it, regardless of the cost. What happens then, I cannot see. It depends on your choices and the choices of those looking for you."

Dahlia walked to the first door and lightly rested her fingers on it. She could feel it. The pull of the pendant, or talisman, as Angel liked to call it. It wanted her to find it. It called to her.

She walked slowly to the next door. Another talisman, but this one brought knowledge that scared her. The talisman and the knowledge called to her, but she sensed the knowledge would break her. She hurried on and touched the third door.

"I feel many talismans behind this door."

"That is the world you just came from. You cannot return there until your fate is bound. Only your mate can do that for you."

"Crew?"

For the first time, she sensed displeasure, or perhaps unease from Angel. "Are you asking me, or telling me?"

"Telling you. Crew. Will he be able to find me in either of these worlds, no matter which I choose?"

"If he is willful enough, strong enough, and clever enough, he will be able to find you in any world at any time."

Dahlia noticed he hadn't exactly answered her question, but she didn't care. Tingles marched up and down her spine. Crew would find her in no time. Maybe she wouldn't have to be alone for very long.

Still, her traitor mouth asked one more question. "What if he does not find me? What happens to me?"

"You doubt him?"

She shook her head, shame heating her cheeks. "No."

"Your imagination is strong, ayasha. Never feed it that which you do not wish to see."

Dahlia remembered the lion and shuddered, knowing that was both exactly what he meant and not at all what he meant.

"You must choose now."

Dahlia put her hand on the second door again, shying away from what she sensed there, then went to the first door and stood in front of it. "Will it be dangerous?"

"All worlds are dangerous, otherwise there would be no discovery, no chances, no possibility of great triumph or sorrow, and without those things, there would be no fun, no chase, no joy, no love."

Dahlia put her hand on the knob but could not turn it.

"Do not be afraid, ayasha. The entire universe and all worlds within it support you. Many beacons and helpers exist to point your way within worlds. I am one such beacon. Your eldest sister is another. Your mate is a third. Your path will be lit from beginning to end, and if you stray from it, there will be chance after chance to find your way back."

But Dahlia was afraid. Complete unknown was behind that door, and Crew was not in that world yet. "What would happen if I stayed here?"

"Ah, that is a choice I have not offered you, because I did not believe you would choose it. If you stay, I will guide you to your *eternal reward*, and you will reside there, permanently. Do you choose it?"

Dahlia shook her head. "No." The way he said 'eternal reward' told her what it was. Heaven. The afterlife. Done, over, finito. She wasn't ready.

"You do relish the danger of these worlds, like all who are here with you. Go, ayasha. I will call for you when it is time. Be as quick as you can, as I will hold the time between the worlds consistent, but I cannot do it forever."

Dahlia grasped the doorknob harder.

And turned it.

CHAPTER 20

Crew stared at Dahlia's body, anguish filling him. He sat back on his haunches and howled out his pain, then shifted into his human form and fell over the top of her, his tears spilling out onto her chest, not noticing the cold against his naked skin. "No. No. I couldn't stop it. I'm so sorry, Dahlia. My fault, all my fault."

A hand landed on his shoulder, then another one on his other shoulder. He didn't have to look around to know it was Wade and Beckett. The smells of their sorrow for him overwhelmed him, lacing over the top of Dahlia's swiftly fading lavender.

"Get away from us!" he shouted, gathering her into his arms, wanting only to smell her, remember her, have no one interfere with his grief. He didn't give a shit about their sorrow. They couldn't help him through it, no one could. He rocked her in his arms and buried his face in her hair, howling, even in his human form.

But then her body began to lose its form. He couldn't feel her skin against his hands, even though he could still see her. She became transparent, fading in the dim light. "No. NO!"

Her body disappeared completely and his arms held only cold winter air. He shot to his feet. "Rhen! he shouted. "Give her back to me, goddammit! I'll curse you, too! I swear—"

He stopped, then turned in a circle, ignoring his packmates who had moved back several feet, wary eyes on him. Her body had disappeared, like his did when he slept. Did that mean?

"Knock me the fuck out!" he screamed, his voice cracking, looking at no one in particular. He ran to Beckett and grabbed him by his shirt, shaking him. "Knock me out, Beck, quick!"

Beckett put his hands up. "Crew, calm do—"

"Fuck that, Beckett! Don't tell me to calm down! You fucking saw her die!" He let go of Beckett and ran to Jaggar, grabbing him like he had Beckett. "Jaggar, do it man, I gotta know."

Jaggar shook his head like Crew was crazy. Oh fuck. He didn't have time for this! He ran to Mac. "Mac, I know you don't understand, but I gotta be unconscious! Knock me—"

Mac's meaty fist came up in a roundhouse blow and caught him in the temple.

His world went dark.

***

Crew came to all at once, rolling off the bed onto the floor and retching on hands and knees, his head pounding. He shifted for just a moment, wondering how much more his brain could take, then shifted back to human form and stood, rushing out of his room.

Mac was at the table, eating cereal again. "Spook! What the fuck is going on? You were only here for a minute earlier, and in the middle of the day. Is she back? Is that why you're naked?"

Crew stumbled to the table. "You haven't seen her? Not all day?"

Mac's face lined with worry. "No."

Crew stared at the ceiling, what hope he had ebbing away. He sat in a chair and dropped his head to the table, his heart destroyed. There was no avoiding fate. When fate wanted you, it could get you anywhere.

"Crew, wolf, you're scaring me."

"She died. She's dead. She was in my other world, and now she's gone."

Crew didn't speak or move for a long time. He could feel Mac's weighty consideration but he couldn't care about it.

"Why did you come running back here looking for her?"

Crew lolled his head, wishing he could really die of a broken heart, because his was shattered and he was tired. "Because her body disappeared."

Mac stood and moved about the kitchen, putting something on the table near Crew. When he popped the top, Crew knew it was a beer. He didn't want it, but he drank it all in one guzzle anyway.

"So when her body disappeared, you thought she came back over here."

Crew didn't answer, dropping his head to the table again with a loud crack. What did he do now? She was gone. In both worlds. There was nothing for him.

Mac cleared his throat. "What if she went to another world?"

Crew squeezed the beer bottle in his hand until it cracked, the jagged glass cutting into his palm and fingers. He dropped his hand to the edge of the table, letting the blood seep out onto the floor. Mac's words made no sense.

Mac cleaned up the glass around him and wrapped Crew's hand in a towel before he spoke again. "Crew, I'm gonna need you to get ahold of yourself and get some clothes on if we're gonna have any chance of finding your female."

Crew raised his head slowly and looked Mac in the eye, screaming internally. "She's dead, I told you."

"I don't believe she is." Mac wrapped the towel tighter around Crew's hand, then began to clean the blood up from the floor.

"Look. I need to tell you something that I've never told you before. You, ah, you know how my mom was always superstitious, right? I know you do, you lived with her for seven years. When you first showed up in our world and told me your secrets, I believed you. I believed all of it. But you made me swear not to tell my parents any of it. So I didn't. I just told them that you had amnesia, and you needed a place to stay. She was nervous about it, so she made my dad take me and her to see The White Lady, to ask about you."

Crew sat up a little straighter, able to think again, just a little, tiny fairy wings beating in his chest. "The augur?"

"Is that what you call her? I call her the only being on the planet spookier than you. I mean shit, you think you come from another world and she thinks she can see the future. You two made a great pair."

Mac gave him a grin, but jumped right back into his story when Crew shot him a black look. "So, we paid her in chickens but my mom made me pay for it out of my own pocket. I had to work off that money for a long time, Spook, but I never told you because I didn't want you to feel bad about it. You did plenty for me over the years, more than made up that debt. So, anyway, we headed out to her cave—yeah she lives in a cave, and it's nasty—and my dad wouldn't even go in. He said female augurs can't be trusted, but my mom wouldn't back down. So me and her went in alone. We sat down on these rocks while she kind of hovered above us on this big rock that looked like a stage. She was walking back and forth constantly, wearing this cliché fortune teller's garb from right out of some stupid movie. She said she could tell us anything we wanted to know, but if we used the word want, the word need, or any pronoun, she would throw us right out on our asses and keep our money, or our chickens, or whatever. She said want, need, and pronouns mess with the spirit messages. So you gotta be super careful how you ask your questions. My mom said something like, 'There is a boy named Crew who showed up at the farmhouse last week. Crew has been sleeping in the barn. Mac is asking if Crew is telling the truth.' 'The truth about what?' the old lady said. 'The truth about wh—.' My mom stopped, and I knew she was about to say 'about who he is,' but she remembered she wasn't supposed to use pronouns, so she thought about it for a moment. Then she pointed to me and said carefully. 'Did Crew tell Mac the truth about the person Crew is and what Crew remembers?'"

Mac grinned, then laughed. "Good thing I went with her, because you told *me* the truth at least. The White Lady didn't miss a beat, she got this super sly look on her face and stared at me. 'Crew told the truth to Mac,' she said, grinning. I didn't know if she was gonna bust me out or not for lying to my mom, but then my mom said, real fast, 'Oh good. Can we trust him?' The White Lady shrieked at that and screamed at my mom to get out, get out, get out, and darn if my mom didn't growl at her, but then The White Lady sent all sorts of spirits at my mom and they were just like dust and wind but my mom was shrieking and beating them with her hands. The White Lady called them off but told my mother their business was done, but she would talk to me alone. My mom looked at me and nodded like I was supposed to know what to ask and then she left the cave. So I'm sitting there and The White Lady is just pacing back and forth and looking at me and grinning, and then she says, 'Your friend, you keep him close and take care of him. He's going to do some important things in his life. When he's at his very lowest point, you bring him to me. You tell him I can help him find his way to what he thinks is lost forever. He'll have to pay with his very dearest possession, but I think he'll find it worth it.'"

Mac stopped talking and stared at Crew, letting it sink in. "I wondered over the years if you'd hit your lowest point a few times, but always decided no, you hadn't quite yet. But when you popped over for just a moment this afternoon, screaming for Dahlia, I dug this out." He threw a faded piece of paper on the table between them.

Crew picked it up and smoothed it out, reading the words The White Lady had told Mac so many years ago.

"I wrote it down so I wouldn't forget it. Spook, I think we can get your mate back."

CHAPTER 21

*C*rew looked around the cave with little curiosity. All he cared about was what The White Lady could do to help him find Dahlia. The knowledge that she might still be alive was too much, like a physical weight sitting on his chest, strangling the air out of him. He wanted so badly to believe.

Too bad he didn't know what the augur was going to want. He had no great possessions, only a little money, but all he had he would gladly give to her if she wanted it. He'd never cared about things, his life was more of an internal one.

"Up here," Mac said.

"Who's there?" a voice called, and Crew thought he recognized it, but could not quite place it. As they rounded a bend in the frigid cave, their boots puffing up dust from the bare ground, apprehension filled him.

She came into view, old and wrinkled as Mac has said,

and still wearing a fortune teller's gown like you might see at a carnival or in a corny movie. But around her shoulders was an animal stole that did not fit. Crew scented. Mink.

Mac stopped short and grabbed him before he continued any farther. "Remember, you can't say any pronouns or 'need' or 'want,'" he whispered.

"That doesn't apply to him," The White Lady said, her eyes shrewd. She hopped down from her rock as if she were in the prime of her life and rushed forward. "I have been waiting for you."

Crew stared down at her, trying to read her and getting blocked at every turn.

"You stay out of my head and I'll stay out of yours," she intoned, her voice hard.

Crew pulled back. She was powerful, and she was more than what she seemed. He sensed many forms inside her, animal and other. He doubted she had much human in her, thinking this was just a form she took because it amused her to trick people. His eyes widened as he realized what she could be. A shapeshifter. A being able to change into any form it wanted, but bound by the strengths and weaknesses of that form. So she could turn into a wolf, bear, dragon, or anything else that existed. He'd heard of them in this world, but hadn't quite believed they existed. But what did that mean her counterpart in the other world was?

She gave Mac a look, then stepped to stand in front of him. "You turned out fine, now didn't you? Put some meat on your bones." She ran a finger down his chest to his belly. "I like meat."

Mac gave her a challenging look and stood his ground, even as she grasped his package. She chuckled. "Yes, mighty fine." She shifted to stand in front of Crew again. "And you.

So powerful." She shook her head. "But so tired. Will you ever sleep again?"

Crew narrowed his eyes. "That's not why I'm here."

"Of course not. You seek your mate." Liquidly, her form shifted until it was Dahlia standing in front of them.

Mac cursed, but Crew only stared, his heart weighing a thousand pounds in his chest. She giggled, and it was Dahlia's giggle that came from her. Crew held himself back from throttling her, wanting to insist she didn't take his mate's form for any reason.

Dahlia's face pouted, the eyes filled with a vicious bitterness Crew knew the real Dahlia had never felt. "You don't want to play?"

She shifted into The White Lady again, and Crew sensed she liked to show off her power.

"You're no fun."

"Is she alive?" Crew asked.

The White Lady stared at him for a long time. He could feel how she was relishing his full attention, maybe even feeding off of it. Her form seemed to grow and glow, while he felt more tired than he ever had in his life.

Mac growled at the old lady, but Crew put a hand on Mac's shoulder. He could take it. When she'd finally taken her fill, she nodded. "If she is, I can help you find her."

Crew sagged and Mac held him up. "Here, take this," Mac said pulling a candy bar from his pocket. Crew unwrapped it, wondering when the last time he'd eaten was. Days, weeks maybe.

He made short work of the bar, but didn't feel better. He put steel in his spine anyway. "How?"

The old woman smiled, seemingly delighted. "All you need is a little help from your friendly White Lady." She held up her hand and a small orange pill bottle appeared in it. She thrust it at Crew.

He took it, reading the label. *Rx for Crew Arcoal. Take the pill after you have finished paying for it. Only then will the way be revealed.*

Crew read it three times, Mac squinting over his shoulder. He faced The White Lady. "What is your fee?"

She smiled at him and her former callousness slipped away for just a moment. She looked almost fond of him. "Ah, but you have already paid with what is dearest to you," she said quietly. "There is but one more part of the payment to finish, and then you will be told how to find your mate. I would tell you now, because you have proven yourself to be a trustworthy and valiant sort, but I do know sometimes even the best intentions can be forgotten when something this important is at stake."

Mac snorted. "Plain language, lady! You aren't writing a crossword puzzle here!"

She gave him a dirty look. Crew touched him on the shoulder again. "It's ok, Mac, I think I know what she means."

The augur beamed at him. "Of course you do. Now, a word of caution. When you take that pill, you are going to be shown two paths. One will take you to a world where you can recover the means to bring your mate and yourself back to your world, and the other will take you to your mate. You must choose one."

"And then what?"

"And then that's it. You choose, and you do what you gotta do."

Mac held up a hand. "Wait, you can't give him a pill that will let him do both?"

"I cannot."

"Then how is he supposed to get his mate back to his world?"

"He's not."

"Then why offer him the choice to go get whatever it is that can get her back? It won't do him any damn good to find it without her."

The White Lady shook her head and Crew sensed she didn't mind Mac's questions at all. Which was good, or he would have been a toadstool or something by now. "That is the way of it and the extent of what I can do. The rest is up to him." She looked at Mac, eyes bright. "And his friends."

The White Lady stretched her hand out to him in slow motion. "Now go," she said, her eyes misty. "You have a little girl to help." Crew felt the power coming and grabbed onto Mac's elbow, holding on tight.

***

Back in their apartment, Crew let go of Mac and checked to see that he still had the pill bottle. He did. Mac cursed and turned in a circle. "What the hell? My truck!"

Crew half-grinned, his heart trip-hammering in his chest. Now to get back home. "Sorry, wolf. She sent us back home. Maybe it's out front."

Mac rushed to the window. "Sonofabitch. It's out there." He held a hand to his head. "See, I told you she was spookier than you, Spook."

"Don't mess with her if you don't have to, Mac. She's powerful."

Mac scoffed. "She's just a little old lady." But Crew saw the unease in Mac's eyes.

Crew tucked the bottle into his shirt pocket, hoping it

would make it home with him. But now, how soon could he get there? "I'm gonna try to sleep," he said.

Mac nodded, then caught his elbow as he headed into his room. "Crew, wait a sec. I got something to tell you."

Crew waited, noting the use of his real name. "Crew, I, ah, I'm not real good at this type of thing, but, well, I kind of get the feeling you won't be coming back here."

Crew raised his eyebrows. That could mean so many things.

"Anyway, I just wanted to say that I'm glad I met you. And I hope you find her. You deserve all the happiness in the world, and I hope I never see you again."

Crew's throat lumped again and he clasped hands with Mac, who pulled him into a hug.

"Me too, wolf, me too," Crew whispered.

Mac let him go and turned away quickly. "I almost forgot, I got something for you." He ran to his room, then returned, his hand held up.

When he opened it, Crew saw the biggest pill he'd ever seen. "It's a bull tranquilizer," Mac said. "Vet says it won't hurt you, but you probably should only take half."

Crew laughed, startled into it, surprised at how much Mac thought to do for him when he wasn't around, then his heart squeezed again as he thought of never seeing him again.

This Mac was a good male, one of the best.

CHAPTER 22

*D*ahlia stood stock still as people rushed around her in the crowded walkway, sunlight bathing them all. The day was warm, much warmer than the world she had left behind, and she sniffed the air, trying to place the unique scent it had. Flowers like she'd never smelled before and a hint of something thicker, like burning metal.

She was in a corridor between two rows of rough tents, with people walking to and fro quickly, some stopping at a tent and talking or bartering, and then moving on with new items in their hands. Their clothing was unique, though also familiar to Dahlia, like something she would see in a medieval movie. To her left, three men in brown uniforms with long, heavy swords at their belts laughed heartily, one taking an apple off a stack on a table and biting into it, not paying the vendor. Dahlia shot a look to the vendor, a young girl in a heavy dress with her hair covered by a plain brown scarf.

She didn't say a word, just followed the soldiers with her eyes. Dahlia stepped backwards, trying to make herself smaller and escape the notice of the soldiers, or anyone, really. She wished Angel could have sent her into this world with appropriate clothing so she didn't have to draw attention to herself. Unless that was the point, to draw someone's attention.

Brave and wild. If ever she needed her mantra, it was now. She was no superhero, no Wonder Woman with a Lasso of Truth, indestructible bracelets, and the perfect line at the perfect time. She started moving, head down, trying to escape notice, pocketing herself between two men wearing pageboy outfits and flowing surcoats, Wonder Woman lines flowing through her head.

You obviously have little regard for womanhood. You must learn respect!

Women are the wave of the future, and sisterhood is stronger than anything!

Another group of soldiers passed her without seeing her and Dahlia noted the swords at their belts. Wonder Woman had been the daughter of a goddess, had divine gifts, and was trained in several fighting styles. Dahlia? She had… she looked down at herself. Nothing. Not even a sisterhood. She pressed her lips together as her eyes started tearing, suddenly realizing she'd been counting on holing up somewhere and waiting for Crew to come and save her. She looked around. Crew wasn't here, and all she had was herself. Time to buck up, buttercup. Quit hiding, quit whining, quit waiting for a man. She might not be Wonder Woman, but she was all she had. Oh, and she did have some super mysterious, unpredictable, and probably dangerous as hell power that she could barely control. Way better than superhuman strength or speed. Right.

She stopped mincing along between the two males and pulled herself up to her full five feet, two inches tall, looking around, meeting gazes, until someone stopped and stared at her. She gave the woman her friendliest smile and lifted her hand in a little wave.

The woman screamed theatrically. "The Dragon Lady, the king's Dragon Lady has finally come."

Dahlia raised a hand to her hair, patting it down, but it didn't feel mussed. Dragon Lady? Come on.

Soldiers swooped in from all directions and Dahlia had what she'd wanted. She'd officially been noticed and was doing something.

Or something was being done to her.

**

Even while she'd been searched for weapons, the soldiers were completely respectful with her. She'd had nothing on her at all, not even her notebook, not thinking to bring anything when she'd followed the plaintive cries of the little girl into the trees next to her house. Briefly, she wondered what would have happened if she would have stayed in her home and called the cops instead. Would she still have died? Of course she would have. That man—demon, her mind insisted—would have found her another way or another time. Or killed that little girl instead of her. She had owed that world a death, and now that it was handed over, she felt light, like she was on an adventure. She didn't know what Crew had to do with what had happened to her, but she sensed he had also known it had been coming and been helpless to stop it.

"Climb up there, maiden," a young soldier told her,

indicating the rock he'd moved his horse next to so she could mount it.

"Why?"

"Our orders are to take you to the castle."

"What if I don't wish to go to the castle?"

The group of soldiers exchanged uneasy looks. Dahlia realized they didn't want to force her, but would if they had to. One male, older than the rest, but barely older than her, stepped forward.

He bowed deeply in front of her. "It has long been our king's greatest wish that if ever you returned to this land, you would be his most honored and cherished guest in his home, which we mean to take you to."

Dahlia blinked hard at his bowed head. The other soldiers behind him also dropped to one knee and bowed low. She couldn't say no to that.

"Ok," she called sunnily, hopping up onto the rock, then putting her hands on the horse's back, eyeing the configuration of what looked more like a piece of rough cloth tied around the horse's middle than an actual saddle. Not that she knew anything about horses or saddles. The horse stayed perfectly still, as if it knew she was a beginner.

She gripped the cloth to steady herself and swung a leg over. The horse shifted its weight but did not move or sway. The young man climbed on behind her and she stiffened at his closeness, but relaxed when he showed no signs of trying to touch her.

The ride went smoothly, Dahlia unwilling to ask any questions, in case she needed to pretend she was this Dragon Lady. She didn't want the soldiers to tell their king she had no idea who she was.

After what had to be at least an hour, Dahlia's stomach

muscles and butt were aching, but just when she was about to ask if they could take a breather, they broke out of a grove of trees and she saw their destination. A castle more beautiful than she ever could have imagined, with ivy growing up the sides and a stone wall built all the way around, tucked into the side of a hill, partially facing a large body of water she thought had to be the ocean by the cleansing smell of salt in the air.

Her hand went to her throat and she twisted at nothing there, her writer's eye taking in every detail. The stocky, thick walls made from sea-worn rocks, the impossibly green grass blanketing the way there, and the tiny windows painstakingly carved into the walls. There were no flashy turrets or showy flags flying, but the castle was no less romantic for that. It was practical, made to keep invaders out and provide shelter for the inhabitants, but not to be an ostentatious display of wealth. She loved it.

The horses wound their way through an ocean-side path until they reached the front gates, which were wide open. Women worked in the large gardens stretching out to the right and the left, all of them stopping to watch and whisper as Dahlia was brought inside. Stars topped markers of graves of varying shapes and sizes that dotted the castle's yard, with children playing tag among the headstones.

The horses stopped near the front door, and the soldier slid off from behind Dahlia, then helped her down, giving her no time to catch her land legs. They rushed inside, the soldiers almost herding her.

"Where is the king?" the oldest one cried to the first person they came across inside, but Dahlia hardly noticed as she took in the interior. Cold, dark halls lined by candles greeted them. A story began to form in her mind and her imagination was off and running with it, causing her to tune out what was going on around her until she found herself inside a great room with a table large enough to seat forty or fifty people, opposite a man who must be the king. She wished fiercely for her notebook, then filed away the story idea, praying she wouldn't forget it. She stood tall and faced the king, waiting to hear what he would say.

He was a tall man, broad through the chest, wearing the same manner of dress the other men in the market had worn, but with a bright red cloth thrown over his shoulder and belted at the waist. No crown. He had a long, straight scar down one cheek. He didn't say a word, just looked her up and down, but not in a sexual manner, and then he glanced to the wall to his left. Dahlia looked, too, then gasped to see a painting of her friend Heather, wearing the exact clothes Dahlia remembered her in two weeks before, the night when Heather had called her to pluck the cats out of the spider webs. *The night she'd found Angel.*

"You are not her," the king said, "but you wear the same style of dress. You have been sent by her?"

Dahlia thought furiously, not sure what to say. Finally, she nodded.

The king's face broke into a wide smile. "Leave us!" he demanded to his guards who stood behind her. When they were gone, he grasped Dahlia by the shoulders. "Are you her daughter?"

Dahlia kept her expression under control, barely. She shook her head. "Sister," she finally said.

The king's eyes widened, then he nodded. "You look so very like her. If you please, could I know her name?"

Dahlia looked again at the painting. Did they look alike? Maybe, around the eyes and the shape of their faces. "Ah, Heather," she said, still eyeing the painting.

"Heather," the king mused, his eyes far away. "Truly a great and powerful name for a great and powerful lady." His gaze shifted to Dahlia's expression and his face fell. He shook his head. "You are here for the amulet. You must forgive me. I had given up hope that your sister would ever return here."

Dahlia's heart sped up. That was exactly what she was here for, and she had been brought to the home of the person who could give it to her!

The increasing sorrow on the king's face made her blood run cold, though, as he gestured to what looked like a clay block set in an alcove on the wall. "It is encased in a magical covenant of its own making that will break only when certain conditions are fulfilled."

Dahlia eyed the clay block. Surely if she was supposed to be here to get the pendant, it would break for her.

She started toward it, but the king got in between her and it. "I am truly sorry, lady, but I cannot let you take it. I have given my word that whoever fulfills the quest for Libeka the Protector's egg will have a chance at breaking the covenant. If they are not pure of intention, the stone will not break for them, and then it will be yours. I swear it."

Dahlia stared at him, swallowing hard. She couldn't take a chance that someone else might claim ownership of the pendant before she could. WWWWD? Wait. She counted the Ws in her mind. Yes, four was enough. *What would Wonder Woman Do* might have to become her new mantra.

"This quest," she said hesitantly. "When does it start?"

CHAPTER 23

*C*rew blinked against the snow that was pressing against his eyelids. He rolled over with a groan, then stood, freezing, half of him wet, wondering how long he had lain there.

Long enough. He checked to be sure the pill bottle was in his pocket and then loped off at a run toward the police station. As he got close, he realized they were all there, waiting for him. The position of the moon told him it was the middle of the night, just morning side of midnight, but the duty room was lit up like it was daytime, and everyone's cars were in the parking area.

He slowed to a walk once inside the parking lot, sending his senses into the interior of the building, counting the warm bodies there. He made his way to a door around the side of the station, wondering how few people he could get away with talking to.

He walked down the corridor, stepping lightly with his boots so that he made no noise, stopping just outside of Wade's office. Trevor and Ella were having a quiet conversation within about the man who had reported Ella's sister missing.

Trevor spoke. "He said he's her boyfriend, and that he moved out here first to find them a house, but she never arrived when she was supposed to."

"What's he like?" Ella asked, her voice soft. Crew could tell she was hiding something related to her sister from Trevor but he stayed far away from her mind. It was none of his business.

"Big. Abrasive. Probably a criminal, but I haven't looked him up yet."

Ella sighed. "Sounds like someone my sister would like. What did you tell him?"

"I told him we would start an active investigation and I'd get back to him as soon as possible. He's not her husband so we have no obligation to tell him anything. I wanted to check with you first."

Crew slipped by the open door, hoping the couple wouldn't see him. In his peripheral vision, he could see they were huddled on Wade's couch, their heads together, their eyes only for each other. Crew's heart hurt at the sight.

He kept walking, heading to the break room, where he could tell most of the rest of the KSRT was, except for Wade and Graeme, who were at the receiving desk.

He stopped outside the door and leaned against the wall, bracing himself for the hundreds of questions that would be fired at him as soon as he walked in. He hated being the center of attention. From in the room, he heard no talking, no anything, except a strange crunching sound.

Inside, Beckett spoke, his voice harsh. "If he never comes back because he's dead, Mac, I'm holding you personally responsible."

The crunching stopped. "Give me a fucking break. I did what he asked."

"You could have killed him. You might have killed him!"

The whole situation felt surreal to Crew, like he was a ghost at his own funeral, and still he couldn't bring himself to go in.

Mac grunted and the crunching started again. His voice was soft but still Crew could understand him, even around the cereal he was crunching.

"If I wanted your opinion, I'd remove the duct tape."

Crew realized the anniversary of when Khain killed the *shiften* females was coming up. Mac always got irritable— more irritable—in this world for a month before and a month after that.

Beckett rose to the bait. "Fuck you, fucker. I mean it, Mac, if Crew doesn't come back, you and me are gonna have more than words."

From down the hall, Graeme turned a corner and came towards Crew. Graeme lifted a hand in greeting when he saw Crew and his eyes asked the question Crew didn't want to answer. Crew shook his head.

A female spoke up and Crew didn't recognize the voice at first, but since Ella was down the hall, it had to be Heather, Graeme's mate. "Maybe it's all that sugar making you grouchy. That's your fourth bowl of cereal."

Graeme stopped in front of Crew and shook his hand, about to speak. From inside, Mac spoke instead, his words erasing Graeme's ability to speak. "Ah. Sister Smokin' speaks.

Were you a nutritionist before you officially donned the title Hotpants Heather?"

Graeme's face turned murderous and he rushed into the room. Crew dropped his head into his hands. Why did Mac even open his mouth in this world?

A scuffle sounded, with a chair being scooted across the room. Heather cried out, "No, Graeme, he didn't mean it!" and a chorus of male shouts overlapped each other. The only thing Crew could understand was, "That's just Mac, don't kill him. We might need him."

Graeme's voice was tight. "Don't say things you'll regret just because you missed the rut tonight, Mac. You went too far."

Mac's voice came out as little more than a squeak. "Easy to say when you're balls deep every night."

Graeme roared and Crew rushed in the room, running to get between Mac and the dragon, peeling Graeme's fingers off Mac's throat.

"Crew!" Beckett called, relief in his voice. Troy barked once, sharply.

Mac rubbed his throat and glared at Graeme, who backed away and put an arm around his female. She smiled up at him like he'd lit the sun.

Crew put a hand on Mac's shoulder. "Thanks," he said, sincerely.

"I'll knock you out anytime, flyboy. Did it work?"

Crew stared back, talking to only him. "It did, but she wasn't there."

"You were looking for your female?"

"Yeah." Crew nodded, trying to think of what to do now.

Wade entered the room, his weary eyes surveying everyone standing there in a loose knot. His gaze settled on Crew. "Explain," he said.

"I met my female yesterday, in the other world I travel to. When she disappeared, I thought she might be there. She wasn't."

Wade nodded once, tightly. "What aren't you telling me?"

Crew felt for his pill. Still there. "I still have a chance to find her. It might have something to do with that little girl, Paisley White."

Wade's face smoothed out. "Good. We were going to ask you to go see her. She's in the hospital with no signs of injury whatsoever, but the doctors can't get her to wake up. They say her brainwaves are active, like she's dreaming, but she lays there like she's comatose. Her mother is out of her mind with worry. I've consulted with nearby *Citlali* and we all think you have the best chance of waking her." He gave Crew a sharp look. "You've dealt with it before, haven't you?"

Crew didn't answer.

***

At the hospital, Wade made most of the males wait at the end of the hallway, while he and Crew went toward the little girl's room on their own.

Wade pushed the door open and motioned Crew inside. There were several people in the room, but the only one Crew could focus on was Paisley White, eyes closed, long dark hair fanning the pillow case like someone had been lovingly combing it out with their fingers. Her essence was strong, deafeningly so, like small children often were, but there was more to it. Crew frowned as he walked toward the bed, his eyes on her delicate face. Wade went past him and talked to the family, keeping between them and Crew.

Crew probed her mind gently, but instead of the fishhook

that had been embedded in his brain, he found a sort of blanket, laid over her senses to keep her asleep and pliant while Khain lured both Dahlia and Crew together.

Gently, Crew lifted the edges of the blanket, and when Paisley didn't flinch, he tugged, pulling the entire thing off of her, taking it into himself. He staggered under its weight, so soon after his recent ordeals, but managed to stay upright. Paisley's eyes opened and looked right at him.

He tried to smile soothingly at her, but it felt strange on his face. She smiled brightly, seemingly untouched by what she had gone through, locked eyes with him and spoke in the most innocent voice he'd ever heard. "Nana says your echo will direct you how to get to where you want to go. Fix your choice clear in your mind, and ask." Crew's eyes widened at the sophisticated speech coming from the young girl.

"She's awake!" a female voice cried and the family almost knocked Wade over to get to her. Crew got only a glimpse of a pretty young woman, the mother, before she gathered Paisley into her arms, sobbing quietly.

Crew backed away, feeling weak as a baby foal trying to find its feet for the first time. The scent of mink entered his nostrils and he looked up sharply. Mrs. White was there, smiling at him. "You found her. I knew you would," she whispered sharply. "Thank you. Thank you for everything." Crew tried to nod, but felt his body sway. She touched him on the arm, concerned, and, at her touch, the demon's blanket evaporated from his soul and his strength came flooding back.

He nodded. "Good wishes to your family," he whispered, then rushed out of the room.

His echo. He had to find his echo. He didn't care if it took weeks, months, he would do it. He had no idea where to look, but he would start with Trent. Trent had an echo and maybe he would have some insight—

Beckett stepped in front of him, stopping his forward momentum through the hallway as Wade ran up from behind. "Crew, I called your name a dozen times."

Crew looked around, barely able to concentrate on any of them. He had his mission and could think of nothing else.

Beckett grabbed him by the arms and shook him. "Crew, let us help you."

"Gotta find my echo," Crew muttered. "I must have one."

Beck's face broke into a smile. "You shoulda said something, dude. I know where your echo is."

CHAPTER 24

*D*ahlia held up her arms while her lady in waiting cinched her corset, then turned her around to finish pulling on her heavy dress. At first she'd been thrilled to try the period clothing, but when she discovered the corsets were tight and the dresses scratchy and heavy, the feeling had faded. They did make her breasts pop, though. She looked down at her usually non-existent cleavage and wondered what Crew would think if he saw her in the outfit.

She stared at the fire in the fireplace of the room she'd been given and wondered if he was still looking for her. She also wondered how much time had passed in the world she'd died in. If twenty years had passed here, while only fourteen days passed there, that was what, a minute or two for every day here? She swallowed hard, realizing he hadn't even started yet, maybe was still in that field where she died. She could be here for weeks over there before he found her, maybe as long as a year?

She remembered what Angel had said just before she'd stepped through the doorway. That he would hold the times between the worlds consistent, and that brought her some small measure of relief, although she couldn't know exactly what it meant.

The king, who's name she'd discovered was Caius, had become cold when she'd said she wanted to join the quest that was to start the next day, to at least be given a chance to compete to win the pendant. He'd sent her away almost immediately, saying he needed to ponder her request and what her showing up meant to the kingdom.

She'd been shown to this room, which was rather nice for being in a drafty castle built from stones, and given the finest food and drink the king had to offer. She'd tried to nap in her bed filled with actual feathers and covered with coarse blankets, desperate to discover where she would go in her sleep, but hadn't been able to. Now it was time for dinner.

Satisfied, her lady in waiting tried to slip simple leather booties on her feet but Dahlia refused. The dress was so long, no one would see her tennies.

Once dressed and perfumed to someone else's satisfaction, Dahlia was led back to the great hall, where she was given the seat directly next to the king. Dinner was a grand affair, and she could tell King Caius was well-loved, which gave her hope that he was a fair man who could be swayed into what she needed.

When dessert was brought out, she scooched her chair a bit closer to him. "Have you considered my request?" she asked.

His wise eyes regarded her. "I cannot, my lady. You see,

women are not allowed to undertake quests. It is far too dangerous, what with them being generally smaller, weaker, and less clever than men."

Dahlia watched him carefully, noting the way his eyes shifted when he said the last part. WWWWD? "Tell me about when you met my sister," she finally said, letting the remark go for now.

His face broke into a tired smile. "It was twenty years ago, almost to the day. The king at that time was an evil man and he raped the countryside for taxes daily, or maybe just for fun." Caius' lips twisted at the memory. "I was a young boy, highly impressionable, and your sister and her dragon saved me and my family from King Dilmer's worst soldiers. I'll always remember how she looked when she told them Graeme the fierce and hungry was displeased with the way King Dilmer ran his kingdom."

Dahlia frowned. Twenty years ago? Dragon?

"I'll never forget what your sister did, speaking so boldly to the soldiers, then giving me everything she had in her pockets. We were a poor family, but the amulet changed everything for us." His eyes took on a far-away look and he gazed over the heads of everyone at the table, seeing that time in the past. "The king was backed by the therianthrope, which made him unbeatable and unseatable. But when the amulet allowed me to—"

Dahlia interrupted him. "Therianthrope?"

"The shape-shifters. Men who can change into any animal they desire, although they most often chose wolves, or lions, or bears, because they love to slay people in vicious manners. They were the king's hired assassins, and if the soldiers weren't scary or bloodthirsty enough for everyday matters, the king would call out the therianthrope. The soldiers never went against his wishes because the rumor was that he was a secret therianthrope."

Dahlia shuddered. Did every world have werewolves?

"One day, after that time with your sister, I was in the field working with the amulet around my neck, under my tunic. My mother gave the amulet to me to wear because I was too young to be in the fields alone, but I had to work and my father had to travel that day. She hoped it would protect me, hoped it would call the Dragon Lady to me if I encountered danger. That day, a therianthrope sauntered through my field in wolf form, one of my chickens in its mouth. I yelled at it before I thought better of my actions, and it dropped the chicken and changed into a bear, then a man, then a big cat, bigger even than a lion, then back into a wolf, and advanced on me. I grabbed hold of the amulet, certain I was about to be killed, and prayed for the Dragon Lady to save me. When nothing happened, I opened my eyes. The wolf in front of me had stopped coming my way, and its eyes had lost all of its cunning, like it no longer had the ability to think or reason in its animal form. It sniffed at the chicken, eyed me, then snatched up its prize and ran away in the direction it had come from. I went home and told my mother and she and my father talked about it long into the night, finally deciding to tell no one. But the next day, an entire force of therianthrope, with a contingent of the king's guards following behind, came to our plot."

The king's face grew grave. "I almost lost my entire family that day, but, in the end, the amulet saved us again. As my little sisters hid behind me, the wolves jumped for the throats of my parents. I held the amulet and prayed for all the therianthrope to lose their shifting ability like the one had the day before, not knowing if I could do any more than that. The amulet glowed with power, heating my hand, and the wolves stopped mid-stride, then ran off in confusion like the other had." He raised his eyebrows and tilted his head. "The guards declared me the new king. I hadn't known that they'd been planning an overthrow ever since King Dilmer had laughed at his Field Marshall who had gone to him with the Dragon Lady's—Heather's—warning."

King Caius beamed at Dahlia. "I was no more than a boy, and I do believe King Dilmer's Field Marshall planned on molding me into a lord who would do his bidding, but my father and mother had other plans. The amulet has always helped when I have asked it to, but I take care to only ask in the gravest of times. I can feel that it is not mine, and if I were to abuse it, it would go dead in my hands, maybe even hurt me. That is why I have not asked it to help with Libeka the Protector. It is clear that is not what it is for."

Dahlia shivered at the power of the pendant, trying to work it all out in her mind. How did Heather get her pendant; the one her mother had disappeared holding so many years ago? Or did Heather have her own pendant, and that was the one encased in that clay block? Would that mean Heather really was her sister? Angel had said she had thousands, but every time she tried to work that math out in her head, her eyes glazed over. Maybe Angel had meant metaphorical sisters.

Dahlia's thoughts clouded as a memory slipped through her, a memory she couldn't be sure was entirely factual, since she'd been so young.

Her mother, cradling her in a hammock as they stared at the boughs of a tree overhead and listened to the buzz of the cicadas in the grass during a hot summer afternoon. "I'm sorry your father's not here with us, Dahl, but you need to know he has a very good reason and he is a very good…" She'd paused for a long time before she finished the sentence, but finally did: "a very good man."

"Where is he, mama?"

"He's working, saving the world, probably, or trying. I didn't know him as well as I had hoped, but I knew enough to know that he was strong and powerful and wanted you very much. Just like I know you're going to go on and do great things."

The memory stopped there, leaving an ache in her heart. Dahlia wondered why she'd never asked Angel who her father was. Angel had mentioned him, saying he'd given her and her sisters internal and external tools to protect themselves, which made more sense now.

King Caius was watching her, his face guarded. Dahlia pulled herself together. "What exactly is the quest?"

"It is to retrieve the egg of Libeka the Protector, the basilisk that lives nearby and protects us from the wolves of the forest. The therianthrope were all turned to wolves who could not shift or think, but their children thrive, when they can get enough food, and it's us they most like to chew on."

"Basilisk?"

"Like a great lizard twice the size of a moose with eight legs and spikes down its back, a natural enemy to the wolves. If a wolf comes into its territory, the basilisk rouses from its cave and kills the wolf or chases it off. It does not harm us intentionally, especially since we take it daily offerings of sweet meats, fruits, and water from the stream, and so we only live within the boundaries of its territory."

"Why would you want its egg? Don't you want more of them?"

Caius sighed and rubbed a hand over the back of his

neck. "The egg is petrified, or must be, because it has not hatched in seven years. Libeka grows old and slow, and if she does not have young before she dies, we will once again find our dogs, any children that wander off, and even groups with not enough weapons, picked off by wolves. If we steal her egg, she will lay another and if it hatches, it will take over her home and protect us. Our small kingdom will be safe from the wolves as long as it lives."

"Why don't you send in your guards?"

"It's not that simple. Basilisk are deadly to humans. If we look her in her eyes, we will die. Even their smell and their hovels are deadly. My soldiers can plug their noses, but they cannot make it to the egg without touching the ground, and her venom permeates their very shoes or any wood they are touching. I've lost many a soldier to this, so I've called together all of the cleverest minds in the land to try to figure out a way that we could not see."

Dahlia narrowed her eyes. "That sounds like something the amulet should be used for."

He challenged her. "And yet, I cannot. I have come to understand the amulet and its energies over the years. It will not do this for me."

Dahlia looked around the table, trying to imagine any of these people going up against a basilisk. It sounded impossible.

"Will you still be king if someone else gets the amulet?" she asked, when her attention made it back to King Caius.

His eyes shifted around the table guiltily and he leaned in close to her. "The burden of a kingdom is great. I do not have many good years left to me, and I must confess that I cannot stomach the thought of spending them in these walls anymore. On the advice of a traveler, I have begun planting seeds of a—what is the word?—a demohcrassy, in the ears of my closest advisors. We have even begun forming a parliament to function under the king. It is my hope that it will thrive if I happen to disappear." His eyes grew bright. "There is a legend of a gateway to the north, ten feet off of a cliff face that will take you to another world if you can manage to get through it. A world with wagons that run by magic and magic boxes with puppet presentations showing constantly, even while you sleep."

Dahlia frowned. "How do you enter the portal if it's ten feet off the cliff?"

He smiled indulgently at her, like the answer should be obvious. "You take a running leap."

Dahlia's hand went to her throat, wondering how many bodies were at the bottom of that cliff.

CHAPTER 25

rew entered Dahlia's house slowly, holding his grief at bay. She wasn't dead. He would find her. If he could just keep that thought fixed in his mind, he could function.

But oh, her scent! The citrusy-flowery essence surrounded him, calming him and incensing him at the same time. He had to find her *now*. Not knowing where she was, if she was safe or comfortable or scared, was killing him.

The white bobkitten, with the black markings on its back that Beckett had described, entered the room slowly from a cat door set into the opposite wall, locking eyes with Crew immediately. Crew probed its mind, but found no intelligence other than ordinary animal. He walked toward it, hearing the other members of the KSRT following him into Dahlia's house.

When he reached the bobkitten, who was about the size

of a regular cat, but still had a very kittenish look to it, he shook his head. The black markings on its back looked like angel wings, not stars. "Beck, this thing doesn't match me."

Beckett hurried forward. "Watch."

He picked the bobkitten up. It twisted in his arms so it could continue to stare into Crew's eyes, but offered no other resistance. Beckett ran his hand up the kitten's back, fluffing the hair in the opposite direction and Crew grunted. That way, it certainly did look like Crew's *renqua*.

"Does he have a message for you?" Beckett asked.

"No message," Crew said, holding out his hands to take the kitten from Beckett. As soon as he had it pulled close to his body it sighed contentedly and snuggled into him, a sound like an idling chainsaw erupting from him.

"Dude," Beckett said, backing away. "Is it going to blow up?"

"I don't know," Crew said, looking down at it, the noise vibrating against his chest. It felt good, soothing, and made him drowsy.

"It's purring, you nimrods," Mac said, slamming the door into Dahlia's home behind him, snow from his boots already melting onto the rug. "That's what cats do."

"Why?"

"I don't know. To hypnotize you or some shit."

Wade and Graeme stood just inside the door in an intense discussion. Wade grabbed Graeme's arm and pointed him towards Crew. "Tell him."

Graeme nodded, looked around slowly, then walked to Crew, who was still holding the purring bobkitten. "I need to tell you about the role of echoes in *dragen* lore. It's very different than what I understand you *shiften* to believe about them. Before I say a word though, I must tell you that none of this can be proven. It's thousands of years of conjecture based on *dragen* belief and experience."

Crew raised his eyebrows, feeling time slipping away, but knowing he needed to hear this. Besides, he had no idea what his next move was.

"Echoes are sometimes messengers, but more often, they can act as psychological and physical portals to other worlds. They normally are assigned to only one traveler, although in this case, I would guess that this echo is assigned to both you and your mate."

Crew's heart twinged at the word mate. "Assigned by who?"

"No one knows for sure. Rhen, maybe. The Light, maybe. Someone else, possibly. Or maybe it's a natural phenomenon that has something to do with the very core of what a traveler is and does." He leaned close to Crew. "Did you know that any traveler who sacrifices themselves so that another may live is offered a chance to enter another world, in lieu of retiring to The *Haven*?"

Crew's mouth dried up and his throat constricted. His Dahlia had sacrificed herself. Would she have chosen to enter another world and that was why he had a chance to retrieve her?

"I see that you didn't. Yes, it would make sense that your mate was offered such a thing. When a traveler chooses that, their echo acts as a kind of beacon so that they can find their way back to the world they died in, if they can locate a portal. Dream travelers also utilize their echoes in this way, using them to find their way to their one true world if they die in another."

Crew opened and closed his mouth, but could force no words out. Beckett draped a hand over his shoulder, clearly fascinated, and asked the questions for him. "What does a portal look like? How likely is it that she could find one?"

"Portals are rare, like I said, but," Graeme nodded to the kitten in Crew's arms, "that little guy could act as one. That wouldn't help her, but maybe it would help you get to her. Once you got there you'd have to find a way back. Generally, all worlds have at least one permanent portal and they are frequently a source of much legend and mystery, and always invisible, very small, and hard to go through accidentally. Some travelers can sense or see the energy of the portal, while others cannot, but are still drawn to them if their intention is to travel."

Graeme held out his hand, palm up. "There is also much speculation that an object small enough to carry in your hand could act as a portal, but only to the most powerful travelers, and only if it was something created specifically for their energy patterns by a powerful being. Rhen could make one. Khain, also."

Crew looked down at the bobkitten, feeling a sudden urgency to get started. He felt in his pocket for the pill again. There.

Graeme looked around the room. "One thing everyone needs to know about travelers, is they generally exist in many fewer worlds than most of you do. *Dragen* are rare, in that we almost always exist in only one world, and that's why we have our dimensional-cracking ability, but if any of you managed to travel to another world, you almost certainly would end up not where you were aiming for, or not where you crossed over, but rather in the mind of your counterpart that already exists there. Travelers usually only exist in two or four worlds, while the rest of you exist in many. Dreams for you can provide a glimpse into your parallel lives, but a true traveler can actually wake up in the body of one of their parallel lives night after night."

He looked back at Crew. "You, Crew, are a fractionated traveler. That is why your body disappears from world to world. True dream travelers don't do that unless they actually go through a portal or die. Fractionated travelers can be created when the mind of a powerful being that has unrealized potential to be a traveler is split under great stress."

Wade crossed his arms over his chest and moved next to Crew. "How many worlds are there?"

Graeme looked him in the eye. "Infinite, all carrying out infinite possibilities at the same time. You could choose to go left tomorrow morning at the light and get hit by a car and die, but your counterpart in another world could choose to go right and still live."

Mac whistled and Beckett pushed his hat back on his head and stared at the ceiling, rubbing his forehead. "Kinda makes our individual lives seem pointless."

Graeme shook his head. "All worlds have a purpose, and all beings in all worlds do, too."

Mac snorted. "What could that purpose possibly be? If we are playing out infinite possibilities, then everything that could possibly happen will happen, so what is the point of it?"

"You need a philosopher to explain that," Graeme said. "It has never interested me. The only reason I know as much as I do is because my brother searched endlessly for the one true world before he died, convinced he could become a god if he found it and partook of the fruits that grow there."

Crew clutched the kitten tighter, his eyes traveling over Dahlia's place, resting on her things, his heart missing her. He had what he needed and wanted to be done with this conversation.

Beckett didn't. "Wait, this isn't the one true world?"

"No. This world sits alongside all other worlds. In *dragen* lore, the one true world is above them, closer to The *Haven*." He looked at Crew closely. "But that's not important, now. If Crew is going to find his mate, we need to leave him alone with his echo." He caught Crew's eye and shook his head. "I don't know exactly how it's done, sorry."

Crew only nodded wearily. He had an idea.

Wade turned to face him, his face grave. He put a hand on Crew's shoulder. "Crew, I know you need your female, but we need you. Promise me you'll find your way back here."

Crew could make no promise, but as he stared at Wade he remembered something important. The White Lady's face entered his mind, grinning slyly.

The rest is up to him, and his friends.

"I'm almost certain I can't get back. You guys have to come get me somehow. An augur told me so."

Graeme frowned. "Female or male augur?"

"Female."

His frown deepened. "Female augurs can't be trusted. They think nothing of telling you what will serve them while pretending it will serve you."

Crew shrugged, eager to be off to find Dahlia. "She's been honest so far."

Graeme's frown deepened and he watched Crew closely, then raised an eyebrow at Wade. Wade stared back, his face grim.

"What else did she say?" Wade asked.

"She's the one who told me Dahlia could be found, and that I had to help the little girl and then I'd be told the way to Dahlia. She said I have to go to Dahlia and my friends have to recover the means to get us home."

He left out the part about him having a choice to go to either place, unwilling to engage in endless discussion about whether it would be better for him to retrieve the means to get Dahlia home instead.

Graeme shook his head. "Did she say anything else? What this thing was? How we were supposed to find it?"

"Nothing."

Graeme nodded thoughtfully and Crew could see his mind working.

Crew left it up to him, only caring about finding Dahlia. Getting back was nowhere near as important to him.

***

Crew circled Dahlia's home, the echo at his heels, taking in everything. He picked up a sweatshirt from the back of a chair and smelled it, taking her scent into his lungs, savoring how it calmed him immediately. On the desk sat her notebook, the one she'd asked for at his place in his dream world, then wrote in so intently with the small smile on her face, while her other hand touched her throat lightly and her hair curled down to the mattress she'd been lying on. He touched his own throat in the manner she always did, imagining her hands on her skin.

He picked up the notebook and paged to the very end to see if she'd written anything that would help him. On the last page were two sentences that hurt his heart and quickened his feeling of loss.

Crew, how can I find you? I've only just met you but I feel like I've spent my life looking for you.

He put the notebook down, unable to read another line. She'd summed up how he felt perfectly. He barely knew her, and yet he knew everything that was important. *I'll find you, Dahlia. I'm coming.*

He strode into the bedroom, thinking he knew what he had to do. The echo followed him. On the bedside table he found a packet of typed and stapled pages with red pen circling a word here, striking out a sentence there.

He picked it up and leafed through it, realizing it was a short story titled *Summer Storm.*

A few paragraphs near the bottom of one of the pages jumped out at him.

He yanked my hair back, then curled his fingers around my throat. He wouldn't go so far as to hurt me, and yet even as the thought crossed my mind, the truth was I didn't know for sure. I'd given myself over to him willingly, told him to do what he wanted with me, both of us knowing his fantasies ran darker than mine.

But did they? My body said otherwise.

He shoved a finger roughly into me and I cried out as my inner core throbbed and clenched at him. He smeared my own wetness up my belly, then handled my nipples roughly, making me groan at the sensation. I went limp in his arms as the first spatterings of rain dropped onto my face.

He lowered me to the ground and flipped me over onto my belly, pressing my face into the warm grass, then pulling my hair into a rough ponytail and yanking it until I lifted up onto my arms to alleviate the pulling on my scalp.

He lowered his mouth to my ear and rasped, "That's right, baby girl, you're mine for the next hour. No one will hear a noise you make, so be sure to scream good and loud for me."

Crew jerked his eyes away from the paper with effort, dropping a hand to his cock that had gone rock-hard before he'd reached the end of the first paragraph. *Was this typical of what she wrote? And what she wanted?* He dreamed of finding out.

He dropped the pages back onto the nightstand, not able to read more or he'd have to take care of himself before he could try out his plan. Which was unacceptable. He had to go *now*.

He took the pill bottle out of his pocket, then sat on the bed. The echo jumped up next to him immediately, shoving its nose at the pill bottle. Crew lifted it over his head and opened it, taking out the pill and dropping the bottle onto the floor. The echo clawed its front paws up his shirt and tried to get to the pill, a strange yowling coming out of its throat but Crew popped the pill in his mouth and dry swallowed it, then lay on top of Dahlia's covers with his boots still on.

The echo climbed up his body and stared into his eyes. Crew got the impression that it was uneasy about something. He stared back, and the echo quieted, then laid directly on his chest, tucking its feet under its body in a way Crew found strangely appealing. The purring began. Crew concentrated on it, noticing how it had no beginning and no end, no rough edges, no intention.

"Dahlia. I want to go to Dahlia. Take me to Dahlia."

His eyes slipped closed.

CHAPTER 26

Darkness. Doors. Time running past. Dahlia's scent coming close, then whipped away from him as he traveled in an opposite direction. The echo staring at him with accusing eyes, then seven words echoing in his brain as he slammed through a closed door and tumbled into the world beyond.

She tricked you. You needed no pill.

Crew woke all at once, like he did in his real world, his senses clear and sharp, but still unable to tell what they were perceiving. He struggled in what felt like a dozen grips on his arms and legs and throat as vicious growling sounded in his ears. The first teeth penetrated his skin and he shifted into his wolf form, twisting out of the holds that gripped him, rising to his full size, snarling and growling his worst.

The wolves that had pinned him to the ground with their

teeth jumped back, then regrouped, the smaller ones covering the throats of the larger ones, as all advanced on him.

Stop! Crew shouted in *ruhi. I will not hurt you!*

The group lost their snarls as one, as most looked at each other uneasily. Crew probed at a few of their minds, finding animal instinct and cleverness plus rudimentary powers of *ruhi*, but little else. Which made no sense. If they were *shiften*, they should have intellect like humans, but if they were only wolves, they shouldn't have any knowledge of *ruhi*. He would have decided they were shape-shifters, but he could tell none had the ability to shift.

The largest male, who was still less than half of Crew's size, spoke in little more than a whisper. *Wolf-god Conri, come to save us.* He dropped onto his belly and rolled over, exposing it to Crew. Crew watched as the rest of the wolves did as their alpha did, some whining.

Crew shifted and stood before them in his human form, looking over the group as a whole, wondering why The White Lady had sent him here. The wolves were scrawny, almost all of them, as if they hadn't eaten in weeks. Some were missing patches of fur and had listless eyes and white gums. He looked around at the concrete walls, dirt ceiling, and cell bars guarding the only way out. "What is this place?" he asked out loud, to see if they could understand him.

The largest male scrambled to his feet and faced Crew, his eyes cast down to the floor. *Conri. Humans dig traps. Fall in when run from basilisk.*

Crew found the hole that led to the open air above, noting the wolf skeletons at the bottom and the scratches on the concrete where many wolves had tried to climb their way out. He pulled on his clothes, then walked below it to look up. Blue sky.

Will the humans come free you or kill you?
No. We starve. Die.

Black anger shot through Crew. No animal deserved to die in this manner.

Do you fight with the humans?
When the basilisk die, then we fight.

Crew walked the length of each wall, stepping over cringing wolves who avoided his eyes.

He glanced out the cell door, then turned back to the wolves, thinking hard. He did not know the situation here, and freeing these wolves could cause problems for whoever lived in this world, but he couldn't leave them locked up to die. It was against his nature. The White Lady would have known that. He did not do this for her, but he would not abstain from the choice because of her.

If I free you, you must promise to find homes far away from humans. You must promise never to hunt their livestock or worry their children or hurt even one of them. You must swear to tell every animal you meet of this trap, so another will never fall down here. Mark it constantly to keep those who do not have the power of speech away. Do you so swear?

The wolves whined and spoke in a rush, their voices overlapping each other. He touched each of their minds in turn, ensuring they all meant to uphold their vow. When he reached a young wolf who still looked relatively strong and healthy, something in his mind made Crew take notice. A scent carried on the wind of his memories of lavender and citrus. He shifted through the wolf's remembrances until he saw what he was looking for. He showed the wolf its memory of the scene.

What is this?
Humans. Outside cave of basilisk.

Crew grew panicked. In the wolf's mind he'd seen a throng of humans gathered around something and could not discern if Dahlia was among them. Why would she be at the cave of a basilisk? But it was the only lead he had. *When?*

Today. When sun high in sky.

Where?

Four howls to the setting sun.

Crew thought quickly, then decided on his plan. He crossed the room to the metal door and tested the strength of the bars, then tested the strength of the setting of the door in the concrete. Both were strong. As he tested, his eyes fell on something laid on a ledge on the far wall of the hallway.

The key.

***

Dahlia crouched behind a large boulder in the putrid-smelling cave and stared at the basilisk, which was almost a hundred feet away, socked into its inner chamber, sleeping. It was terrifyingly large, twice as large as a moose, like the king had said, with iridescent scales instead of fur, and jagged, clay-brown spikes in a ridge along its back. It's face was a lizard face and it gave Dahlia the creeps, especially as venom dripped out of its slack mouth and sizzled when it hit the floor.

She'd gotten permission to enter the quest, not exactly proud of the way she'd done it, but heartened that she'd been able to, all the same. WWWWD was working for her.

She'd gotten the king drunk, pouring him glass after glass of the thick, sweet wine his maids had brought out after dinner, all the while asking questions about his life.

When she'd learned about his late wife and his two younger sisters, she'd finally had the courage to ask him, "Do you really believe that women are less clever than men?"

He'd faltered, then shook his head. "Not all."

An hour later, she'd had her promise, and another she hadn't even realized she was going to ask for. He'd agreed to put two women on the parliament if he could find two who would agree to it. She didn't think he'd have the trouble he seemed to think he would.

She'd returned to her room high on her victory and managed to fall asleep only when the sun had brought first light to her window. She hadn't slept long before being awoken to dress for the quest, and as far as she knew she'd had no dreams and didn't wake in another world.

The quest hadn't started till noon, giving her plenty of time to fight with her lady in waiting about the dress everyone thought she was going to wear. Dahlia insisted on wearing either her own clothes or clothes meant for a man, but King Caius wouldn't allow it and his tight expression when he told her so made her think he was not happy about the promise she had wrung from him, even having him sign a piece of parchment that said so. She'd known he wouldn't break his word once given, even if he had been drunk and coerced, and she'd been right.

She knelt on her heavy, stiff dress and cursed it's cumbersome nature. The soldiers had told her if even one thread of her clothing grazed the basilisk venom, it would travel to her skin along the cloth and she would die screaming. So much for her plan to get the basilisk out of the cave somehow, then tiptoe over to the egg. It wouldn't have worked anyway. She could scarcely find one inch of un-slobbered-on ground. She'd entered through a back entrance that was too small for the basilisk to fit through, which was the only reason she'd been able to get so close.

She looked up the walls of the cave, wondering if she could perhaps scale them somehow, but they were smooth. If she had rock climbing equipment maybe she could do it, but she wasn't a rock climber.

As the shadows in the area she was crouching in lengthened, Dahlia began to panic. She was no closer to getting the egg than she had been when she'd first arrived at the cave. She knew she could get the basilisk off the egg, but then what? There was absolutely no way possible to get to the egg without risking her life. A discarded wooden box that had once been a wagon across the large cavern attested to that. The venom had eaten through the metal wheels, then the wooden seating, and sealed the fates of the men inside.

She'd had visions of returning victorious within only a few hours, wowing even the king, but unless she could create a tornado that would pick up the egg and bring it to her, she would face the same defeat everyone had before her.

She chewed on her lip and thought about that. A tornado wasn't a good idea, it would whip the venom everywhere, but what if she could create a being of some sort that would pick up the egg for her? Could she do that? Or grow vines from the ceiling and drop them to the egg, have them grasp it, then somehow move to where she sat? Did she have that kind of control over the objects her imagination spawned? Only one way to find out.

Dahlia closed her eyes and concentrated, jumping when a familiar male voice spoke from behind her.

"If I had known one of your skills was basilisk slayer, I wouldn't have worried about you so much."

CHAPTER 27

*D*ahlia whirled around, heedless of the dangers of the cave. "Crew!" she shouted, shooting to her feet and running into his arms.

He lifted her, twirled her, and their lips met before her feet landed back on the ground. He was here! He'd found her!

In his kiss, she sensed all the worry and fear he'd gone through, thinking he would never see her again. He kissed her like he was marking her, claiming her, memorizing her. The cave disappeared, as did all of her worry and planning. Crew had found her, and that meant everything would be right from now on.

He lifted her again and walked her forward to sit her up on the rock she'd been hiding behind, so she had to angle her face down to kiss him and he had to angle his up. He kept one hand anchored on her hip to steady her and pulled off the scarf covering her hair with the other, pulled out the tie around her simple chignon, then shook her hair free, pulling it around his face.

"Dahlia," he murmured. "I missed you."

Her heart light, she smiled against his face as his lips planted tiny kisses over her top lip, bottom lip, cheekbones, chin, and eyebrows. "I knew you'd find me."

"How could you possibly have known that?"

"Angel told me you would search for me."

He pulled back and looked at her? "Angel?"

She placed her hands on his shoulders, feeling the muscles there, then running her fingertips over his skin just to make sure he was real. "It's hard to explain, but there's this bobcat who—"

"Oh, the echo."

Her brow furrowed in confusion. "The what?"

He smiled at her and she loved how it turned his face from sexy-intense to sexy-sweet. "We have a lot to talk about."

She smiled back. "We do." She kissed him again, heat building inside her, regardless of the danger of the situation.

He maneuvered her head back with the hand in her hair and kissed his way down her collarbone to her overflowing breasts. He pulled back and drank in the sight. "I love this dress on you," he said, "but I'm surprised to see you in it."

"King Caius wouldn't let me wear pants. He says it's not proper for a lady. He's the reason I covered my hair, too."

Crew's eyes flashed. "This king no longer has any say or sway over you. "

Dahlia laughed and patted his cheek. "Don't hurt him. He's been very helpful."

Crew frowned. "Then how is it that you are in this cave contemplating that beast?"

Dahlia wrapped her legs around him. "I'll explain later;

right now, I just want to tell you hello properly. If there's one thing I regret from our night together, it's not sleeping with you."

Crew growled and kissed her harder, his free hand moving from her hair to her skirts, trying to find its way underneath them. "And you would do that here, in the basilisk's lair?"

She pouted. "I guess I couldn't even if I wanted to. I just realized I can't get this undergarment off without taking the entire dress and corset and everything off."

He growled again at the thought. "That's because you don't have claws."

Dahlia giggled. "Ooh, don't, they aren't mine, and I don't think the lady I borrowed them from has many pairs," she said, thinking of her strict and dour lady in waiting who had worn the same dress both days Dahlia had seen her. Besides, did she want their first time to be in this rank-smelling hole?

She stared at Crew as he stared up at her, his lips turned up in a smile, his eyes saying everything she felt. She leaned forward to rest her forehead against his, unable to touch him enough. "I'm so glad you found me."

He stiffened, then spoke quickly. "I owe you an apology."

"For what?"

"It's my fault you died."

Dahlia pulled back and frowned, trying to imagine how he could possibly think that. There'd been no way out of it. If he had fought, the little girl would have died.

He took a deep breath. "That being who killed you?"

"Khain, the demon."

"How did you know that?"

"Angel told me."

"Right. Of course. Khain did it because I challenged him

many years ago, when you were just a little girl. He marked me and used me to find you, after he promised me that he would kill you."

She stayed quiet for a few moments, thinking the words over, staring into Crew's eyes as tension kept him stiff. She finally spoke. "I know that you believe it's your fault, Crew, but everything that's happened to me in the last few days tells me otherwise. Just like you told me you believe in fate, I'm now starting to believe that everything we do serves something greater than us, whether our actions are what that something envisioned or not. I think you're innocent."

He frowned. "I'm not innocent, Dahlia."

"Ok, then, what if I told you that if I had to do it all again, and I could choose not to die, but that would mean I would never meet you or could never have you, then I would choose for Khain to kill me again, exactly as he did."

"You would?"

Dahlia nodded, seeing the loosening of something behind Crew's eyes. Something that had been there for a long time. "Yes, he could even kill me a second time if it meant—"

Crew's eyes went wide and he covered her mouth. "Don't say that. Don't ever say something like that."

Dahlia remembered what Angel had said.

Your imagination is strong, ayasha. Never feed it that which you do not wish to see.

She shook her head hard, then whispered into his palm, "I take it back."

***

Crew knelt behind the rock with Dahlia, smelling her scent and thrilling at her nearness. When he'd spotted the guards outside the cave he'd had a momentary panic when he'd wondered if they could have done something as barbaric as sacrifice her, but as he'd snuck past the incompetent young-sters, he'd scented her and known she was alive and in deep thought, her mind worrying a problem, but in no immediate danger.

Then when he'd seen her, waist tiny over flaring skirts, shoulders bare and tempting, hair covered, he'd had a hard time believing it was her, but there was no mistaking her scent and the way it made him feel.

"Aren't there others trying to do whatever you are do-ing?" he whispered, wondering what mad king would send a female up here by herself.

"I sent them into another part of the cave after a fake basilisk."

"You... How?"

She grinned at him, running her hand along his leg, seemingly unable to stop touching him. It gladdened his heart even as it made him unable to concentrate.

"Ah, we really do have a lot to talk about. I'll try to ex-plain later, but right now, just help me think of a way to get the egg that's under that basilisk. Those green piles on the floor, they're venom and it'll go right through your shoes and clothing. Besides, if you get too close to the thing, it's scent will kill you, or if it looks right at you that will kill you, too."

Crew stared. "How big is the egg?"

"I don't know. I haven't seen it yet. Don't you want to know why I need it?"

"I'm sure you have a good reason," Crew said absently, his mind racing.

"I know I can get the basilisk out of the cave, if we just had a way to get to the egg."

Crew grunted. "I think I have a good shot at getting the egg over here, if you can get the basilisk off it."

Dahlia turned to him, her eyes wide. "Crew, you can't go in there. I mean it. What if you can't heal yourself in time?"

He gave her a gentle smile. "Trust me, Dahlia. I won't go in there." He nodded at her. "Let's see what you've got."

Her lips quirked at the challenge and a glint entered her eye. "Ok, big boy, you asked for it."

She turned straight ahead again and Crew watched her curiously as she closed her eyes and her brow furrowed. Her right hand raised to her bare throat and twisted at nothing there, making Crew grin. He had to lean forward when she started whispering to herself to make out the words, but still they didn't make any sense.

"Now what would a female basilisk find sexy in a male? Big? Scaly? Mean?" Her face tightened and he could see her eyes moving behind her eyelids. He didn't dare interrupt her as power flowed out of her, more mental power than he'd ever felt in his life. She was more powerful than ten *citlali*! More powerful even than he was?

Across the cave, a mighty roar rent the air, jerking Crew's head that way. The basilisk woke up, lumbering to its feet and shaking its head, venom flying, as another one, slightly bigger, slogged into the entryway of the cave, gave his head a shake, then turned and exited. The first basilisk followed with a roar of her own, but Crew thought it was an eager noise.

"How...?" No. He knew how, or suspected. He changed his question as Dahlia opened her eyes and grinned at her work. "Is it real?" he asked.

She shook her head. "I don't know."

"How long will it last?"

She met his eyes. "I don't know."

He turned to the egg, that lay within a dirty, messy nest of sticks across the poisonous cavern. It was about the size of a football. He hefted it with his mind, lifting it an inch off the surface it lay on. Heavy, but doable. "We better hurry then. Try not to interrupt me."

He moved the egg over the ledge of its nest, then down off the platform and across the room, keeping the speed steady and slow, so he didn't wobble it or drop it in a pile of deadly drool. He ignored Dahlia's gasp as she realized what he was doing, breathing only in tiny, shallow gasps until the thing was close enough to grab.

He wanted to float it directly into Dahlia's hands, but he couldn't take the chance it would hurt her. He plucked it from the air instead and examined it until he was satisfied it was safe.

"Your egg, my great basilisk conqueror," he said, holding it out for her to take, feeling the silly grin on his face, glad it was back.

It felt right.

CHAPTER 28

*E*lla walked on the path through the forest, hand-in-hand with her mate, her soul light with the beauty of winter. Heavy snow weighed down the branches around her, absorbing all the sounds in the area, making her feel like she and Trevor could be alone on the planet, until a fat bird landed on a branch above her and scolded her. She looked up and smiled at it.

Heather and Graeme's cabin appeared as they rounded a bend. Ella heard banging from behind the cabin and assumed they were working on the reptile atrium Graeme was building for Heather off the side of the cabin. Ella shuddered, thinking of all those lizards having free run of the house, even though Heather had assured her they would prefer to stay in the atrium.

Movement caught her eye to the right and she spotted Graeme walking through the woods, his head down, as if in deep thought. The ground beneath him was bare of snow. As she watched, the snow on the ground six feet in front of him melted as he drew close. Even the snow above him melted instantly and dropped to the ground as rain as he walked, but the heat coming off him evaporated much of it, making him look as if he were walking in fog. She wondered how much heat was coming off him.

Trevor also watched him as they continued to follow the path around the back of the cozy cabin. Heather was there, her hands clasped tightly around a metal container the size and shape of a thermos.

Heather placed it down on a metal work bench in front of her and ran to greet them, a smile on her face.

Trevor lifted his chin towards Graeme in the woods. "Is he ok?"

Heather's face grew worried. "He's been like that since we returned from Dahlia's house last night. He hasn't slept. He's convinced we're missing something big and if he doesn't figure out what it is, we won't be able to bring Crew and Dahlia home."

Trevor headed that way. "I'll talk to him."

Heather gave Ella a hug. "Good to see you." Then she put her hands out, indicating everything on the workbench. "Don't touch anything, it's all hot enough to burn you." She indicated several pieces of opaque glass at the end. "Except for those. Those are cooled now."

Ella picked one up. It was small, and square, only about the size of a piece of paper folded in half, but over a half inch thick. She examined the air bubbles and swirls within it, then held it up to the sky trying to see through it. She could, but everything was distorted on the other side. "What is it?"

"It will be a part of the walls of the atrium. Graeme is going to make it almost entirely out of windows that he makes himself from sand and limestone."

Ella's mouth dropped open. "That's the most romantic thing I've ever heard."

Heather giggled. "I know, right?" She ran to a heavy-duty shelf and pulled it open, lifting out a windowpane that looked to be about two feet wide and two feet high. She held it up. "Look how gorgeous."

Ella's eyes ran over every detail. The pieces of glass were irregular-sized, but all cut into square or rectangle shapes, then jigsawed so closely together that only an inch of wood ran between each. The resulting pattern, or lack of a pattern, was beautiful.

Heather walked back to the thermos and picked it up, rolling it in her hands, then peering inside.

"What are you doing?"

"I'm trying to see if I can get the sand and limestone hot enough to melt. Graeme is encouraging me to work on my fire. He says it's important to be able to control it before I get pregnant, because the fire-lust can get out of control in pregnant females."

Ella tilted her head, and tried to see in the thermos without getting too close. "But you're not *dragen*."

Heather nodded. "That's what I told him. Graeme thinks it doesn't matter. He's convinced I'll behave exactly like a *dragen* female when pregnant." Heather put the cylindrical container down on the workbench in front of her, glanced at Graeme in the forest, and moved closer to Ella, her face grim. "I don't want to tell him, but I'm afraid we'll never get pregnant."

Ella pulled her into a loving hug. "You will, I know you

will." She held her sister at arm's length and peered at her. "Are you trying to get pregnant?"

Heather smiled. "We're not trying not to."

Ella squealed and jumped up and down, pulling Heather with her. She dropped her hands to her lower belly, which still showed little signs of rounding, and said excitedly, "That would be so wonderful if we had babies at the same time." Ella grew serious and looked at Graeme and Trevor talking in the woods. "I think Graeme's smart, telling you to work on your fire skills, though. Did I ever tell you what happened to me in the *Pravus*?"

Heather shook her head. "I've heard bits and pieces, but not all the details."

"My body generated some sort of power that repelled Khain, maybe hurt him a bit. I'm not totally sure how it happened, but I've been thinking that you and I have been given these powers for a reason, and we need to strengthen them. Or at least learn to control them."

Heather nodded, her eyes wide. "Oooh, let's do it."

Ella grabbed her hand and squeezed it. "Okay then, do you want to start tomorrow? In the yard behind the house?"

Heather glanced to the males, who were walking side-by-side, Trevor having taken off his light jacket and thrown it over his shoulder. "Should we tell them? They might worry."

"I don't think we'll be able to hide it, and I know they already worry. Maybe they'll worry less if we can show them some sort of competence."

Heather crossed her arms over her chest and grinned. "It's a date. I'm excited."

"You should come to the house for dinner tonight. Since the KSRT induction ceremony has been postponed until Crew comes back, we wanted to do something for Troy and

Trent and Graeme. Trevor already asked Graeme but said he didn't think Graeme was into it. But we never see you."

Heather smiled shyly. "We've, ah, we've been busy."

"I know, newlyweds and all that."

"It's more than that, we ah, we were both virgins."

It was Ella's turn to look shocked. "Even him?" She said pointing towards Graeme.

Heather nodded.

"But he's nine hundred years old."

"Nine hundred and thirty-six, actually." She stared into the forest, the love in her eyes spilling over. "His mother was the last female dragon and he would've killed any human he took, so he never did."

"Wow," Ella breathed. "What's he like now?"

"Insatiable."

Ella laughed. She could imagine. A screeching noise drew their attention and they both stepped away from the cabin so they could see the open meadow beyond the edge of forest. Smokey ran from the house, straight to the back of the property, bounding through the snow with Angel chasing him gleefully. The two housecats and one wild animal had gotten along immediately, but Angel had been standoffish with everyone else. From around the front of the house, a bigger black shape streaked after them. It was Troy, barking madly, and Ella wondered if Angel had warmed to him. Trent followed, but at a slow, almost tired, walk. He sat in the snow and watched the three animals play.

Heather motioned towards Trent. "What's his story?"

"He's an old soul. A thinker." *And I wish I knew if he was happy.*

Heather seemed nervous as she stared at the wolves. "I

heard him tell Trevor that you are worried about something and he needs to ask you about it, that it's something big."

Ella turned to her quickly. "Oh no. I wonder how he knows." She grasped her sister's hand. "I need to tell somebody this. Promise you won't tell anyone, even Graeme?"

Heather grimaced. "I guess I can promise not to tell if he doesn't ask me directly."

Ella nodded quickly. "That's good enough for me. My sister is pregnant."

Heather shook her head. "The one in the hospital? Is that bad?"

"I don't know if she was pregnant before Khain took her."

Heather bobbed her head in understanding. "Oh no. Can Khain get humans pregnant?"

Ella dropped her eyes. "There's a good chance that I am at least one quarter *shiften*. It stands to reason that she could be, too. Khain can get *shiften* pregnant."

Heather grabbed her shoulders. "That's not good. You *have* to tell Trevor."

Ella threw back her head. "*I know.* If only I were sure if it was Khain's or not, because I know what Trevor is going to want to do if he even suspects it is. I just found out that she had a boyfriend and he's reported her missing, so I've gotta talk to him to find out if he knew she was pregnant. If he did, that solves everything. If he didn't…"

Heather's eyes were far away and, as Ella gazed at the sister she'd only known for two weeks but already loved more than the one lying in that hospital bed, she remembered something. "Graeme said a portal could be something small enough to hold in your hand, what about our pendants? I haven't touched mine since it sent me to some other world." She grimaced, remembering the absolute fear she'd felt as those horses had approached her at high speed when she should have been home in her own bed.

Heather turned to face her slowly, and Ella could almost see the lightbulb over her head. "You're kidding me. I don't think he knows that. You have to tell him the story."

But Graeme and Trevor were already striding toward them with purpose, Graeme's expression hopeful and Trevor's resolute. Trevor had already told him.

***

Heather watched as Trevor pulled the pendant out of the safe slowly, being careful to touch only the chain it was secured on. He turned to Graeme and put it in his hands.

Graeme ran his fingers over it but frowned after a few moments. "I get nothing." He turned to Ella. "I need you to handle it."

Trevor stepped between them without giving Ella a chance to answer. "No way. She's pregnant. I told you what happened the last time she touched it. We aren't taking that chance again."

Ella's face showed relief while Graeme looked resigned, but frustrated. Heather held up her hand, her eyes ping-ponging between all three of them. "I'll try. Will it work for me?"

Graeme turned to her, his eyes unreadable. He stared at her for a long while before he answered. "It might." His eyes flashed. "Listen to me. Fix in your mind exactly what you want it to do. You only want information from it. You don't want it to take you anywhere, you don't want it to do anything, except talk to you. Make sure your intention is crystal clear."

Heather felt a thrill go through her. Her mind cast back

to her own pendant, and she wondered where it was now and what the boy Caius had done with it. "Got it, boss." She held out her hand for it.

Graeme grasped her by one wrist and put the pendant in her hand, holding tight to her. Warmth spread from the object through her body, feeding her thrill. She remembered the fire she had started when she'd first discovered her own pendant in her mother's jewelry box and she took a deep breath, trying to contain her spiking fire-lust. She could feel it, aching to take control of her. Ella gasped, causing Heather to open her eyes and look down. The jewels in the face of the snarling wolf were glowing a bright orange-yellow.

Heather closed her eyes again and concentrated on her question as pictures she could not quite interpret flashed through her mind.

Can you take us to Dahlia?

She saw Dahlia in her imagination, wearing some sort of an old, dressy costume and carrying something heavy in her arms. The image faded and was replaced by another. Dahlia riding astride a horse, her head thrown back in laughter, again wearing that dress that looked straight out of the middle ages.

She opened her eyes and faced Graeme, her fingers curling around the pendant. She didn't want to give it back. "I can see Dahlia, but I don't know if that means I could go to her."

Graeme turned away from her and paced through the room, hitting one hand against the other. When he spoke, his accent was heavy as if he were only talking to himself. "I dinnae believe we are supposed to go to Dahlia. The augur said Crew had to go to Dahlia and his friends had to recover the means to retrieve them from wherever they were." He turned and fixed Heather with his eyes. "Ask it if we can find Dahlia's pendant."

Heather gave Graeme a secret smile, thinking he looked impossibly sexy when he was concentrating, then she closed her eyes and did as he asked. An image of a pendant flashed in her mind, different than the one she had in her hand, but more similar to it than her own, which had a dragon instead of a wolf on one side. She saw the pendant she assumed to be Dahlia's hanging on a nail in an enclosed dark space. She tried to get more information but the image only spun.

Heather opened her eyes to relay what she had seen, but frowned when Ella's expression turned scared and Trevor got between Ella and Heather, then grabbed for her, but his hands seem to go right through her. She looked down at her body, hearing a stuttering, whooshing noise in her ear like a wagon with one square wheel traveling at an impossibly high speed. She held onto the pendant tighter and looked around, only able to see Graeme for a moment before she disappeared out of Trevor and Ella's house completely.

CHAPTER 29

ahlia stared down at the egg, unable to believe they'd done it. She never would've been able to without Crew.

"That was impressive," she said as she curled the egg into her chest and headed down the dark corridor towards the exit. "Can all werewolves do that, move things with their minds?"

Crew jogged to catch up with her, then stared down at her as he walked beside her. When he spoke, his voice was amused. "Werewolves don't exist, Dahlia."

She frowned at him. "Are you making a joke? I saw you change, remember?"

He grinned. "I'm not a werewolf. I am a *shiften*, able to change into my animal at will. The moon does not control me." He thought for a second, then spoke again. "I will concede that during the full moon, some *shiften* feel more irritable, more aggressive, and all are more sexually-charged."

Dahlia giggled. "Kind of like a *shiften* period?"

His grin grew and her expression turned pensive. "What does it do to you, personally?"

He grabbed her hand to pull her to a stop before they reached the end of the corridor, tucking her hair behind her ear with the other and tearing her heart open with his intense stare. "I look forward to showing you."

When Dahlia could move again, they left the cave, squinting against the light, the egg held in Dahlia's arms. The soldiers sitting on rocks a few feet away stopped their talking and stared, mouths open.

The leader recovered himself first. He stood and ordered one of his soldiers to, "Hie on to the market, as fast as you can, tell the king it is done." He approached Dahlia, his eyes on the egg, his hands open.

Crew stepped between them and crossed his arms over his chest. "She keeps it," he snarled.

The soldier dropped a hand to his sword hilt. "Who are you?"

Fear shot through Dahlia. She pulled at Crew but he did not move. She stepped next to him, speaking to the soldier. "My husband. He just got here. The king would like him safe and well-treated."

The soldier did not take his hand from his sword, as he continued to stare aggressively at Crew. "How did you get in there with her?"

Crew challenged him. "Walked in under your noses, while you and your hens were clucking about the price of beets at the market."

Oh, perfect. Hotheaded didn't begin to describe him. Dahlia pulled at him. "Crew, can I talk to you for a second over here?"

Crew allowed himself to be pulled away. She stood on tiptoe and pulled him down by the shoulder so she could whisper in his ear. "What are you doing? They're on our side."

"Dahlia, it seems like they've all been perfectly kind to you, and because of that, I won't humiliate any of them, but this is the way of males. You must not interfere or they will not respect me. If they don't respect me, our way in this world will be much harder than it has to be, and eventually I'll have to make them fear me. It's been different for you because you are a female, but now I'm here."

Dahlia stared into his eyes, noting their warmth as he gazed at her. So different from when he looked at the soldiers. She nodded. "Got it. I apologize."

He kissed her quickly. "No need to be sorry with me, doll. Always know that."

Dahlia shivered at his sentiment, wanting to show him how glad she was that he was there, but the eyes of the soldiers were on them. They returned and she stood back a step, letting Crew speak.

"Where are we taking this rotten thing?"

***

With narrowed eyes, Crew watched the soldiers mount their horses. He turned and stared suspiciously at the horse Dahlia had ridden up on and they were supposed to ride back on together. He walked in front of it and tried to lock eyes with it. The gentle mare whinnied nervously, and splayed her front legs, her ears rotating madly. Dahlia stepped forward to try to soothe her, smiling discreetly. She'd never been on a horse before when she'd first arrived in this world either, but

Crew seemed almost scared of it. Definitely nervous. Didn't he realize the horse was more scared of him?

She got close to him. "It's ok. The ride's not bad once you get used to it."

Crew shook his head and pulled her close. "My animal doesn't like it. My animal wants to run alongside."

Dahlia glanced at the soldiers who were paying them no attention, then lowered her voice. "I don't think that's a good idea. I'll tell you why later."

He nodded. "Does it have anything to do with wolves who used to be shapeshifters?"

Dahlia gave him a sharp look, nodded once, then turned to watch one soldier on horseback urge his horse into a trot, then a canter.

Crew's mood darkened. Dahlia pulled him towards the horse. "Don't worry, we don't have to go that fast. They'll wait for us."

With a look of resignation on his face, Crew reached a hand out to touch the horse. Dahlia thought the horse was going to bolt until Crew's fingers reached it, and then the horse calmed at once. Crew grabbed a fistful of mane and swung a leg up and over until he was seated on the horse, grimacing and shifting in his seat. "Squashes the balls," he muttered.

Dahlia grinned. He looked like an expert already if he could get over the ball squashing. He held out a hand to pull her up and she grasped it, squeaking as he lifted her straight into the air and deposited her in front of him.

They pushed the horse into a trot a few times, but mostly stayed at a walk. The ride to the market took almost an hour, but when they were still twenty minutes away they could hear the celebration. When they finally stopped their horses and dismounted, Crew lowered Dahlia to the ground first, then slid off with a groan of satisfaction. "I'll never do that again."

Dahlia didn't have the heart to tell him that the castle where they would be sleeping would also require them to ride on a horse. She frowned, wondering if they would indeed be staying in the world that night. They had no way home that she knew of. The portal off the cliff-face was a no-go, in her mind.

The soldiers led them to a stage that had been built in the center of the marketplace. Crew challenged the stares of the curious citizenry who gaped openly at her and him with his strange clothing. Dahlia tried to smile at them. The faces were not as friendly as she had hoped.

King Caius rushed to meet them, wearing a thick gold crown on his head for the first time that she'd seen, a broad smile on his face. She held out the egg to him and he took it, then gave it to a soldier and tried to embrace her. In a flash, Crew was there, his hand on the king's chest, stopping his forward motion, his lips pulled back in a snarl.

King Caius stepped back and motioned for his soldiers to sheath the swords they had pulled when Crew had touched him. Dahlia noticed a man standing next to him and slightly behind him that she'd never seen before. His face was long and sour, his hair unkempt and receding. His lips twisted as he watched the king greet them, making him look angry that they'd succeeded at recovering the egg.

"Who are you?" King Caius asked Crew, pulling himself up to his full height, which was almost as tall as Crew.

"Her mate," Crew snarled as Dahlia said, "My husband, Crew." As soon as Dahlia saw the king's face soften, she shifted her gaze to the man next to him. His eyes widened with surprise and then narrowed, then he wiped his face clean of all expression. Dahlia shifted uneasily and looked back to the king.

The king held out his hand to Crew and they shook, Crew not softening at all, the king watching him carefully. "Good Sir, you are very blessed to have such a wife, and I thank you for admitting her to our services. She has saved my kingdom from grave dangers."

Crew nodded, then stepped backwards and put a protective arm around Dahlia. The king would no longer look her in the eyes. He motioned to the sour man next to him. "This is Lord Theobald, who has just been appointed Head of Parliament."

Lord Theobald bowed at the waist an inch or two, then stood back, as if scrambling out of Crew's reach. Crew didn't even look his way, his eyes locked on the king.

King Caius took the egg from the soldier who was holding it and walked to the center of the stage as a courtier struck a great bell, sending a resounding noise out over the crowd, which quieted at once.

King Caius held the egg over his head in both hands, his voice strong and clear. "Dahlia the Clever and Crew the Strong have retrieved the basilisk egg. Show them your thanks!"

The crowd responded with a great roar, holding their arms above their heads, some throwing flowers and coins up onto the stage. The king addressed them again. "And now it is time for a celebration. Eat, drink, and be merry, for today is declared a holiday."

The crowd erupted again and the king returned to Dahlia and Crew.

The king smiled at Crew and again avoided Dahlia's eye.

"Whatever I can do for you, name it. If it is in my power, it is yours."

"The pendant, King Caius. That is all we need," Dahlia said quickly.

Crew held up a hand. "And a room, somewhere private to sleep."

The king nodded. "Of course. I will secure you a guard to the castle, and Crew, your lady can show you to your sleeping quarters. But won't you stay and celebrate with us?"

Crew shook his head once and said, "We have other things to attend to."

Dahlia's cheeks heated but her imagination felt no such embarrassment. It already had Crew naked and holding her to the bed, taking care of the regret she had voiced earlier.

***

Crew got on the horse with much less fanfare the second time, but Dahlia could tell he still did not like it. As they rode slowly through the forest, a soldier ahead and a soldier behind, Crew relaxed enough to look around. He lifted his head to scent the air. Dahlia shifted in her seat to see his face.

He smiled at her and her insides melted. "This seems like a nice place to live," he said. "I could get used to this world."

Dahlia leaned back to give him a kiss. "I was thinking the same thing."

By the time they reached the castle, Dahlia's muscles were aching again, but Crew seemed limber as he jumped off and helped her down. As he stared at the castle and took in the view, she wished she had her notebook to record his reaction. The way he nodded when he viewed things he liked and the way his lips thinned when he viewed things he didn't like.

LISA LADEW

The intensity in his eyes as he gazed out over the water on the back side of the mountain. She could write entire sonnets on just the way his back stiffened and his chin jutted out when any men looked at him... or at her.

The guard led them directly into the great room, speaking softly with the soldiers already there, then motioning that Dahlia could take the clay block. Apparently the king's instructions had been that she could have it whether the covenant broke for her or not.

Dahlia led Crew to the alcove where the clay block sat, surprised that the king hadn't wanted to come back to see if she were able to break the covenant. He truly was a king of the people and she knew they would be sad to see him go.

Dahlia touched the block softly with one finger, having no idea if she was pure in intention or not. A high chiming noise sounded and the thing cracked in half instantly, revealing the shining pendant immediately.

Crew pulled the pieces of the block away and cast them onto the floor. "Is that what you were sent to get?"

Dahlia nodded and grasped the pendant lovingly. From the front, it looked much like the one that had left her life so many years before, but when she spun it around, a snarling dragon greeted her, its eyes purple.

"A dragon?" She could hear the surprise and upset in Crew's voice.

"It's not mine," she whispered. "It's Heather's."

"That's all right, then," he said.

She cradled the pendant in her hand and could feel the pull of worlds within it, its power apparent, even to her who had no experience with such things.

"Do you have a pocket?" Crew asked. She nodded. "I

don't think you should be holding it in your hands. It makes me nervous."

"Okay," she said, dropping it into the deep pocket in the folds of her dress, pressing her hand to the very bottom first to sure there were no holes. She could not lose such an important item.

She almost reached in her pocket again to pull it out and give it to Crew for safekeeping, but a voice sounded in her head.

No. It stays with you.

CHAPTER 30

Heather opened her eyes to darkness, frowning because it had been daytime when they'd entered Trevor's house to retrieve the pendant from the safe. One look at the sky told her she had traveled outside of her own world, to one with almost no stars in the sky and a moon that looked to be three times the size of the sun in her world. She shivered violently and grabbed the pendant hard in both hands, focusing on it as if her life depended on it. "Take me back home, take me back home," she demanded, squeezing her eyes tightly shut and praying that the next time she opened them, she would see Graeme's face.

The stuttering, whooshing noise came again, and she kept her eyes squeezed shut as she felt a cold wind blowing her hair. She didn't open her eyes again until she heard Ella's voice. "She's coming back. Thank goodness."

Trevor spoke up. "That was nothing like when you went.

You were there one minute, and gone the next. You didn't slowly fade in and out like that."

Graeme was at her side and she uttered a prayer of thanks when she finally felt his arms around her. He pulled her to face him and gazed at her, his eyes traveling from the top of her head down to her toes. "Are you ok?" She nodded, still shaken. He addressed Trevor. "It makes sense. If this pendant was made for Ella and allows her to travel between worlds, the energy patterns of her sisters could be similar enough to allow them to use it, but not in the same smooth fashion that it would afford to her."

Graeme pulled her even closer and looked in her eyes. "Where did you go?"

Heather shook her head, still shivering. "I don't know. Somewhere that it was nighttime." Graeme smoothed her hair and ran his thumbs across her forehead, tracing just above her eyebrows. "Could you see anything?"

She nodded. "There was something in front of me like a house, but I didn't pay attention, I just wanted to get back."

"Did you sense any danger?"

She shook her head, embarrassed that she hadn't taken a look around.

Graeme ran his thumb over first one of her eyebrows, then the other, then smoothed a hand over her hair again and massaged the back of her neck. "Tell it you want it to take both of us to the same place you just returned from."

Heather pulled back, not sure she was willing to do so, now that she had seen what the pendant could do. "What if we get separated?"

Graeme shook his head. "I could sense you. I would've followed you if you hadn't immediately started to flicker back into this world. Getting to you would not be pretty, but by my estimation, there is nowhere in this universe I could not follow you."

Heather nodded slowly. "I'll try, but hold on tight." She grabbed his hand in hers, then closed her eyes and asked the pendant to take them both.

Stutter, stutter, whoosh, a great wind and even more pulling as the pendant took them both, and then Heather almost fell to the ground. Graeme caught her and pulled her upright, while staring straight ahead. Heather turned to see what he was looking at.

A woman stood there, bouncing on the balls of her feet, her hands clasped together, a huge smile on her face as her long brown hair blew with the night wind. "You came back!" she shouted, clapping her hands, then throwing her arms out to her sides and spinning a circle. "I so hoped you would. I've been feeling that something great and wonderful was going to happen soon and here you are."

Heather smiled. She seemed harmless enough, and enthusiastic. "You saw me come the first time?"

The woman shook her head. "No, but I knew you were here."

Heather shook her head, confused. "How did you know I was here if you didn't see me?"

The woman crooked a finger at them, motioning that they should follow her. "Come, I will show you." She walked through the cutest handmade white picket fence Heather had ever seen, following a stone path up to a quaint but perfectly modern-looking house, not quite what Heather had expected after what Ella had said about the world she'd been transported to.

The woman turned and faced them again. Heather estimated her age to be somewhere between forty and fifty years old, but the constant smile on her face made it hard to tell. "I almost forgot my manners, my name is Deborah, but you can call me Deb, or the moon lady, if you like. That's what my neighbors call me. They think I'm crazy." She whirled and headed back into the house without waiting to hear their names.

Heather looked at Graeme, and his dumbfounded expression made her bite back a snicker.

Once inside, Deborah walked to the back wall of an open kitchen and stood by a patchwork quilt that seemed to be glowing. She put her ear to it. "Come here, sweetie," she said motioning to Heather. "Come hear it."

Heather looked at Graeme and he nodded. She caught the look he sent her. *She's not dangerous.* Heather walked next to Deborah and pressed her ear to the quilt. She did hear something behind it, a sort of soft, chiming noise, like someone had run their finger around a chanting bowl and left it to vibrate.

Heather held out her hand and opened her fingers so Deborah could see what she had there. "Does whatever is making that noise look anything like this?"

Deborah stared at the pendant for a full minute, her face going white, then slowly raised the back of her hand to her forehead and slumped to the ground in a faint.

"Oh," Heather breathed, and reached for her. Graeme stepped forward, but before either of them could reach her, Deborah rolled onto her stomach and pushed up to her feet, holding on to the wall.

"Deborah, sit down," Heather told her, her brow furrowed.

Deborah held a hand to her head again, then moved to the brown couch against the far wall and sat down. "I'm sorry, don't mind me, I have low blood pressure and sometimes it gets away from me. I have to admit I've encouraged it, though, because my late husband, McManus, God and the angels rest his soul and keep him from Satan's roost, loved it when I fainted. It made him randy as the neighbor's dog, and I loved that."

Graeme snorted a surprised laugh and Heather glared at him, then burst into giggles. She tried to hide them behind her hand, then asked Deborah if she needed a glass of water.

"Oh no, dearie, you just lift that quilt up and get out what's in the cupboard behind. I guess that's what you came for."

Heather nodded at Graeme and he did as Deborah asked. He brought the pendant to Heather and showed it to her. It was similar, but not the exact same as the one she had in her hand. As the two pendants came closer to each other, the pendant in Heather's hand emitted the same noise as the one in Graeme's. Heather looked up at him questioningly. Graeme shrugged. "I'll get them close, but make sure you don't touch both at the same time. I'm not sure if it will do anything to you, but I'll pick safe before sorry."

He moved the pendants closer together and the chiming sound intensified to a peak, and then cut off altogether just before they touched.

Heather smiled at Deborah, examining the features of her face, and wondering if what she suspected was true. Before Heather had figured out how to ask the question, Deborah smiled brightly at her. "So you'll be taking me home now, then?"

Heather looked to Graeme nervously.

Graeme spoke to Deborah. "Where is home to you, Deborah?"

She nodded at the pendant in his hand. "Where that

pendant brought me from, twenty-one years ago. I would say Earth in the twentieth century, but this world, for all its differences, is also called Earth and also in the twentieth century, twenty-first now, actually."

Graeme nodded to Heather and whispered in her ear. "We can probably do it, but it's up to you. I just need to know how she got hold of this pendant."

Heather whispered back, "I think I know."

She turned to Deborah again, but Deborah asked her own question before Heather could say a word. "Are you two together?"

Heather smiled and nodded.

"Of course you are!" Deborah clapped her hands together and shot to her feet again. "I can tell you are by the way you look at each other." She put her hands on her hips. "If I could give you one piece of advice, it would be to never let your sex life go stale. Me and my late husband, McManus, God and the angels rest his soul and keep him from Satan's roost, always tried new things, right up until the day he died. He was much older than me, but he was a very open-minded man, just the same. Food play, foot play, bondage, role play." She lifted up her fingers and put one out, grabbing it with the fingers on her other hand like she was going to start counting out more kinds of play, but Graeme put a hand up, stopping her, his face tight.

Heather giggled again. "Food play?" but Graeme's eyes flashed. He didn't want to know.

"Oh, sorry," Deborah said. "I know, I'm wildly inappropriate. My late husband, McManus, God and the angels rest his soul and keep him from Satan's roost, always told me so with a smile on his face. He said he loved it, though, it kept him young."

She stood. "But you, young man, don't need me to keep you young, so I'll shut up now."

Heather shot an amused glance at Graeme, then turned back to Deborah. "Deborah, do you know Dahlia?"

Deborah stared at her, then rushed around the couch to grab her into a hug as her tears began to fall.

"Dahlia is my daughter. I hoped you knew her, but I couldn't bring myself to ask. Please, can you tell me how she is?"

***

Heather held on tight to Deborah as they skidded back through whatever space they had to maneuver through to get to their real world. When they arrived, Deborah was a dead weight in her arms. She laid her gently on the floor, ignoring the stunned looks on Trevor and Ella's faces, then stood and looked around for Graeme.

Deborah opened her eyes and shot to her feet, her smile wide as she headed for Trevor and Ella to hug them both.

"Where's Graeme?" Heather muttered, turning in a circle, looking around at the walls of Trevor's basement. "He should have been here by now. He said he was leaving right after us."

Worry sat heavy on her chest as she gripped the pendant in her hands. What if the other pendant had somehow stopped him from doing that dimensional-tearing thing he did?

But then he came down the stairs, his boots pounding on the wood. "Sorry, I was off by a few feet. Landed in the driveway."

Heather breathed a sigh of relief, then turned to introduce Deborah to Ella and Trevor. "She's Dahlia's mom. I told her we are waiting for Dahlia to come back from the other world." She raised her eyebrows and shook her head, indicating they shouldn't mention that none of them knew exactly where that was.

Trevor shot a nervous look up the stairs. "Oh, that's wonderful, Mrs. Ah-"

"Deborah, call me Deborah, or Deb, or the moon lady, if you like. That's what my neighbors call me. They think I'm crazy."

Trevor nodded his head slowly, his eyes big. Heather had to wonder if he'd ever had a full-blooded human in his house before. He spoke slowly to her, like maybe she didn't speak English very well. "Deborah, perhaps we should take you to Dahlia's house? You could wait there for her. We'll bring her straight to you if she shows up here first, but I don't think she will." He looked to Ella for help.

Deborah nodded happily. "That would be great. Fantastic. Stupendous. She's half angel, you know."

No one spoke. No one moved. No one breathed.

Deborah tittered and nodded, looking at the four of them in turn. "Oh, yes. Her father came to me one night dressed in Harrison Ford's body, because between his Han Solo and Indiana Jones characters, I thought he was the sexiest man alive at that time. I told him he didn't need to put on the mask for me, and I knew what he was underneath, but he just laughed at me and said he wanted to please me enough that I would let him make a baby with me." Her gaze went to the ceiling and her eyes went soft. "He sounded like wind chimes when he laughed."

Graeme turned to Heather. "I never imagined the angel would talk to them. We need to ask your mum her experience."

Mouth still open as she stared at Deborah, it took Heather a few moments before she could respond, but when she realized what he'd said, she shook her head vehemently and flashed him a look. "No way, Graeme, you can't imagine what she's like. Just believe me when I tell you that, if she knows you exist, you'll never get rid of her. She'll literally try to live inside your shirt pocket. That's if she doesn't keel over with a heart attack first, at me asking her about sex with an angel."

Ella finally managed to get her breath, looking at Trevor as she spoke. "Deborah, maybe you'd like to stay for dinner?"

CHAPTER 31

*C*rew pulled Dahlia impatiently to the stone stairs heading toward the direction she'd indicated her room was in, turning to make sure the soldiers were no longer following them. When the hallway was empty, he spun her against the wall, bracing the back of her head with his hand, and gathered her to him, breathing hotly into her mouth. "I've been imagining this since I first scented you inside that cave, since I first knew I'd found you again."

Dahlia sighed and melted into him, opening herself to him completely. *Good girl.*

He reached his fingers around to the back of her dress, unlacing the first ties there. "Will anyone come down this hallway?"

"Crew, I don't know. I haven't been here long and I don't leave the room at night."

He glanced in each direction, then decided not to risk it. He put a hand behind her shoulders, then bent to catch her behind the knees, and picked her up. Her smile made him glad to be a male, and glad to be alive and to be hers, no matter what world they were in. She locked her arms around his neck.

"You're mine," he growled, walking swiftly in the direction of the room she'd pointed out. "And I'm going to show you exactly what that means as soon as I can get those clothes off you."

She sighed again and her hand went to her throat as her hair tumbled over his arm and swayed freely in the air. In his mind, he saw her peekaboo nipples from the night they'd shared, after she'd pulled her hair over her shoulders to cover them. His already stiff cock hardened and lengthened until he groaned from the need and pressure.

At her door, he got them inside, setting her on her feet just long enough to bar the door, then picking her up again and holding her as he surveyed the room. He carried her to the bed on the far side of the room and set her down gently, kissing her until she melted like butter, pressing her body against him. She didn't seem to be in any hurry to get anywhere and he approved. They knew each other sexually already, a bit, but he still wanted this first time to be special, for both of them.

As he kissed her, he continued to work on the ties at her back, until her dress loosened and he was able to pull it down and off her. She stepped out of it and he threw it onto the bed, staring at her in wonder. Underneath the dress, she wore a one-piece white undergarment, at least two more skirts, and a stiff piece of fabric that cinched her waist and held her breasts up to the ceiling.

"Sweet baby Jesus," he whispered and Dahlia laughed merrily, the sound ringing off the stone walls.

"Crew, you shouldn't say that."

"I'm sorry. I didn't—." He couldn't form a thought in his head. She was too gorgeous for words.

"I forgive you," she said demurely, spinning in a circle. "If you help me take all this off, I'll put this piece back on for you." She tweaked the corset thing and smiled at him.

Crew made fast work of it all. She turned around so he could only see her lovely backside, then pulled the fabric back on and indicated he should fasten it. He did with slipping fingers, unable to concentrate on the knots when so much of her skin was on display.

Still facing away from him, Dahlia pulled her hair forward and took a moment to position it exactly how she wanted it, then turned to face him slowly. While she turned, he could count every time his heart beat by the six strong throbs in his cock. His animal howled inside him and he let it, but didn't loosen his control of his actions one bit. It wasn't time for that.

Her hair covered her nipples again, so that he could scarcely see the pink peaks of her creamy skin through it. He licked his lips and almost forgot what he was supposed to be doing. Almost.

He locked eyes with her, then pulled his shirt over his head and dropped it to the floor, kicking his boots off, then shedding the rest of his clothes as quickly as possible. He loved that her eyes went to his cock and her fingers closed like she had to touch it. Her tongue came out to wet her lips.

"I'd forgotten how big..." she started.

He hooked his fingers inside the one piece of clothing she still wore that covered only her belly, accentuating above and below like arrows pointing out where he should go, then pulled her to him. "Don't say that, doll, don't start to imagine it's going to hurt." He slid his hands over every inch of bare skin he could find, tweaking her nipples, pulling at her hair, kissing the spots that seemed most sensitive. She groaned against him and he thought he'd never heard anything that sounded quite as beautiful.

He picked her up, kissing her as he walked her to the bed and laid her down, stopping to watch as she spread her hair out like a fan around her. Pure sex, that's what she was, sent to torture him in the most delectable manner he'd ever experienced.

He knelt before her on the side of the bed, hearing her quick intake of breath as he kissed her inner thighs and her soft, "oh," as she realized what he was going to do. He sensed he was her first in this manner and that thought made him fiercely glad. He would show her how a male should treat a female. How he would treat her every day for the rest of their lives.

He started slowly, his intention to drive her mad before he took her where he ultimately wanted her. He kissed her softly as her whimpers and moans directed him where to go, and where to stay away from… for now.

She wound her fingers into his hair and tried to grind against him, but he resisted her, curling his arms around her legs for better control, keeping his pace and pressure light and teasing until she cried out.

"Crew, oh my God, I can't. You have to—"

He didn't stop long enough to answer her, instead using the flat of his tongue exactly where she wanted it, stroking her in her softest spot again and again until her legs trembled and she screamed his name. Her wetness drenched his face and he loved it.

When she pushed him away, he stood and took his cock in his hand, pushing against her, holding tight to his control, still unwilling to hurt her even a little.

Her eyes were closed and her hands limp upon the bed, her fingers curled, her calming scent of lavender everywhere. He smiled to see her so open, so trusting, so relaxed. When he pressed his cock into her opening ever so slightly, her eyes flew open and locked onto his. "Shhh, doll, don't tense." He pressed in another millimeter, relishing the feel of her hot, wet, tightness. He'd known she would be like this. Like liquid velvet wrapped in silk. *His.* He eyed her creamy shoulders, then pulled his gaze away.

He gritted his teeth and focused, not wanting to lose himself to the pleasure of the moment. Dahlia's eyes closed and her hands fisted the rough blanket beneath her.

Crew leaned forward, laving first one nipple then the other, not moving an inch inside her, until she relaxed and put her hands in his hair again.

He worked his way up to her sensitive neck and ears, then murmured, "That's right, relax. I promised you I would never hurt you and I never will. You're in control. I'm not moving till you do." He held his lower half perfectly still, kissing her lips, her eyelids, her temples and cheeks, gratified as she began to relax again underneath him.

When she wiggled her hips, he knew he was golden, but still he didn't move. She opened her eyes, kissed him back hotly, then tried to pull him forward, her nails digging into his ass. *So fucking sexy.*

"You ready?"

Her eyes were wild. "Yes, Crew, yes."

He moved forward just an inch, tightening his hold on himself. "I want to be certain you're ready."

She wiggled again and tried to scooch down the bed and drive him deeper into her. Crew locked his hands around her slender arms and pinned her to the bed. "What are you doing, doll?" he drawled, his hips like steel, unbendable, unmoveable.

Her eyes flashed. "Are you teasing me?" she shot at him, her fingers curling into her palms.

"I might be," he said, "just a little. But mostly I want you to want my dick so much you draw me inside your tight little pussy. Maybe beg me a little."

Her eyes went wide at that and he suppressed a grin. He loved her innocence. And her opposing heat. He wanted to read more of her stories, her fantasies on display, to see if any of the lines she used in them would fit him.

Her lids lowered until she was gazing at him under long lashes. "I want you," she murmured. "But if you try to make me beg you might regret it."

A sudden wind picked up in the closed room, ruffling his hair. Crew looked around at nothing and smiled, giving her what she wanted, easing into her as she sighed and the wind disappeared. He praised fate and everything that brought this female to him. He couldn't have picked a more perfect mate if he'd used a dating service.

He whispered into her ear again as he eased his way inside her and she accepted him, her walls stretching to fit him like a glove. He kept his hands clasped around her arms, pulling her slowly onto him.

"I can't say I wouldn't love to hear you beg me, but we'll save that for another time."

***

Dahlia's cheeks heated and so did her insides. Now she was glad they hadn't had sex before, because nothing could top this. This unhurried, sweet but spicy interplay. She wanted it to go on forever.

Crew groaned as he finally seated himself fully inside her. She lifted her hips experimentally, loving the fullness, how he stretched her to her limit and every slide of his skin against hers sent her towards another climax. Heaven. That's what this was. Heaven on earth… or wherever they were.

He pulled out, then moved back inside her just as slowly, his strong hands pulling her to meet him. Her gaze traveled over his chest muscles, his tattoos, the thick veins that encircled his arms and hands. She leaned to one side and bit his forearm, hard, not knowing where the urge came from and not caring.

He met her gaze then and gave her a sexy grin that she filed away in her mind for later in a mental file called Biting Crew. She would do that again.

His hands dropped from her upper arms to the curve of her hips and his fingers bit into the flesh there as he pulled her roughly against him. She cried out and so did he. She watched him unabashedly as he threw his head back, closed his eyes, and groaned out his pleasure.

Crew locked eyes with her and pulled out, then thrust into her again. He'd been right, she felt no pain. Only intense sweetness. He grinned at her, almost cockily, and she grinned back, knowing she never would have been able to imagine this playful side of him the first time she saw him. She didn't know which she loved more, his intensity, or his clandestine mischievousness.

All thoughts were driven from her head as his pace increased and the sound of their frenzied meeting filled the room. She urged him on as she felt herself rushing toward climax, as he steered her there expertly. The pleasure built in intensity and she closed her eyes, her fingers clawing at his skin, her head thrown back.

"Crew, yes!" she cried out, as another, stronger orgasm took her over, obliterating all thought, all knowledge of her as a being separate from him for just a moment, and thick pulses of pleasure rushed through her midsection so quickly, she couldn't tell where one ended and another began.

Crew pumped into her hard, then stiffened and groaned out his own release as she felt his hot seed spill inside her.

She opened her eyes wide and stared at him in shock.

CHAPTER 32

You came inside me," she said, still staring at him with wide eyes.

Crew pulled out of her slowly, his mind not registering what she'd said at first. "I did."

He looked around for something to clean her up with, finding what looked like clean towels in a chest near the wall. He tossed the used towel on the floor and flopped onto the bed next to her, curling her into his arms.

But she still looked shocked. "I thought you would at least pull out. I would have said something, but…"

He was confused. "Why would I pull out?"

She hit him on the chest with one small hand, her face incredulous. "So as not to get me pregnant, you dink."

He pulled her hair around to the front of her and draped it across her neck and breasts, propping himself on one elbow to take her in. "I want to get you pregnant."

Dahlia's mouth dropped open. "You what? We've known each other for three—" She tried to count on her fingers but frowned and Crew knew she wasn't sure how to count the night together in his dream world, or the night she'd died, or even the time in between.

She shook her head and erased the air with her hands. "Exact days don't matter. It hasn't been very long."

His heart filled with love for her. "You're my mate," he said simply. "It's what we were meant to do. Our young will be beautiful and strong and I love them already."

Her hand went to her throat as she thought about it. He could tell she'd never considered if she even wanted babies, but he knew she would love the idea soon. Crew laid his head down on the bed and massaged her hip, the warmth of her body already exciting him again.

She raised up on her hands to stare at him. "Then why didn't you bite me? Don't you do that?"

It was Crew's turn to be surprised and consider. "You mean claiming you?"

She nodded and rubbed her shoulder. "Yeah, isn't that something werewo—I mean *shiften* do?"

Crew rubbed a hand over the back of his neck, looking up at the soaring stone ceiling above them. "It is. We call it claiming, and once I do it, it bonds us together in a deeper way than a promise or a ceremony could ever do. I wanted to claim you the other night when we were together, but I held myself back then, because I didn't know if you would accept it. Tonight... well, tonight I didn't think about it."

His gaze shifted and he knew he was lying. He grimaced. "I take that back. I did think about it, and I'm not sure why I didn't do it. Maybe because I didn't know you knew the concept and I didn't want to scare you." He heard the lie in his voice this time and he grimaced again. "That's not true either." He gazed into his mate's eyes. "I'm not sure. Can I think about it for a second?"

She nodded, and he relaxed, satisfied that she wasn't upset with him. He closed his eyes and shifted through his inner feelings. Contentment deeper than he'd ever known. Desire to take her again. Fierce joy that she was who she was. A far off worry about what would happen when they returned to their own world. He circled about that one and prodded it, teasing out all of its factors.

Finally, he opened his eyes to look at his mate. "Are you afraid that when I do claim you, we'll go back to our world?"

For just a moment, her eyes took on that haunted look he remembered from when he'd first met her, and then she nodded. "Angel told me I can't return to our world until you bind my fate. He didn't say how you would do it, but I guess I assumed the bite would be how." She pouted slightly. "He also said you couldn't read my thoughts."

"I can't. I just get broad impressions of how you feel and what you want, and I didn't even realize how strong it is with you until you asked me why I didn't claim you. I guess the answer is I didn't claim you because you aren't ready to go back to our world and you think the claiming will send us there."

"You can do that with everyone?"

He nodded. "Almost everyone. But I try not to. And it's strongest with you."

"Does it get... tiring?"

He grinned. "My entire life has been tiring, but no longer."

She relaxed her head onto her arm and stared at him, a small smile on her face. "What do you mean?"

He traced his fingers lightly across her hip, then down her backside, dipping them under the corset, then swirling off to her lower belly and thighs, not looking her in the eyes. "You soothe me. Your thoughts, your scent, the fact that you are strong and clever and sweet and gorgeous in exactly the way I like my females. Your spirit always calmed me, made me want to stay still and let you come to me, but ever since I entered this world to find you alive again and acting like a warrior, that feeling has been greater. I could sense your anxiety before you died, and now it's gone, and your soul is stronger for it. Strong enough to soothe both of us."

Dahlia didn't speak for a long time and when he looked at her, her eyes were shining and her face was constricted. He lifted his hand to her cheek. "Oh, doll, I'm sorry. What did I say?"

"The sweetest thing I've ever heard in my life."

***

Heather beat Graeme into their cabin, flipping on all the lights, raking her gaze over her lizards to be sure they were fine, then ran to their kitchen table, pulling Ella's pendant out of her pocket and gently placing it on the table, then looking up at her bond partner impatiently. "Put Dahlia's down, too."

Graeme did and the pendants chimed once, then fell silent. Heather looked from one to the other, then back up at Graeme. "You sure we should do this now?"

He nodded. "Now that Deborah is settled, we should at least try. We don't know what they are going through wherever they are. But Deborah didn't need to be around when we did it."

Heather nodded slowly. "Shouldn't someone know?"

"Wade knows. Trent and Troy know. Trevor knows. But we are still on our own."

Heather licked her lips. "Come grab hold of me. I'll try holding one in each hand."

Graeme nodded, crossing to her and grasping her arms. "Fix in your mind what you want before you touch them."

Heather concentrated, then picked up first Ella's pendant, then Dahlia's. She frowned and grasped them tighter, her lips thinning.

After a few moments, she put them down on the table and turned to Graeme in disappointment. "Nothing. I get nothing."

He nodded, his brow furrowed. "They aren't ready for us. Crew hasn't found her yet, maybe. Don't worry, leannan. We'll try again soon."

CHAPTER 33

I can't believe we haven't left the room in three days," Dahlia said. "We don't have a TV, or the Internet, or anything."

Crew plucked a handful of grapes off the tray of food they'd been brought and returned to her, popping a few in his mouth, his eyes twinkling, his look heating. "Are you bored?"

"No, Crew, not bored," she said. She loved how they had all day to lie around and enjoy each other. She loved that there were no demons in this world who would kill her on principle. "Don't look at me like that. I'm getting sore. I'm not sure how much more I can take."

He flopped down on the bed next to her and ran a finger down her naked chest. "A good pounding will take care of that."

"Crew!"

He laughed and ate another grape.

She could no longer say she wasn't as experienced as she wanted to be with all things sexual. Crew had introduced her to positions and moves she'd scarcely imagined before. She couldn't wait to improve the sex scenes in her stories.

They hadn't just spent the time exploring each other's bodies, but also had talked endlessly, exploring each other's minds. They'd talked about dream worlds, deaths, dragons, books, movies and TV, wolves, gods, her father, his past, his family, prophecy, his powers, and her power. She'd learned so much about his preferences, like he liked classical literature and movies while she preferred contemporary, and he had a photographic memory.

Neither of them had traveled anywhere in their dreams the last two nights. Every morning when he woke up, he said he'd never felt so rested in his life. Plus, they'd agreed to hold off on the claiming until he sensed she was ready to go home. Dahlia figured he would probably know before she did.

He grasped her hip. "Why haven't you asked the king for a parchment or something? They have to have some sort of paper here."

Dahlia shrugged. "I've been trying to train my mind to remember my ideas better. I keep imagining a big file cabinet and putting stuff in files that are marked so I can come back and find them later."

He nodded. "I bet that's like weightlifting for your brain. Could you create something with your imagination right now if you wanted to?"

"Like what?"

"I don't know, like a flower."

She frowned. "Do you want me to try?"

He nodded and she concentrated, closing her eyes, thinking of a flower. What kind of a flower? A tulip. She'd always thought they were pretty. She imagined one in as much detail as she could come up with and opened her eyes, but nothing had appeared. He stood up and looked around the room, then shook his head.

"Oh, wait, I forgot the most important part." Emotion. She closed her eyes again and tried to think how to bring emotion to a flower. Maybe she had to imagine a scene in which she could attach emotion to the flower. She smiled as she thought of Crew bringing her a handful of wildflowers. She watched as he picked every one of them in the field, passing over ones that weren't good enough for her, dreaming of the way she would smile at him and kiss him when he presented them. She saw each spray of baby's breath and every purple petal clearly in her mind and felt the love that would spread through her as she realized that he'd done it only to make her happy.

Crew grunted and she opened her eyes. In his arms was the biggest bouquet of wildflowers she had ever seen. "I did it," she said quietly.

"Not only did you do it, you overdid it." He put the flowers down on the table next to their food and picked one up to smell it. "Sweet, almost too sweet, like it's not real." He ran his fingers over the petals. "The texture is just right."

He put the flowers down and turned back to her. "Can you do something alive? Like a bug?"

Dahlia made a face. "Ew."

"Something innocuous, maybe a ladybug."

"Yeah, but what if there are no ladybugs in this world and me bringing one in decimates some bug that's keeping all the crops alive."

Crew held out his thumb. "I'll smash it after I get a look at it."

Dahlia frowned. "I don't want you to smash it."

"Then do a spider, then you'll be glad that I smashed it."

She laughed and closed her eyes, but before she even tried, she knew she wouldn't be able to muster up one emotion that would bring her a ladybug, and she didn't want to figure out an emotion that would bring her a spider.

She opened her eyes. "Maybe something alive isn't a good idea."

"Are you pulling it in from somewhere? Or are you creating it?"

She shook her head. "Not sure. Creating it, I think."

"You should practice. When we go home, it will make me feel much better if I know you have control over this power of yours, Dahlia." She turned away before he could see what was in her eyes, but it didn't matter. He had a window into her heart.

He didn't speak for a few moments and when he did, his voice was soft. "You don't want to go home." It was a statement, not a question.

She shrugged. "You have people there. Friends. All I have is Angel."

He got back down on the bed with her. "You have your sisters."

"That's true, but I'm nervous to meet them. I mean, I already know Heather but not very well. What is Ella like?"

Crew shook his head and ran his fingers through her hair, pushing it back over her shoulder and away from her face. "I honestly don't know, I haven't talked to her much."

Dahlia let Crew cradle her close as she tried to imagine what going home would be like.

From outside their tiny window, a great commotion sounded.

Crew jumped up to look outside. "It's a messenger. He's meeting with someone in the courtyard. He looks excited. Oh, the king just stuck his head out another window."

Heather sat up and she could hear the words.

"Libeka the Protector has laid another egg. She sits on it now."

The king shouted back down to him. *"Declare a celebration this very eve in the market!"*

Crew turned back to her, eyebrows raised. "Is that all these people do, party?"

Dahlia stood up and looked around for her clothes. "I'd like to go," she said, wondering if Crew could see her ulterior motive. If he did, he didn't say a word.

"Anything you want, doll."

***

Crew lifted her off the sweet female horse they'd been given to ride to the market on, then swung his leg over and slid down easily, looking as practiced as a cowboy. He learned quickly.

His sleeveless jerkin he'd borrowed rode up, and she was treated to a heavenly view of his ass in the tight leggings that he hated but all the other men wore. She'd only been able to get him to wear them instead of his jeans by promising not to wear the one-piece undergarment she couldn't get off without stripping down under her dress.

As he'd helped her get dressed, she'd been able to see his fantasies of bending her over the bed and her skirts falling up and over her body written all over his face. She was totally into it. As soon as they got back.

He faced her and adjusted himself. "You're lucky I love you. I wouldn't wear this for anyone else."

Dahlia's chest felt light and her mouth grew dry. "You... love me?"

He frowned. "I haven't said that before?"

She shook her head, her heart soaring.

"I do. I think I have since I first saw you at the rut. Maybe when I saw you outside it."

Dahlia raised her hand to her throat. "You didn't know me then. It was lust."

He shook his head slowly. "It wasn't. I could feel your spirit. It wouldn't have mattered if you had a squeaky voice or talked too loud, or liked to pick your nose and wipe it on the furniture."

Dahlia tried to make a face at that, but she couldn't twist her smile into anything else.

He brushed her hair back from her face and gazed into her eyes. "You might have been a disgusting nose picker, but you would have been *my* disgusting nose picker."

Dahlia laughed. "Crew!" She caught his hand and held it to her heart. "I love you, too."

His eyes bored into her. "I know. I actually thought we'd already done this. Sorry."

She gave a shaky laugh. "Okay, since you're so smart, what do we do now?"

He pulled her towards the music, mostly drums and a light guitar-sounding instrument. "We dance."

They entered the marketplace, surprised as usual by the overdone frivolity of everyone there. There were two areas with people dancing and Crew tried to pull her to one, but she tried to pull him to the other. "Let's join the circle dance," Dahlia urged.

Crew stared at it, his eyes intense, then shook his head. "Dahlia, I can't."

"Sure you can, silly. Just do what they do. It looks like a cross between the hokey pokey and square dancing." She tried to start forward, but Crew caught her and held her arm.

"Dahlia, if any man in that group touches you, I'll kill him."

That stopped her. She looked around, alarmed. "But why?"

He gritted his teeth. "I haven't claimed you yet. Until I do, I can't control my impulses."

She raised a hand to where her shoulder met her neck, the spot where he'd indicated he would bite her, and stared at him, then tried to smile. "Got it."

She led him to the couples dancing and they tried to join in and follow the movements of everyone else.

Within only a few moments, Dahlia felt eyes on them. Crew growled deep in his throat and she stared at him, thinking this had been a very bad idea. Lord Theobald the Grim, as Crew had taken to calling him, emerged from the shadows, and she could see him in the light of the bonfire. He stared at them, his eyes shrewd, then he stepped forward and addressed her, bending low.

"If it please the lady, I would like to partake of a dance with her." Dahlia shook her head. Was he stupid?

Crew stepped in front of her and bared his teeth at the man. "It doeth not pleaseth the lady-eth."

Dahlia felt like giggling and holding her hands to her head at the same time. He was such a smartass. But one with absolutely no filter.

Lord Theobald nodded curtly, as if he had expected as much. "Then perhaps, you would show the crowd your swordplay? I have to imagine you are a master swordsman. The king has informed me of his intention to ask you both to fill seats on our newly formed parliament, and as such, I should like to get to know you better."

Dahlia wondered if that was even true. She pulled on Crew's arm. "We shouldn't have come," she whispered. "Let's go back."

Crew held up a hand to her, his eyes staring intently at Theobald. "I'll show you something," he said, his voice low.

Dahlia groaned, not quite able to understand how dancing had turned into something that had her belly churning in fear.

Lord Theobald led them through the crowd to an open area where two men were fighting with wooden swords in front of a small group of spectators. He motioned them past the two men to a thick wooden post as tall as Crew, buried securely in the ground. Its sides were chipped and marred from sword blows.

Dahlia could hear whispering as some of the crowd watching the two men dispersed and made their way to surround the new spectacle.

Lord Theobald raised his hand to a soldier, who carried over a sword three times as thick as the one he had on his belt, holding it close to his body like it was very heavy. He tried to hand it to Lord Theobald, but he shook his head and indicated Crew.

Crew grabbed it with one hand and sliced the air with it, his eyes locked on Theobald, his muscles showing no sign of strain. Dahlia rubbed the hollow at the base of her throat, her imagination taking off with what might happen next. Would someone come over and try to fight Crew? The only reason she wasn't trying to pull him away was because she knew he would never go. But Crew knew nothing about handling a sword. Was Theobald trying to prove something?

He only stood there, arms crossed over his chest, waiting for Crew's next move. Crew's eyes narrowed, then he walked to the wooden post. He hefted the sword in his hand again, then grasped two hands around its hilt, almost like he would a baseball bat. He raised his arms high and sliced at the pole diagonally and down, grunting as metal met wood, chopping it completely in half.

Dahlia gasped, as did most of the women in the crowd. The top half of the post thudded as it hit the ground and fell over.

Crew jabbed the sword into the dirt, his eyes challenging Theobald, as he held out a hand to Dahlia. She ran to him, lifting her skirts so she wouldn't trip over them.

As soon as they were out of Theobald's hearing range, Dahlia whispered to Crew, "I'm sorry I wanted to come out here. Let's go back."

He shook his head. "No need to be sorry with me, doll. He's showing his hand, and that's always a good thing."

CHAPTER 34

The ride back to the castle was quiet, only the noises of the night and the clip-clopping of the horses echoing off the trees in the forest. Crew didn't say a word and Dahlia didn't mind. She was lost in thought herself. Why did someone always have to be an ass? Of course she knew the answer to that, because that someone was unhappy.

Once inside the room, Crew's mood stayed dark and she could see his mind working. He picked at the evening snacks they'd been brought, but mostly looked out the window, a frown on his face. Dahlia undressed, her own mind working out her own problems, trying to come to an understanding or maybe an agreement with itself.

When she got into bed, he finally joined her, taking her more roughly than she was used to, then draining a glass of ale before falling asleep. Her stomach was unsettled so she'd refused the wine that had been brought up for her, and he'd drunk that also.

It took Dahlia over an hour to finally fall asleep and when she finally did, she dreamed of falling over a waterfall, Crew nowhere in sight and unable to save her.

***

Crew tried to wrench his eyes open but they felt glued shut. Rough hands grabbed him around his elbows and shoulders and pulled him to his feet. His head hung, because his muscles would not react to his commands to hold it upright. Drugged. Someone had slipped him a tranquilizer somehow. He fought against it, knowing if he just had enough time he could force his body to metabolize whatever it was. Or to function anyway, he had plenty of experience with that.

A female cry reached his ears and he stiffened, trying to hear more. It was Dahlia. "Let him go!"

Using all the strength he had, Crew forced his eyelids open. The room was filled with soldiers, and two of them near the door had King Caius in a prisoner's grip. Dahlia was also being held, but by only one male, who had a knife to her throat. *He would die for that.*

Across from him, Lord Theobald held up the pendant and it swung in the light from the fire, sparkling prettily.

Lord Theobald strode to the king and thrust the pendant in his face. "Tell me its power. How can I make it strip the shape-shifter of his ability? How can I lock him into one form?"

Dahlia screamed and struggled against the soldier who held her tight. Lord Theobald addressed him. "Be careful with her. If the shape-shifter wakes up, we'll need her to control him."

He turned back to the king. "Answer me!"

The king shook his head and pressed his lips together. Lord Theobald nodded to one of the soldiers who stepped forward and rammed the king in the chest with the hilt of a knife. The king fell to the ground, his hands on his chest, coughing and trying to breathe.

Crew felt his mind clearing slightly and his muscles attempting to return to his control, but not fast enough. Wind ruffled his hair and he looked up, trying to force his eyes to settle on Dahlia. Her face was set with fury.

"It's working," Lord Theobald called, his eyes locked on the pendant. It was glowing. He strode towards Crew, but his steps faltered as more wind whipped through the room. He looked around the room, then out into the windless night, a confused frown on his face.

Crew looked back to Dahlia once more, gratified when her eyes seemed to glow with the pendant. He raised his head and tried to speak to the two soldiers who were pinning his arms. His voice came out weak, but they could hear him. "Let me go, before my mate gets any angrier. Maybe she'll spare your lives."

Lord Theobald looked at him and Crew grinned at the confusion on his face. Some things were just too perfect.

The soldier holding Dahlia screamed and Crew saw that the knife he'd been holding had turned into a deadly looking emerald-green snake and sunk its fangs into his arm. The soldier let go of Dahlia and batted at the snake. Dahlia turned, her eyes narrowing as she faced Theobald. "That's mine," she said, her eyes on the pendant, her hand out.

He clutched it closer to him and yelled at two more soldiers. "Don't just stand there. Get her!"

They started forward, but Dahlia was too quick for them. The emerald-green snake grew to the size of an anaconda and wrapped around their feet, tripping them, then coiling around them.

Theobald stared at his soldiers and the snake, then muttered something. Crew wasn't sure if it was 'witch' or 'bitch', but he didn't think Dahlia would mind either. He grinned, relaxing in the holds of the soldiers who had him, starting to enjoy himself, especially as more of the drug suppressing his mind and body wore off.

"You know," he started conversationally to the soldiers who had hold of him. They were staring at the snake squeezing their compatriots to death with wide eyes, then both let go of him and stepped away, trying to pretend they'd never been in on any of this. He addressed them anyway. "You made a mistake thinking I was the dangerous one. That delicate flower over there is about to bend you both over this bed and shove snakes up your—"

"Crew!" Dahlia snapped. "The pendant."

"Oh, right." He took two steps towards Lord Theobald and snatched the pendant out of his hand, then stepped over snake and soldiers to stand next to his female as all the soldiers who were able ran from the room.

"Can you help the king?" she asked.

"What about Old Fat-and-Bald?"

"I don't think he's a problem anymore." Crew looked up just in time to see Theobald drop to the floor in a dead faint and Dahlia's snake head over to cuddle him.

Crew helped the king to his feet as the man coughed alarmingly.

When he got himself under control, King Caius surveyed the three men on the floor, rubbing his chest, then cursed in

Theobald's direction. "He's been planning this for months. I can't believe I trusted him."

Crew grunted. "Me neither. Maybe let the people vote next time."

Caius shook his head. "The problem is, I don't know who I can trust. Those soldiers he brought with him were among my inner circle."

Crew stared at the king for a few moments, then said. "I can find out who you can trust. Gather everyone. The entire castle staff, anyone you want to put on the parliament, and all of your soldiers. I can tell you at a glance."

The king only stared for a few moments, then nodded sharply. "It will be done."

***

Several hours later, the roosters crowed proudly outside as Dahlia and Crew made their way back to their room, hand in hand. Crew had touched the mind of every person the king had put in front of him and gave the king a 'yay', 'nay', or 'could be swayed by money or promises of power'. The castle staff was suddenly much lighter, but the king could trust them all.

As soon as they were inside, Dahlia pulled him into a hug. "Thank you for doing that."

Crew shrugged, his amber eyes intense with heat. "It was only right."

"I've had some time to think, Crew, and I'm ready to find our way home."

His gaze bored into her. "You're certain?"

She nodded. "I've been thinking about this all wrong, thinking if we could stay here, maybe we could somehow skip out on all that demon and prophecy stuff, maybe avoid the danger totally." She dropped her eyes. "I was hiding from it, and that's never a good idea. Especially when every world is dangerous."

Crew took her chin in his hand and brought her eyes up to meet his. "Delaying isn't hiding, Dahlia, you just needed a little vacation. A little time to clear your head. Are you positive that you're ready to go back now?"

She bit her lip and nodded.

"Good," he rasped, his voice suddenly thick and heavy as his lips dropped to hers, kissing her deeply and with such passion that her core heated instantly. She felt something inside of him unfurl and let go, and only later realized it had been his tight control of himself. "Because I can't wait one more second to do this."

He kissed her again, then lifted her and carried her to the bed, breaking the kiss to put her down and turn her around. She fell onto the bed and pressed her face into the blankets as he lifted her skirts and threw them over her head. He retreated for a moment, and then she felt his thick cock at her entrance. He was inside her in only one thrust and she cried out at the intruding pleasure of it.

He wrestled with her skirts until he could see her again, and she tried not to tense, knowing what was coming. He pulled her hair into a ponytail and tugged it toward the bed, baring her shoulder.

A vicious, growling snarl came from him and Dahlia had one second to be scared before his teeth sank into her unblemished skin.

"Oh!" Dahlia cried as an orgasm that hadn't been close a moment before forced its way through her, wringing every ounce of pleasure out of her that her body had to give. Crew pumped into her twice more, sending more furls of sensation through her, then he stiffened and groaned, and she felt his hot seed shoot inside her, even it bringing pleasure.

The stiff sound of cloth ripping reached her ears, but she couldn't worry about it as more pleasure took her higher, then feathers wrapped around her, lifting both her and her mate from the bed into the air. She cried out again, mystified, but feeling completely safe. Crew wrapped his arms around her from behind as they first raised, then lowered back to the bed, and the feathers disappeared.

"What in the hell was that?" Dahlia panted.

"That was some badass lovin'." Crew said, pulling slowly out of her, then looking around for something to clean up with. "You're welcome."

She laughed. "No, you're welcome." When she turned to see him, her blood was running down his chin. The sight didn't gross her out at all, like she'd been afraid it might. It made her wonder if he could do it again. She'd come too quickly, next time she wanted to savor it more, if that was possible.

"No, I mean the feathers." She touched the bite where her neck met her shoulder. It seemed to be healing already.

He climbed onto the bed with her, face clean, and smoothed her hair back.

"That was your daily reminder that you're half-angel, just in case you do something silly, like forget."

CHAPTER 35

Heather ran to catch up to Ella, leaving Graeme behind to talk with Trevor as they all walked through the driveway to the van that would take them to the police station along with their daily guard. She grinned as snow melted underneath her feet the way it did Graeme's. She could only put out about half as much heat as he did and only if she concentrated super hard, but it was enough to bring a smile to her face.

Ella smiled at her. "No word?"

"Nothing. I'm starting to get antsy. The pendants seem like they're dead." Heather stuck her hand in her pocket and pulled out Dahlia's pendant. Graeme had Ella's. "Graeme says they aren't, but I can't help but worry."

Ella dropped her voice. "Trevor's worried, too. And Wade is sick out of his mind. Lorna said he hasn't slept for days."

Heather pouted and shoved the pendant back in her pocket. "If only they would just tell us Crew and Dahlia are ok. Then we could wait a little—"

A bright light filled the sky and Heather and Ella raised their hands to cover their faces. Their guard came streaming out of the temporary shelter that had been built in front of the house for heat and electricity for them. Heather could hear their rough exclamations, but she couldn't see them because her retinas were scorched.

A thick longing for her bond-partner twisted through her and she dropped her hands to her belly for just a second, then turned to look for Graeme as the light faded.

Ella grabbed her. "Do you feel it?"

Heather didn't want to admit anything. "What?"

"Like you have to jump Graeme or die trying?"

Heather nodded slowly as Trevor and Graeme came running up to them. Ella grabbed her shoulders. "That's what I felt when you and Graeme had your bonding ceremony." She looked up into the sky. "He's claimed her. I know it."

The light began to disappear from the sky, more slowly in some places, until only a glowing arch was left.

Mac spoke up from behind them. "It's like a rainbow of sex. A funky sexbow."

Heather glared at him, still irritated with him from the other night. Bruin, the big *bearen* Mac seemed attached to at the hip, elbowed Mac and grinned. "Makes me feel tingly in my girly parts."

Mac snorted. "You have girly parts? That explains a lot."

Bruin's smile didn't fade. "Fuck you, Scooby-Doo."

Trevor turned to hide his smile, pulling Ella with him and whispering into her ear. Ella giggled and hid her face in her hands.

Graeme grasped Heather's arm and she smiled, imagining what he was going to say. "Check the pendant."

Ok, that wasn't as sexy as she thought it would be.

"Hurry, before the light fades completely," he said, his eyes searching the sky. Heather pulled it from her pocket and held it up. "Graeme, its eyes are glowing."

He grabbed her arm in a tight grip. "Let's go."

***

Dahlia watched Crew relax and unwind before her eyes as he told her about the wings and what they had looked like. She hadn't even realized how much tension he'd still carried until he began to let it go. Frequent sex helped him a lot, but now that she was good and claimed, he looked like he'd turned back the clock. Half of his worry lines were gone, smoothed out.

She looked around at the room she now wondered if they'd ever leave. "We're still here. I guess it wasn't that easy."

He touched her face, her hair, her shoulder. "We'll find another way. Don't worry."

"The king said there's a portal to another world somewhere to the north, but it's ten feet off a cliff-face. You have to run and leap for it."

Crew grinned. "That's my doll, always looking for the most danger she can find. When we get home, I'll have to take you to a twelve-step program. Or just accept that you have the spirit of a *wolfen*."

She laughed and punched him lightly on the arm. Heather's pendant chimed in her pocket. She looked at Crew questioningly and dug through the folds of her skirt to fish it out.

The noise was much louder when it escaped the fabric of her skirt. "Crew, look," she said, turning it so he could see the glowing eyes of the wolf.

A noise sounded in the hall. A scuffling, bumping sound and then a woman's giggle. "I bet they're in there," the female voice said.

A male's Scottish brogue cut through the door. "We should give them a few minutes."

The giggle sounded again and Crew jumped off the bed, shooting Dahlia a shocked look. He pulled on his pants and crossed the room as Dahlia scrambled to right her skirts and pull the torn dress back into place.

Crew ripped the door open. Dahlia saw only a male's broad back pressing a female against the wall, but she noticed at once that their clothes were modern.

"Graeme!" Crew shouted.

The male whirled about, and his face broke into a smile. "We found you."

Heather peeked around Graeme and, when her gaze landed on Dahlia, she shrieked and ran into the room, catching Dahlia around the shoulders and hugging her, squeezing the very breath out of her.

"Hi," Dahlia finally managed when Heather let her go and stepped back. The only people in her lives who had ever greeted her like that had been her mother and Crew. And now her sister. And to think, she'd almost entertained the thought of not going back. She held up Heather's pendant. "This is yours."

Heather's mouth fell open. She looked around the castle. "Is this the world where I left it with the little boy?"

Dahlia nodded. "Time moves faster here. That was twenty years ago in this world."

"Twenty years!" Heather took her pendant and gazed at it. "Caius, the boy? Is he—?"

"He's the king now. Your pendant helped him do a lot of good stuff for the world."

Heather turned to look at Graeme. "Did you hear that?"

He nodded gravely. "Aye."

Heather dug something out of her pocket and handed it over. "Here's yours."

Dahlia felt her heart seize in her chest and her throat wouldn't work. Her pendant. She touched it gently, remembering the last time she'd seen it. Her mom—the thought hurt so much and she turned away from it, cradling the pendant in her hand, trying to keep herself together. A strange buzzing filled her head as she waited for Heather to tell her about her mom.

But Heather's eyes were still crawling over the castle. "King, huh, I'd love to see him."

Graeme shook his head. "I dinnae ken if that is a good idea. Ask Dahlia what she feels."

Heather waved her hand. "It's cool. You're right. Maybe I can just leave him something. Something to say I was thinking about him." She dug in her pockets, pulling out only some keys, her phone, and an orange whistle of some sort. She tossed it on the bed. "That's perfect. It's a survival whistle with a compass and a signal mirror. I got it for your mom, but I can get her another one. She's a super sweet lady, but she sucks at directions. She got lost this morning in the meadow behind the house—" She broke off and frowned at Dahlia. "Dahlia, what's wrong?"

Crew rushed to her and Dahlia went limp on the bed as blackness rushed up to meet her, willing herself not to faint, not to lose it completely.

But she did.

CHAPTER 36

ahlia came to slowly, blinking her eyes as Crew held her by the shoulders and blotted water onto her face. She stared at him gratefully. "I'm ok. I can sit up."

He helped her up and Dahlia grabbed Heather's hand. "My mom. Tell me."

Heather spilled the story in only a few minutes and Dahlia's world collapsed just a little more. Confirmation. Somehow, she'd always suspected she'd been responsible for making her mother disappear. The worst fear she'd buried in her life had just come true.

She tried to speak. "Is she?—Does she?—Is she mad at me?"

Heather's brows furrowed. "Mad at you? Has your mom ever been mad at anyone?"

Dahlia cocked her head, hearing something that she

wasn't sure if it was in her mind or somewhere outside the castle's walls. A yowling, like an animal… then she knew.

She turned to Crew. "Angel, he's calling me."

He nodded. "I hear it, too."

"Time to go, kiddies. Got all your stuff?" Graeme said.

"Oh, I just want to change into my—"

But before Dahlia could finish the sentence, they were being pulled across time and space. She reached for Crew in the split second she had before her bare feet touched the snowy ground. He caught her hand, landing on the ground next to her, looking around at the Illinois winter from the middle of someone's driveway. He smiled down at her. "Well, that was easy." She tried to smile back, but her heart still pounded.

Heather and Graeme appeared next to them, their entrance into the world just as simple as Dahlia and Crew's had been. Heather grabbed Graeme's hand. "My pendant was way better than Ella's or Dahlia's."

He grabbed her hand and kissed it. "Of course it was, leannan."

A male voice sounded behind them. "Crew, what the fuck is that on your face?"

Crew stood up straight and wiped a hand across his face, turning to greet several men Dahlia did not recognize. She could guess about one of them, though. The guy in the camo cap had to be Beckett, Crew's best friend in this world.

"Never mind, it was a smile. Never seen you wear one before," Beckett said.

Crew flipped him off, then caught him in a bear hug and clapped him on the back, then shook the hands of the other men, leaving stunned expressions on their faces. "Get used to it, Beck, you're gonna be seeing it from now on."

He turned to Dahlia and picked her up in one smooth

motion, then pressed a kiss to her lips as the guys in the driveway whistled and cat-called. "If you'll excuse me, I need to get my female out of the cold."

Dahlia still couldn't speak. She looked around, wondering exactly where they were. One more guy caught her eye. "Mac," she cried, forgetting herself for just a second, forgetting what world they were in. She owed him so much thanks. She turned to Crew first. "Does Mackenzie like you in this world, too?"

Mac's eyes narrowed and he came close. "Where did you hear that name?"

Too late, Dahlia realized her mistake. "Your... your sister," she said in a small voice.

Mac's face tightened and he faced Crew. "My sister is alive in that world you go to?"

Crew nodded and his expression tightened. For the first time, Dahlia saw him as his friends knew him.

Mac didn't say anything for a few moments as everyone seemed to hold their breath. Finally, he spoke, and his voice was softer. "Is she an adult?"

Crew nodded again.

"What—what is she like?"

Crew opened his mouth, then closed it again, then opened it again, like he wasn't sure what to say, but Dahlia knew exactly how to describe Mackenzie.

She caught Mac's eye. "She's fierce."

Mac clenched his lips together and his eyes glistened. He nodded to Dahlia once. "Thank you," he whispered.

Then he turned and walked away, not towards any buildings or cars, but just away. When he crossed the street, he walked straight into the forest, plowing furrows in the snow with his boots.

Everyone in the driveway watched him go.

***

Dahlia clung tight to Crew as he carried her into the house. "That was sweet," he said to her, his small smile that was meant just for her back on his face.

He put her down just inside the doorway and she looked around. The house was beautiful.

A woman's voice called from the top of a stairway to her left. "Ella, is that you? I have to show you this snow angel I made. You can see it best from up here!"

Dahlia clutched at her throat. "Mom?" she whispered. Crew steadied her from the back. Someone pounded down the stairs and Dahlia looked up, her legs threatening to give way under her.

Her mother came down the stairs, a smile on her face, looking impossibly beautiful and sweet and just like Dahlia remembered her. Dahlia barked out a rough cry and covered her face with her hands.

Deborah stopped. "Dahlia," she said softly, then her feet pounded down the rest of the stairs so fast Dahlia was afraid she would fall.

"Dahlia, baby, I've missed you so much." Her mom gathered her into a hug bigger than the one Heather had given her. Tears streamed down Dahlia's face, but still she couldn't look at her mom.

"Baby, look at me. Sweetie, how have you been, oh, I love you so much, baby."

Dahlia couldn't get her voice to work. Her tears were thick and heavy and strangling her. Her mom rubbed her hair and rocked her back and forth and finally Dahlia found the courage to speak. "Mom, I'm so sorry."

"For what, baby? You didn't do anything."

Dahlia lost it again. Her mom didn't even know. She gathered her courage and all the strength she had and said, "I sent you away all those years ago. It had to be me. When I touched the pendant, that made you disappear. It's my fault. All my fault."

She let the tears fall freely behind her hands and waited for her mother to realize it was true. Deborah peeled her hands away from her face and looked her in the eye, her expression kind. "Oh, my baby girl. It's not your fault. It was never your fault." She stopped talking for a second, then seemed to gather courage and start again. "When I told you that I thought your father wanted me to show you the pendant, it wasn't exactly true. When he left it with me, he told me not to give it to you till you were old enough to understand what it meant, and he left it up to me to decide when that was. It was my fault, Dahlia. All my fault. Never yours, sweet girl." She pulled Dahlia close. "It's been an adventure, and if I could do it all over again and never leave you, I would, but then you wouldn't have a half-brother."

Dahlia hiccuped and tried to stop her flow of tears. "A what?"

Her mom held her at arm's length, and she dropped her hands and met her mom's eyes. "We've got a lot to talk about, baby girl. I hope you can forgive me for leaving you."

"Of course, mom, it wasn't your fault either."

"Agreed. No one's fault. And look at you, standing here short as me and beautiful as a flower and with this fine man by your side."

Deborah held Dahlia with one hand, and pulled Crew into a hug with the other. "Hi, Crew. Thank you for taking care of my baby girl. I'm Deborah, but you can call me Deb, or the moon lady, if you like. That's what my neighbors call me. They think I'm crazy."

She pulled back and touched him on the cheek. "Or you can call me Mom."

CHAPTER 37

*D*ahlia walked slowly around her home for the last time before the movers came. She touched her notebook and pen in her pocket, still glad to have them back with her.

She and her mate were breaking ground on a cabin behind Trevor's house that afternoon, and they would be staying in one of his guest bedrooms until it was finished, the one her mother wasn't sleeping in.

They'd been back in the world for four days, and she and Crew had had a small mating ceremony that had doubled as a wedding the day before, then spent the night almost alone here, at her old house. She said almost because the six burly cops surrounding the house and coming in occasionally to use the bathroom hadn't wanted to bother them, but their presence was definitely felt.

Dahlia whipped out her notebook and pen and waited

for the words to flow through her, then wrote swiftly as they did.

If I have to be in a world where the ultimate evil would like nothing more than to find me and kill me, I'm glad Crew has such strong and loyal friends. I can tell that each and every one of them will die before they ever let anything happen to me or my sisters.

She waited a moment to see if there was more but there wasn't. She flipped back a page to reread her thoughts about the wedding, a small smile on her face.

My mom being there was the cherry on top, the icing on the cake, the gilding on the lily, and the feather in the cap. She cried the whole time and pulled everyone into a hug several times. I couldn't look at her or I would start to cry, too.

I can't understand how I got so lucky. I've never been so happy in my entire life.

She went back a page.

Crew wants small. I want small. I can tell Ella wants to throw us a party as big as the one she had, but I know that would make Crew uncomfortable, and me, too. Heather said small is good, and my mom just cried. So we are going with small. Crew says another one true mate has been found already, even if the male doesn't quite believe it or know it himself, so maybe Ella can throw a big party for them. He won't say who the male is, but by the worry on his face and the strange things he said in his dream last night (I hope it was a dream!), I think it is Beckett.

She frowned, remembering. Crew had tossed and turned so badly he'd woken her up. She'd shaken him and tried to wake him, but he'd opened his eyes and looked right through her, holding his hand straight out.

"Beckett, she's not who you think she is. Follow her."

When she'd finally gotten him to wake, he'd brushed it off as a nightmare he couldn't remember and made a joke that it was his first nightmare since he was thirteen years old.

She turned a few more pages slowly, and reached her first thoughts since she'd gotten her notebook back.

I can't believe that Ella is Fern from my dream world!!!! !!!! It's like I haven't lost her at all, except she doesn't remember me like that. Beginning to believe in fate more every day.

Stranger than that, they'd discovered they'd known each other online, in this world. Ella had read her stories and they'd talked via instant messenger most days, mostly about wolves, although neither had known the other's real name.

Crew's voice called to her from her bedroom. "Doll? Are you all packed up?"

She shut her notebook and slipped it back in her pocket. For a few moments, at least.

***

Crew kissed her on the cheek and eyed the construction going on in Trevor's back yard, a bunch of big males gathered around a table. "I'm gonna head out there and see what's going on."

She smiled at him and nodded, then walked through the house, listening to the rare quiet. As she reached the kitchen window, she saw Ella and Heather in the back under a large tree with snow-covered branches. A large circle of snow around them was melted down to the bare, wilted grass and neither woman had a coat on. Dahlia slipped the window open a crack so she could hear what they were saying.

Ella held a stick in her hand and was giving Heather a pep talk. "Focus, Heather, I want the fire on the end of stick. You gotta get it burning. Then I'll drop it and you do that puff of hot air thing you do to catch it and make it fly backwards."

Heather put her hands on her hips. "I hate practicing on you. Trevor will slay me if I burn you."

"Have you burnt me yet?"

Heather's voice was pouty, like a young girl caught in mommy's makeup. "No."

"You focus better when I hold it. Just like I was able to lift you off the ground before. I can't lift anything else that's near as heavy as you are. Just you."

"Are you calling me fat?"

Ella's voice was teasing. "Probably not, since you're taller than me and still weigh less than me. But if you want me to call you fat, I will."

Dahlia slid the window closed and headed out to where her sisters were training.

When they noticed her the smiles on their faces welcomed her home.

"Ladies," she said. "I think I know the secret to what you two are trying to do."

She paused for effect, until Heather rolled her eyes. She laughed and stepped forward, looking up towards the sky, trying to think of something to wow them with.

The way she was feeling, it had to be something joyful. Clouds shaped like kittens, maybe, or flowers bursting through the snow, blooming four months too early.

"About that secret. It's emotion. Watch."

She closed her eyes and opened her imagination, excited to see what happened next.

Notes from Lisa xoxoxo

(If you read OTM3 first, be sure to go back and read OTM1 and OTM2, there's a lot of back-story in those books.)

Crew was so fun to write, and boy did I enjoy watching his and Dahlia's journeys. Crew never saw it coming, and when it all turned around for him, he jumped in with both feet. I hope you enjoyed reading him. I am a bit nervous about all the world hopping and I can't wait to hear from a few people whether it was too much or not (crossing fingers it wasn't).

So, what's next for OTM? Beckett's coming next (what's his big secret?), then maybe Mac (is his otm gonna be sweet or spicy? What do you think?). Then we'll have to see what happens. Don't ask me, I don't have a clue, but I hope it's sexy and fun and a little bit dangerous ;)

62216080R00160

Made in the USA
Lexington, KY
07 April 2017